GETTING
MOTHER'S
BODY

GETTING MOTHER'S BODY

A NOVEL

SUZAN-LORI PARKS

Random House
New York

Copyright © 2003 by Suzan-Lori Parks
Songs copyright © 2003 by Mama's Helper Music

All rights reserved under International and Pan-American Copyright
Conventions. Published in the United States by Random House, an imprint
of The Random House Ballantine Publishing Group, a division of Random
House, Inc., New York, and simultaneously in Canada by Random House of
Canada Limited, Toronto.

RANDOM HOUSE and colophon are registered trademarks of Random House,
Inc.

ISBN 1-4000-6022-2

Printed in the United States of America

BOOK DESIGN BY DEBORAH KERNER/DANCING BEARS DESIGN

FOR FRANCIS AMMON — THE FIRST
TEXAN I EVER MET.

AND, OF COURSE, FOR PAUL.

GETTING
MOTHER'S
BODY

BILLY BEEDE

"Where my panties at?" I asks him.

Snipes don't say nothing. He don't like to talk when he's in the middle of it.

"I think I lost my panties," I says but Snipes ain't hearing. He got his
eyes closed, his mouth smiling, his face wet with sweat. In the middle of
it, up there on top of me, going in and out. Not on top of me really, more
like on top of the side of me cause he didn't want my baby-belly getting
in his way. He didn't say so, he ain't said nothing bout the baby yet, but
I seen him looking at my belly and I know he's thinking about it, somewhere in his mind. We're in the backseat of his Galaxie. A Ford. Bright
lemon colored outside, inside the color of new butter. My head taps
against the door handle as he goes at it.

"Huh. Huh. Huh," Snipes goes.

In a minute my head's gonna hurt. But it don't hurt yet.

"Where—" I go but he draws his finger down over my lips, hushing
them so I don't finish, then he rubs my titty, moving his hand in a quick
circle like he's polishing it. I try scootching down along the seat, away
from the door, but when I scootch, Snipes' going at it scootches me right
back up against the door handle again. I wonder if my baby's sitting in
me upside down and if Snipes' thing is hitting it on its head like the
door handle is hitting me on mines.

"Ow," I go. Cause now my head hurts.

"Owww," Snipes go. Cause he's through.

He lays there for a minute then pulls himself out of me and gets out the car. He closes up his pants while he looks down the road. Zipper then belt. In my head I can see all the little seeds he just sowed in me. All them little Snipeses running up inside me looking for somewheres to plant. But there's a baby up in me already, a Baby Snipes. Baby Snipes knocks down the Little Snipes Seeds as fast as they come up.

"How you doing?" Snipes asks.

"Mmokay."

I turn from my side onto my back, raising up on both elbows. My housedress is all open and the baby makes a hump. Snipes turns to look at me, his gold-colored eyes staying on mines, seeing the hump without really seeing it. He ducks into the front seat, getting his Chesterfields out his shirt pocket, and standing there with his back to me, smoking in just his undershirt.

"Penny for yr thoughts," I go but he don't turn around or say nothing. I sit up, buckling my bra and taking a look around for my panties, first in the front seat then running my hand between the backseat and the seat back, thinking my panties mighta got stuck in between but not finding nothing. Then I do feel a scrap of something and give it a yank. Big red shiny drawers. Not mines. Snipes turns around and sees me holding them.

"My sister's," he says smiling and putting on his shirt. "I let her use my car sometimes."

I stuff the drawers back where I found them, first leaving a little red tail sticking out, then stuffing them back in all the way.

"I didn't know you had no sister," I says. "I don't know nothing about you."

"Whatchu need to know?" he says.

"What's her name?"

"Who?"

"Yr sister."

"Alberta," he says. Then he turns away showing me the side of his face, shaved clean and right-angled as my elbow. He's smiling hard, but not at me.

"Clifton, can I ask you something else?"

"I'll get you some more panties, girl, don't worry," he says.

An hour ago, when Snipes came to get me, I was doing Aunt June's hair. I heard his whistle. He weren't stopped at the pumps. He was stopped across the road, standing against his car looking cool, waiting for me to come outside but waiting cool, just in case I didn't show. I seen him and run across the road without even looking to see if cars was coming and he picked me up and swirled me around. Just like Harry Belafonte woulda.

"You ain't been around in almost a month," I said, breathless from the swirling.

"I been working, girl," he said. He got a custom-coffin business. He makes and sells handmade coffins in any shape you want with plush lining inside and everything. While we drove he showed me his sample book with three new photographs, proud, like folks show pictures of they children. A oak Cadillac, a guitar of cherry wood, and a pharaoh-style one too, all big enough to get buried inside, the new ones not painted yet so folks can pick out they own colors.

"People been talking," I said.

"What they saying?"

"Stuff," I said. "They saying stuff." We kissed as we drove down the road and then I started laughing cause he was tickling me and getting me undressed and showing me his sample book and driving all at the same time. His left hand on the wheel, his right hand between my legs. Then we pulled off the road. Then we did it. Now we done.

"I'll get you a whole damn carload full of panties, girl," he says. "Them panties you had on is probably along the side of the road somewhere between here and Lincoln." He smiles and I smile with him. I remember taking them off. The wind was whipping and musta whipped them out the window while we drove. But that was an hour ago.

Now I look down the road, seeing if I can see them. I see somebody down there walking in the dirt and the shimmer from the heat.

"I don't wanna go home without no panties," I says.

"You worry too much," Snipes says.

All the car doors are open and the wind goes through, drying the sweat off the seats.

"I gotta know something," I says.

"Whut?"

"The man's supposed to ask the girl," I whisper.

He don't speak. ·

We been together since March. Now it's July. I wanna give him a chance to ask me.

"You said I wouldn't get bigged the first time we did it," I says.

"Was our first time your first time?" he says.

"You gonna marry me or what?" I says. The words come out too loud.

He don't speak. He cuts on the radio but it don't work when the car ain't running. He gets out, closing the back two doors, leaving mines open and getting back behind the wheel.

"Sure I'm gonna marry you," he says at last. "You my treasure. You think I don't wanna marry my treasure?"

"People are talking," I says.

"They just jealous," he says and we both laugh. "Billy Beede got herself a good-looking man and they all jealous."

When we quit laughing we sit there quiet.

"You my treasure, girl," he says. "You my treasure, capital T, make no mistake."

"I'm five months gone," I says. Too loud again.

He wraps his fingers tight around the wheel. I want him to look at me but he don't.

Someone comes up, stopping a foot or two from the car to stare at us openmouthed. It's Laz. He got his wool cap down around his ears and his plaid shirt buttoned to the chin.

"You want yr ass kicked?" Snipes asks him.

"Not today," Laz says.

"You don't stop looking at me and my woman, I'ma kick yr black ass," Snipes says.

Laz looks at the ground.

"You don't get the hell outa here, I'ma kill you," Snipes says.

"Being dead don't bother me none," Laz says. He got a bold voice but he ain't looking up from the ground.

Snipes jumps out the car and they stand there toe to toe. Everything Snipes got is better than everything Laz got.

"Go the hell home, Laz," I says and he turns and goes. Snipes throws a rock and Laz runs.

"Goddamn boot-black-wool-hat-wearing-four-eyed nigger proba-bly wanted to see us doing it," Snipes goes, getting back in the car and laughing and holding my hand. "Peeping and creeping boot-black-winter-hat nigger."

"Laz is just Laz," I says.

"His daddy runs the funeral home but Laz ain't never gonna be run-ning shit," Snipes says, laughing hard and squeezing my hand to get me to laugh too and I laugh till his squeezing hurts and I make him let go.

"Today's Wednesday, ain't it?" Snipes says. He looks down the road, seeing his upcoming appointments in his head. "I'm free towards the end of the week. Let's get married on Friday."

"Really?"

"Friday's the day," he says, taking out his billfold. He peeks the money part open with his pointer and thumb, then he feathers the bills, counting. His one eyebrow lifts up, surprised.

"That's what you call significant," he says.

"Significant?"

"What year is it?"

" 'Sixty-three."

"And here I got sixty-three dollars in my billfold," he says smil-ing.

He pinches the bills out, folding them single-handed. He reaches over to me, lifting my housedress away from my brassiere and tucking the sixty-three dollars down between my breasts.

"Get yrself a wedding dress and some shoes and a one-way bus ticket."

"I'ma go to Jackson's Formal."

"Get something pretty. Come up to Texhoma tomorrow. We can do it Friday."

"You gonna get down on yr knee and ask me?"

"You come up tomorrow and I'll get down on my knee in front of my sister and her kids and ask you to marry me. Hell, I'll get down on both knees. Then we can do it Friday."

"How bout today you meet Aunt June and Uncle Teddy?" I says.

"Today I gotta go to Midland," he says.

"It'll only take a minute."

"I don't got a minute," he says. He looks at me. He got lips like pillows. "Have em come to Texhoma Friday. They can watch us get married. I'll meet em then."

"When they come up you gotta ask me to marry you on yr knees in front of them too," I says. "They'd feel left out if they didn't see it since you'll be asking me in front of yr sister and her kids and yr mother and dad—"

"My mother and dad won't be making it," Snipes says.

"How come?"

"They's passed," he says. He starts up the car, turning it around neatly and pulling it into the road, heading back towards Lincoln. On Friday my new name will be Mrs. Clifton Snipes.

"I was ten when Willa Mae passed," I says.

"Willa Mae who?"

"Willa Mae Beede. My mother," I says.

Snipes takes his hand off the wheel to scratch his crotch. His foot is light on the gas pedal. There's a story about my mother. All these months I been seeing Snipes, I didn't know whether or not he'd heard it. Now I can tell he has.

"They say yr mamma went into the ground with gold in her pockets," Snipes says.

"You believe that?" I says.

"I'm just telling you what they say."

"And I say Willa Mae Beede was a liar and a cheat. Getting locked up in jail every time she turned around. Always talking big and never amounting to nothing."

He takes his foot all the way off the gas to look me full in the face. We coast along. "She was your mamma, girl," Snipes says.

"Willa Mae passed and it didn't bother me none. I was glad to see her go," I says.

"How come you call her Willa Mae?"

"Willa Mae is her name," I says.

He turns his eyes back to the road and we pick up speed. We go fast. The hot air swishes through the car with all the windows down. I put my hands on the sides of my head, keeping my hair in some kind of shape.

"Willa Mae's pockets of gold ain't nothing to sneeze at," Snipes says. He sorta yells it over the loud whoosh of the air.

"Shoot, Snipes," I says. "Willa Mae Beede was the biggest liar in Texas. She didn't go into the ground with shit." I feel mad then I laugh. After a minute Snipes laughs too.

"Any jewels she had was fake," I tell him.

"It makes a good story," he says.

"A good story's all it makes."

He checks his wristwatch. We come up on the road that leads to the Crater and he pulls over.

"I gotta let you out here."

"Can't you take me all the way home?"

"I gotta get to Midland."

Sanderson's is only a mile away. I can walk.

"Penny for your thoughts," I says.

"Nothing on my mind but coffins," he says smiling, looking down the road, hands easy now, two fingers of each balanced on the wheel. "Doctor Wells is dying. I'ma talk him into getting buried in a black doctor's bag made outa oak."

"That sounds nice," I says.

His arm grazes my belly as he reaches over to open my door for me. I get out then lean through the window so he can give me some sugar. My dress gaps open. He looks quick at his sixty-three dollars.

"We getting married on Friday, Billy Beede!" Snipes hollers, taking off, driving north, waving at me as he goes.

I walk home the other way.

SNIPES

I don't know how the hell I get into these messes.

This mess I'm in now started with me needing three dollars' worth of gas and a Coke. Just goes to show.

"That's a nice car you got," she said. "What's it called?"

"It's a Galaxie."

"Like the stars and stuff?"

"It's just a Ford, girl," I said. I was on my way home. It was getting late. The man who'd sold me the gas had gone inside through the filling station and into what looked like a trailer out back. The girl was lingering.

"You like cars dontcha?" I said.

"Not really," she said.

"You wanna go for a ride?" I ast her.

"It's late," she said.

"Maybe some other time then," I said. And I went on.

But I came back the next day. Don't ask me why cause I don't know. Billy Beede got a good head of hair and a nice smile tho there's plenty of gals with that. I heard folks say her mamma died rich, but I didn't have no designs or nothing on her money. I was just headed back to see her.

"You wanna go for a ride?"

"I'm supposed to be watching the place. My aunt and uncle's getting groceries in town."

"We'll only go down the road," I said. And we went.

I thought it would be hard to get her. But it was easy. Right on the side of the road the first time and on the side of the road, every other week or so after that, whether I had business in Lincoln or not. From March until today. The first time I went slow. I told her I loved her and that she didn't need to worry about nothing cause couldn't nothing happen the first time.

She only told me a few things about herself—that she had a talent for hair and used to do hair in town. I kept my cards close to my chest too. I only talked coffins. I coulda tolt her how I got a mother and father living in Dallas. I coulda tolt her that. I coulda tolt her other things. But I wasn't wanting to let too much of my life loose cause letting yr life loose can turn a good time bad. Just goes to show, cause now the little bits of my life I done let loose at her has gone and made a mess.

Maybe Doctor Wells will go for my doctor-bag coffin. He wants to go out in style and I'll give him a good price.

I'ma have to cross Lincoln off my list. It don't bother me. Jackson's Funeral ain't never gonna buy nothing from me no way. Still.

Shit.

I don't know how I get into these messes.

LAZ JACKSON

I wished I coulda caught them doing it. If I coulda caught them doing it, then my anger woulda come up and I woulda tolt Snipes that Billy Beede belongs to me and I woulda been so mad I mighta maybe kilt him. I seen them in the car. I got all the way up to the windows without them seeing me. But they was through doing it already and when I seen them sitting there I didn't feel mad I just felt sick.

Now I can hear Billy walking in her shoes. Clop clop. Like a horse. Walking down the road. I'm laying flat on my back. Flat on the ground and right alongside the road. I got my hands acrosst my chest, I'm all laid out to rest. When she walks by she's gonna pay her respects. She'll have to.

"I'm getting married on Friday," she yells out to everybody, to no one. "Billy Beede's marrying Clifton Snipes!" It would be nice if she yelled out how she was gonna be marrying Laz Jackson.

Now I don't hear nothing. No more clopping.

I could get up but don't. Billy's on her way towards me and I'm gonna lay here till she passes by. Her man left her on the side of the road and now she's walking home. But I don't hear no more clopping. She got off the road and is walking in the dirt or she took her shoes off and her feet on the hot ground must be burning up pretty good about now.

I can smell her coming: 12 Roses Perfume, sweat, hair grease and something else. A thick smell: the smell of almost-milk. Now her smell is right on top of me. Pressing down against my smell of sweat from running from the rock Snipes threw. He hit me on the back of the head.

It hurt but it ain't bleeding. I keep my eyes shut but I know Billy's standing right above me looking.

"Whut the hell you laying there for?" Billy goes.

"I'm dead," I go.

"No you ain't," she goes.

"Am too," I go. "Laz Jackson is dead and you oughta be crying."

"If you dead how come you running yr mouth?" she goes.

I open my eyes looking up at her. In one hand she's holding her shoes, pink-colored pumps against her blue housedress. Her other hand's holding her dress tight to her leg so the wind don't lift it up.

"Your feet hurt?"

"No," she says.

"They look like they hurt," I says.

She bends down, putting her shoes back on, her eyes holding on to mines, making sure I don't look up her skinny black legs and see nothing. She stands on one leg while she puts the first shoe on, then, balancing hard, she puts on the other shoe.

"I'm getting married Friday," she says.

"To me?"

"Hells no," she says. Then she looks to Midland. "Clifton and me been planning our wedding for months now." She says it loud, like she's saying it to me and to Snipes too.

I sit up, rising from the dead. If I had me a car and was sitting in it, the way I'm sitting would be towards Midland. My car'd be faster than his, as black as his is yellow. I'd go down there and run him off the road. *Who bigged you?* I wanna ask Billy but I know who: the one she calls Clifton Snipes.

"You think yr mamma'll give me a good price on a dress?" Billy asks me.

"You gotta ask her yrself," I says.

She looks down the road, towards Midland again, then she looks towards Sanderson's filling station where her and her aunt and uncle stay at. They run the filling station and live in a mobile home out back. Sanderson's ain't theirs though, they just run it.

She starts walking, in her shoes again. Clop clop clop clop. I get up and walk after her. I seen up her smock. *Where yr panties at?* I ask her. Not out loud, just in my head.

"I was reading in the *Encyclopaedia Britannica* that there's more dead in the world than there is living," I says out loud.

"So whut," Billy says.

We come up on the station. Four hundred yards. She throws her shoulders back and lifts up her chin. Someone on the porch, her Uncle Roosevelt, is standing there with Dill Smiles. They wave at us but Billy don't wave back.

"There's more Negro in the world than there is white," I go but she ain't listening.

"I want that wedding dress your mamma's got in the window. The one with the train," she says.

"That dress is high."

"Snipes is paying for it. He gived me enough money to get any dress I want. Plus shoes."

"Mamma closes up around five," I says.

She glances up at the sky. It's after four.

"Shit," she goes and takes off running towards the filling station, as fast as her shoes and belly lets her, one hand still tight down at her hem, the other hand balled in a fist and working like a piston.

I keep walking, taking my time, looking at the sun, at the dirt, towards Midland, towards Sanderson's. My fly is buttoned wrong. I button it right. My glasses are dirty. I clean them. Without my glasses on everything is a blur like I'm standing still and the world is moving. I got six different suits. Snipes, he got one or two but don't never wear them together at the same time. He comes around every month to show my daddy his sample book and him and my daddy talk. It's always the same.

"We don't know nobody who wants to be buried in no coffin that looks like a banana," my daddy tells Snipes.

"I got an appointment with Doctor Wells over in Midland. Doctor Wells says he'd like to be buried in a doctor's bag," Snipes says. "And look here, I got Cadillacs, guitars, Egyptian styles, and this here's an airplane," Snipes goes, turning his picture pages. "I made each one myself," he says.

My daddy can't be moved. "Jackson's Funeral Home ain't the most respected in Butler County for nothing. White or black, we the most respected. You seen the sign out front. 'Established in 1926.' We'll be fifty years come 'Seventy-six," Daddy tells him.

Snipes got on a yellow shiny shirt to match his face. He's wearing a suit jacket that don't match his pants. That's his style. His shirt is dark with sweat and when my daddy turns him away he will fold up his sample book and stand outside at his car, taking a clean shirt out and tossing the sweated shirt in the trunk. I seen him do it last time he came through.

"Jackson's Funeral is gonna be fifty in twelve years," Snipes says smiling, still trying to make a sale. "That's a heritage to be proud of."

"Thirteen years," I says, correcting him. So far I ain't said nothing but that.

"You all planning for the future," Snipes continues, not embarrassed by his wrong adding. "Custom coffins is the future, I'm telling you."

"You talk like you know it all but you can't even count," I says.

"We thank you for stopping by," Daddy says, shaking his hand and Snipes goes. I know where he's headed. He's going over to see Billy Beede. She won't give me the time of day but she'd fly to the moon for Snipes. I watch him go.

Ten years ago, when I was ten years old, my mother and dad told me all the facts of life. They divided life into its two basic parts, Life and Death, and each took a part, explaining it all while we ate dinner. Mother took death, Daddy took life. They'd took the opposite parts when they'd explained it several years before to my brother Siam-Israel, but Siam-Iz went bad, so they switched around their parts when they got around to telling me. Neither of them went on too long. The whole of it was through before Mamma got up to get what was left from the night before's pecan pie.

Roosevelt's on the porch with Dill. I can see them both good now. Dill is holding a letter, working it like a fan.

"Billy oughta want to hear this letter," Dill says.

"June'll read it when Billy gets back," Roosevelt says.

"June oughta read it now," Dill says.

"She says to wait," Roosevelt says.

I stand there looking at them. I tip my hat to both. "Mr. Beede. Miz Smiles," I says.

"How do, Mr. Jackson," Roosevelt says.

"Ain't you hot in that wool hat?" Dill asks.

"I'm all right," I says.

"Billy's out back washing up. She says she's gonna pick out a wedding dress," Teddy says. Roosevelt Beede goes by Roosevelt and he goes by Teddy too.

"She marrying you, Laz?" Dill asks but Dill knows Billy ain't marrying me so instead of saying nothing I just give her the finger. She makes her hand into a gun and pretends to shoot me dead.

"Yr ma might close her shop before Billy gets there," Teddy says.

"I'll hurry home and ask Mamma to wait," I says.

"We thank you," Teddy says. And I walk on.

I got six suits. Snipes got that yellow car. I got Billy's panties, though, in my coat pocket. I move them up to my breast pocket, letting them poke out just a little, like a handkerchief.

"Oh, Laz, why was you born, why was you born, Laz?" I ask myself.

"To find Billy Beede's panties by the side of the road," I says.

JUNE FLOWERS BEEDE

I never seen Billy wash so fast. Come running up in here, standing out back, pumping water into the tin bucket.

"Get me my special soap," Billy says. That's easy for her to say, but I only got one leg. Billy's got two. I crutch inside the office, getting down on my only knee to reach a little shelf underneath the counter where she keeps her soap, her perfume, and her small tin box. All her treasures lined up there. Right underneath the shelf is where she stores her pallet every morning. The tin box got a lock on it. Billy wears the key around her neck.

When I crutch back outside, Billy got all her clothes off and is hunched over the bucket, splashing her face and armpits.

"I'ma get me that dress in the window. The one with the train," she says.

"How much it cost?" I go.

"I dunno but I'ma get it," she says.

"Don't go stealing it," I says. She stops her washing to look at me, cutting me in two with her eyes.

"Snipes gived me more than enough money," she says lathering on the soap, using too much even though she's in a hurry. The white soap against her vanilla-bean skin makes her look like a horse that's been running.

"Your mother woulda stole it," I says.

"I ain't no Willa Mae," Billy says. She lathers soap on her face then rubs it off hard with a rag. She don't favor her mother. Couldn't be more different looking. Willa Mae was light and fine featured. Billy is dark. But on the good side, Billy got a way with hair and could make a living at it if she wanted whereas Willa Mae didn't never amount to nothing.

"You went out with your Snipes and you forgot about my hair," I says.

"I'll finish it after I get my dress."

One side of my hair is nicely pressed and the other side's still wild. Billy's hair is nice on both sides.

"Your mother woulda loved to see your wedding day," I says.

"Why you gotta keep bringing her into it?" Billy says. She wipes herself down with her dirty housedress as I hand her a clean one, one of my castoffs, green and faded, but clean and with a good zipper up the front. I'm a size or two bigger than her but the dress fits her tight, especially around the middle. Willa Mae had plenty of "husbands" but weren't never really married, and now here's her one child, Billy, only sixteen with a baby inside her and no husband yet. When I was sixteen I lost my leg. I'd like a new leg, but even if we could get the money together for it, I ain't yet seen one in my color. Me and Roosevelt don't got no kids. Billy's soap smells like roses.

"The apple don't fall that far from the tree," I says, just to bring her down a notch.

"I ain't no goddamned apple," Billy says.

ROOSEVELT BEEDE

"I used to be a preacher but I lost my church. God is funny," I says.

"Sounds like you preaching now," Dill says.

"You gonna give Billy her letter?"

"She's in the back washing," Dill says. Just then Billy comes running outside. Dill waves the envelope at her.

"A letter for you," Dill says.

"Let's read it when I come back," Billy says, jumping over the two porch steps and going down the road.

Me and Dill watch her go. She left a smell of soapy roses. June is out back. I hear the bucket splash. She's watering her flower garden with Billy's wash water.

Dill holds the letter up to the sun, trying to get the news through the envelope.

"You know that letter ain't to you," I says.

"The letter's from Candy and Candy's my ma," Dill says.

"It still ain't to you," I says.

Dill's voice gets sharp. "It's addressed to Billy c/o me but in all these years these letters been coming I ain't never opened one yet," Dill says. Dill's long-legged and coffee-colored with Seminole features and soft hair cut close. Straw hat pulled down low and always wearing mud-speckled overalls and a blue work shirt and brown heavy boots. Dill's a good head taller than me and a bulldagger. I wouldn't want to fight her.

"Candy's probably just asking for payment like she always do," I says.

"Probably," Dill says.

I dip some snuff, holding out the tin to Dill after I've had mines. Dill don't dip but I offer it anyway. Dill don't never ever dip and Dill don't hardly ever drink. Willa Mae's buried in Candy's backyard so Candy writes asking for money to keep up the grave. She sends the letter to us by way of Dill. Candy's Dill's mother but she don't never write Dill nothing.

"Ma could be saying something new this time," Dill says.

"I doubt it," I says.

"You never know," Dill says.

"Sounds like you do know," I says.

"Yr saying that I opened it," Dill says. Her left arm goes stiff, with her hand making a fist. She knocked down someone with that fist once. They didn't get up for two days. My sister. But for what I can't remember.

"I'm just running my mouth, Dill, I don't mean to mean nothing," I says.

She shakes her fist free of whatever made her want to hit me.

"I coulda opened it and read it seeing as how it's partly addressed to me and I can read. But I ain't," Dill says.

"Course you ain't."

"I'll bet you on what it says in here," Dill says.

"I don't got shit to bet with," I says. It's funny but neither of us laugh.

"Let's bet you'll take up preaching again," Dill says.

I don't say nothing to that.

We sit there watching Billy turn into a speck as she hurries down the road to Jackson's Formal. Mrs. Jackson sells dresses and together with her husband Israel they run the Funeral Home too. Laz helps out. When people start they lives they ain't nothing more than specks. And when Billy came into our life, coming up the road in Dill's old truck, coming back from LaJunta and the tragedy, she weren't nothing more than a speck on the road, and then a truck, and then Dill in a truck and then Dill in a truck with little Billy. We thought Billy was gonna live with Dill like her and Willa Mae did when Willa Mae was living, but Dill didn't want Billy around no more so Billy's been living with us since she was ten.

"LaJunta, Arizona," Dill says, reading the postmark. I hold my hand out for the envelope and she hands it to me. A circle with some lines running through it and some marks and a stamp. Below that some marks that say "Miss Billy Beede c/o Dill Smiles, Lincoln, Texas." But the lines could say "Mr. John F. Kennedy, President of the United States, Warshington, D.C." for all I know. I never did learn to read. June and Billy read good though. Dill reads pretty good too.

June comes outside. Her crutch tapping the floor like someone's knocking. She looks at Dill's truck, a shiny blue Chevrolet, parked off to the side of the pumps.

"That yr new truck, Dill?" June asks.

"Bought it with pig money," Dill says.

"We could read this now," I says, fanning the envelope, "it would spark up the day."

"We'll wait," June says. "It's addressed to Billy so it's only right to wait for her."

"Like Billy gives a crap," Dill says. "She was glad when her mother passed, said so herself."

"She didn't mean it," June says.

"You and Roosevelt don't got no kids and Billy's your niece, that's how come you think that way, but I'm telling you Billy was glad when Willa passed. Billy said 'good riddance' and clapped her hands. I was there. I heard and seen it all," Dill says, retelling us the tragedy.

We sit quiet. If I could give June children I would. If June could give me children she would.

"Candy's got the grave to keep up plus she runs that motel," June says.

"How much money you think Candy's gonna want from us this time?" I ask.

"Do it matter?" Dill says. "You can't send her none nohow."

"But we always write her back polite," June says. "And Candy always finds a way to hold on."

"She don't ask me for money cause she knows I won't send her none and I won't write her back polite neither," Dill says.

"The bank's gonna take her motel one of these days," I says. I should know. I had a church, a nice church over in Tryler before me and June comed here. It was the most beautiful church you ever seen. And the bank took it.

"Ma always finds a way to hold on," Dill says.

"Plus she got Even helping out now," June says. Even is Candy's daughter. Dill's sister but by a different daddy.

"Ma always finds a way to make do," Dill says.

"How come she asking us for payment, then?" June asks.

"She's what you call resourceful," Dill says.

June says "huh" to that.

A car comes up, out-of-towners. White. I give them two dollars worth of gas.

"You got a restroom?" the lady asks.

"No, ma'am, we don't."

"We shoulda stopped at a Texaco," the man says. And they go on.

"You all should build a restroom," Dill says.

June says "huh" to that too. If we could get the money together to build a restroom June would be the one to clean it. It would be Billy's chore but Billy ain't as timely at her chores as June is, even though June only got the one leg.

"Ma asked you all for fifty dollars payment last time," Dill laughs, "this time she'll probably ask for sixty."

"Candy can ask all she wants," June says. "I got a whole dictionary full of words I can say no to her nice with."

"I know the pain of losing a structure," I says. When the bank told me they was gonna take my church I went to the bank and got down on my knees.

"I know the pain of losing a structure too," June says.

We sit there for a while. Not saying nothing. The white out-of-towners leave a cloud of brownish dust in the road.

"It's worth it, keeping on good terms with Candy, even if we can't never send her nothing," I says.

Dill picks up my thought, "You mean cause of the treasure? You mean cause Willa Mae's buried out there with her pearls and diamonds?"

"No. I was thinking more along the lines of, what with Candy being your mother and you having partly raised Billy some, that makes Candy practically family to us and we should keep on good terms with her," I says, but I am thinking about the diamonds and whatnot. I can't help it.

"Yr just thinking about the treasure," Dill says, smirking at me.

I stay quiet.

June adds her two cents. "I'm thinking all that treasure Willa Mae got in her coffin ain't doing no one no good," she says. She clumps along the porch, reaching the steps and sitting down, laying her crutch by her side. There's a blank space where her leg used to be. I ain't never seen her with two legs. When I met her she had just the one. Folks say I was smart marrying a woman with one leg cause a woman with one leg ain't never gonna run off. But I didn't marry June on account of that. June's a good woman. Today she's salty but most days she's sweet.

"What you think of Billy's Snipes fella?" Dill asks.

"We ain't met him yet," I says. "She says he stays at Texhoma. We should be going up there for the wedding."

"We should be going to LaJunta and getting Willa Mae's treasure," June says.

"Leave my sister in the ground," I says.

"I ain't saying take her out the ground," June says yelling. "I'm just saying take her treasury out the ground." Then her voice goes soft. "Just enough to get me a leg," she says.

"You got a point there," I says. I look at Dill, waiting for her say. Getting at least some of my sister's treasure has crossed my mind more than once. Dill would tell us how to get there or we could just look at a map. LaJunta's in Arizona and Candy's motel is called the Pink Flamingo. That wouldn't be no trouble. June suggested the very thing about six years ago and Dill told June that if she went treasure-hunting, she would be going against the wishes of the dead. Dill's the one who heard Willa's dying wish and Dill's the one who put Willa in the ground, so to my mind, if Dill don't give the OK and we was just to go out there and dig, it would be like stealing.

Dill speaks through her teeth. "Yr waiting for me to say go head but I ain't gonna say it," she says. "Willa Mae was proud of two things. Her pearl necklace and her diamond ring. Getting buried with them two things was her dying wish. I coulda took them, I coulda stole them from her while she was breathing her last breaths, but I weren't about to go against her dying wish. So I put her in the ground and I put her jewelry in the ground with her," Dill says, saying "jewel" and making it sound like "jurl." "Willa Mae wanted to be buried with her jewels and that's what she *still* wants," Dill says.

"How you know what Willa *still* wants?" June says.

"She ain't changing her mind once she's dead," Dill says.

"She might," June says. June reads and knows things.

"I know Willa Mae better than you and I heard her dying wish," Dill says, making a fist and bringing it down slowly on the arm of her chair. That ends that.

"Dill Smiles, you the most honest person I ever met," I says.

June says "shit" to that and gets up, with more difficulty than usual, to go clumping back inside.

"You the most honest person I know," I says again and Dill nods her head in thanks. Dill Smiles don't open no mail that ain't addressed to her and Dill Smiles don't flout no dying wishes of the dead. Dill Smiles is the most honest person I know, even if she ain't nothing but a bulldagger.

BILLY BEEDE

Mrs. Jackson stands beside me. She got a tape measure hanging around her neck and one of them red pincushions, stuck full of steel pins and shaped like a tomato, tied to her wrist. We both looking at the dress in the window, the one with the train. It cost a hundred and thirty dollars.

"How much it cost without the train?" I ask her.

"The train's on there for good," she says.

"What if it weren't?" I says. "How much would it cost if the train weren't on there for good?"

Mrs. Jackson looks at the dress then at me, sizing me with her eyes. Except for my baby-belly I'm on the narrow side. Her eyes hang on my belly and when I catch her staring, she looks through her front show window and up into the sky. It's after five o'clock. When I came up she was standing at the door waiting for me. While I was washing up, Laz had told her I was on my way. I wiped the toes of my shoes fast across the backs of my legs, left then right, to get the dirt off. She let me in then turned the "Open" sign to "Closed."

"I don't think it'll fit you," she says softly.

"It'll fit," I says. "But all I got is sixty-three dollars."

"Mr. Jackson don't like me spending all my time making these dresses then losing money by selling them cheap," she says.

"Sixty-three dollars ain't cheap," I says. I want to tell her how I'd have more money if her husband woulda bought one of Snipes' coffins and how, since her husband keeps turning my future husband away, she owes me a deal. I want to say all this but something in me tells me to stay sweet.

"It's all hand-sewn," she says. "That's not a machine-sewn dress and it's not some dress from the Sears catalogue. That there's a once-in-a-lifetime dress."

I see something in her, something I'm not sure of at first. Something my mother might call The Hole. It's like a soft spot and everybody's got one. Mother said she could see The Hole in people and then she'd know how to take them. She could see Holes all the time but I ain't never seen one. Until now. Words shape theirselves in my mouth and I start talking without thinking of what I need to say. It's like The Hole shapes the words for me and I don't got to think or nothing.

"When you got married, what'd yr dress look like?" I ask Mrs. Jackson.

The hard line of her mouth lets go a little.

"It musta been pretty," I says.

"That dress is an exact copy of my wedding dress," she says smiling. "I was fifteen. One year younger than you are now." She looks at the dress then back at me then at the dress again.

"You make your dress yrself too?" I ask.

"My mother made mine for me," Mrs. Jackson says. And then she goes quiet.

The Hole shapes more words in my mouth, all I gotta do is let them out. "Willa Mae, you know, my uh—"

"Your mother," Mrs. Jackson says, saying "mother" out loud for me.

"Yes, ma'am, well, she's passed, but she sure woulda loved to see my wedding day, seeing how she was always jilted and never lucky enough to get married herself."

We stand there quiet, both looking at the dress.

"Let's see what it looks like on you," Mrs. Jackson says. She hurries to get a stool then stands on it, pulling down the window shade. I take off my clothes while she strips the dummy. By the time she gets the dress off I'm ready. With the shade down it's dark inside her store. She can see my baby-belly but not too good. She holds the dress for me and I put my hand on her shoulder and step into it. A row of seed buttons up the back. High collar and long sleeves, blind-you white satin with lots of lace. Plus the long train with a hand loop to hold it off the floor. *Be small, baby,* I says, talking to my baby without opening my mouth. *Be small, baby, be small.*

The dress fits.

"Look at you," Mrs. Jackson says. Her voice is thick like she is about to cry but I can't tell for sure in the dim light.

I look down at my pink pumps. "I used to wear these when I worked over at Miz Montgomery's," I say. "I guess they'll do."

"Pink shoes with your wedding dress will not do," Mrs. Jackson says.

"I can't afford no nice ones," I says.

"You wear size 6?" she asks.

"Size 5," I says.

She goes to the back, walking backwards and turning her head this way and that to get a good look at me. When she's out of sight I do a slow twirl. Snipes didn't say nothing about the rings and he don't know what size I wear but I guess we'll get them when I get up there. I can't expect him to think of everything. He had his new coffins on his mind today, plus that dying old Doctor Wells.

"The baby looks like it's growing pretty good," she hollers from the back.

"Yes, ma'am," I says. No one has said nothing about the baby but I guess, since she knows I'm gonna have a husband to go with it, it's OK to mention now.

"You lucky you got such small feet," Mrs. Jackson says coming back into the main room with a shoe box. "I don't carry many shoes but I did have these."

"I don't got enough for shoes," I says.

"Try them on and hush up," she says.

I pat myself on the back for having the intelligence to wash up before I came here. Sometimes smelling good can make all the difference. Mrs. Jackson brings me a chair and I sit, trying on the shoes like a lady would. When I get them on she helps me up.

"Look at you," she murmurs.

"Do I look all right?"

"Your poor mother," she says.

"I only got sixty-three dollars," I says.

"And here it is 1963," she says.

I pick up my pocketbook, fish through it and hold the bills in my hand.

"Can you promise me something?"

"Whut?"

"Don't go telling all of Lincoln, Texas, how you got yrself a hundred-thirty-dollar dress and a pair of twenty-dollar shoes off of Mrs. Jackson for sixty-three dollars. People would accuse me of playing favorites."

"Yes, ma'am."

She takes the money from me, counting it quickly, then sticking it underneath the pincushion on her wrist. "And when I say don't tell no body I mean don't tell no body, you hear? If word gets back to Mr. Jackson, Lord today, I won't never hear the end of it."

"Yes, ma'am."

"Now turn around and style it for me," she says.

I tell the baby to stay small again. It stays small. I turn all the way around one way then around the other way.

"I look all right?"

"You as pretty as you can be," she says. "Just as pretty as you can be."

WILLA MAE BEEDE

This next song I'ma sing is a song I wrote about a man I used to know. It's called "Big Hole Blues."

My man is digging in my dirt
Digging a big hole just for me.
He's digging in my dirt
Digging a big hole just for me.
It's as long as I am tall, goes down as deep as the deep blue
    sea.

He says the hole he's digging is hole enough for two.
He says the hole he's digging is hole enough for two.
He says he'll put me down there in it
And put my boyfriend in it too.

He says he's just pulling my leg, but I got to play it safe
He says he's just pulling my leg, but I got to play it safe
I done packed up all my clothes, I'm gonna leave this big old
    holey place.

Everybody's got a Hole. Ain't nobody ever lived who don't got a Hole in them somewheres. When I say Hole you know what I'm talking about, dontcha? Soft spot, sweet spot, opening, blind spot, Itch, Gap, call it what you want but I call it a Hole. To get the best of a situation you gotta know a man's Hole. Everybody's got one, just don't everybody got one in the same place. Some got a Hole in they head. Now, you may think "Hole in the head" is just another way of saying stupid, but "Hole in the head" means more than that. It means that they got a lack and a craving for knowledge. Not just the lack, now, but the craving too. A man could have a Hole just about anywheres: in the head, in the wallet (which means he burns his money), in the pocket (which means he don't got no money to burn but would like some), in the pants, in the guts, in the stomach, in the heart. You offer a person with a Hole in the head some knowledge and they gonna be in yr pocket cause you done gived him the opportunity to taste what he craves, but if a person's got a Hole in they *heart* and you offer them knowledge, you won't be able to sway them none. A Hole-in-the-heart person craves company and kindness, not no book.

MRS. FAITH JACKSON

I've never seen a girl so happy as Billy Beede walking out my store right now with her wedding dress and them matching shoes all wrapped up in my white store box. Mr. Jackson can say what he likes but it's the formal-wear business that's about making people happy. He says the funeral business is about making people happy but I've never seen no one smiling at a funeral. He doesn't think Lincoln's got the economy to support a formal-wear store and, tell the truth, I don't turn a profit. If it weren't for people dying, we would be out on the street. But, seeing as how folks do continue to die, I can, every once in awhile, afford to sell a hundred-thirty-dollar dress and a pair of twenty-dollar shoes for sixty-three dollars. Seeing as how the Funeral Home is doing so well, and folks is always continuing to die, and Jackson's is the most respected Home, black or white, in the county, which means folks come out of their way to have us help them in their time of grief, and seeing as how Billy has her dead mother buried all the way out in Who-Knows-Where, Arizona, and seeing as how her Mr. Snipes, the man Jackson says is trash, has done right and asked her to marry him, I figure I can sell my show-case dress for the price she can afford.

Laz is gonna be broken up about it. He's had his cap set on Billy Beede for the longest. Too long, I told him when he said he'd seen her running with Snipes. Much too long, Mr. Jackson said when we all seen Billy's belly. Just cause you set your cap on someone, don't mean she'll set her cap on you.

You have to make the best of what God gives you, that's what I say.

That's how I live my life. Married Jackson when I was not but fifteen. I was in the family way, but not like Billy Beede. My Israel had already spoken for me, and my mother and dad both were living. I was showing but I could walk around this town with my head up. Not like Billy Beede: shoulders pinched together, her head hanging down like a buzzard.

Me and Israel didn't plan on getting married so early but we did. I had hoped to have a slew of girls. We had two boys. I had hoped Siam-Israel would run the Funeral Home with Israel, and Laz would be a doctor and deliver babies. That woulda dovetailed nicely, you know, cradle to grave with the funeral business we've already got. Nothing worked out like I hoped. Siam is doing time over at Huntsville and Laz, well let's just say that Laz is doing his best. Doing the best with what we got. That's the most that any of us can ask.

DILL SMILES

They call me bulldagger, dyke, lezzy, what-have-you. I like my overalls and my work boots. Let them say what they want. It don't bother me none.

I take the letter back from Teddy. We're still waiting here on his porch for Billy. She ain't come back yet.

"Billy'll be home directly," Teddy says.

I lean my chair, tipping it back to balance on the two hind legs, like a stallion rearing up. Then I right the chair and get on my feet. "I don't got no time to waste," I says.

"I ain't said nothing bout yr new truck," Teddy says quickly.

"It's a 'Sixty-two. It ain't brand-new."

"Looks like you just drove it out the factory," Teddy says.

"It's just shiny," I says. It's last year's model but the fella never drove it.

"You got all the luck, Dill."

"I do all right."

"Bet it runs good."

"I don't got no time for no jalopy."

"Course you don't," Teddy says. "A Beede would have the time but a Smiles would not."

I sit back down, taking the letter out of my front overalls pocket and resting it on my lap. We sit there quiet. Waiting.

"You gonna give me one of them new pigs you got?" Roosevelt asks.

"You can buy one, same as everybody else," I says. My good sow Jezebel farrowed last night. Got up in my bed to do it too. She's spoiled.

"Thirteen piglets and no runts. Dill Smiles oughta give Teddy Beede a free pig," Teddy says.

"Thirteen's unlucky. Why you want an unlucky pig for?"

"Thirteen ain't unlucky for you," Teddy says admiringly. "You got nothing but good luck, Dill, you got the luck of the Smiles."

"I don't got nothing like good luck."

"Yes you do," Teddy says using his greezy voice. He must really want that pig.

"I ain't arguing witchu," I says.

"Gimme a pig," Teddy go.

I shake my head no.

"Hell, Dill, I'm practically yr brother," he says.

"I ain't no goddamn Beede," I says and we both laugh.

We see a speck coming down the road. Too small and too slow for no car. It's Billy.

"You think she got her dress?" Teddy asks.

"She's Willa Mae's child," I says.

"Meaning whut?"

"Meaning by hook or crook Billy got herself a dress. Mighta got herself two or three dresses."

"Billy don't favor Willa," Teddy says.

"Billy don't favor me neither," I says.

Teddy cuts his eyes to me, getting a good look at my profile without turning his head. I'm doing the same to look at him. His pecan-colored cheek is fleshy. Gray grizzle around the chin where he ain't shaved this morning. Willa Mae told me once that I looked like an Indian nickel. Teddy's mouth opens a little. I've brought him to his limit.

"Go head, Teddy, say it," I says.

"I'm just taking a breath," he says. He coughs and puts his eyes back front. *Why the hell should Billy favor Dill Smiles?* That's what Teddy wants to say, but he wants me to give him a free pig more than he wants to give me a what for.

The Billy-speck coming down the road gets bigger.

"She's whistling," I says. We both hear it.

"Guess she got that dress," Teddy says.

"Billy don't favor Willa Mae but she's got her mother's heart and ways," I says.

"Not completely," Teddy says. "Willa Mae didn't never like to work, but Billy had that good job over at Ruthie Montgomery's."

"Billy *had* a job," I says.

"Well, Billy was doing pretty good in school," Teddy says.

"Then she quit," I remind him.

"Willa Mae was always singing her songs and flaunting herself. Billy can't even carry a tune," Teddy says.

"What you got against yr own sister?" I ask him. "What you got against Billy taking after her own mother?"

"Willa Mae ended up in the ground," Teddy says.

"We all end up in the ground," I says.

The tune Billy's whistling don't sound like a song. Just a bunch of notes and not in a steady rhythm. Then I recognize it. She's whistling around something Willa used to sing. I can't recall the words though.

"You got more luck than anybody in Texas," Teddy says.

"I've had my share of bad luck too," I says and Teddy nods cause he knows.

"Where did I come here from?" I ask him.

"Dade County, Florida," Teddy says.

"Dade County, Florida, and don't you forget it," I says.

I came here from Florida with the promise of work from Mr. Sanderson, and when I found out the work was just field work alongside the wetbacks and the no-counts, I didn't go back. I stuck it out. I worked harder than all the women and most of the men and saved up enough to start my pig business. Teddy remembers that. And when Willa Mae Beede came home to Lincoln looking to move in with Teddy, her married brother, she ended up living with me instead. Me and her was like husband and wife, almost. When Billy was born, it was me, Dill Smiles, who took care of Willa Mae and her bastard child both. And when Willa Mae left me for good that last time, it was my mother's house in LaJunta where she decided to die at. I drove out there. Billy was standing in the corner of the room like a little dark ghost. Willa Mae was dying in a bed of blood. She'd tried to get rid of her second baby and botched it. She told me she was sorry for the wrong she'd done me and that she wanted to be put in the ground with her pearl necklace and her diamond ring. I gave her my word. Then she died. I was with her. Teddy knows.

Teddy and me can see Billy good now. She's carrying a box balanced on her head and holding it with one hand, like they carry stuff over in Africa.

When Teddy Beede looks at me, he sees what I want him to see: Dill Smiles and Dill Smiles' luck, which, to Teddy's mind, springs from the bounty of Dill Smiles' fairness, which in turn, springs out of a long swamp of unlucky years that hardworking Dill Smiles has bravely lived longer than. To Teddy, because I've lived longer than my bad luck did, I'm now allowed to enjoy thirteen healthy piglets and a shiny new-looking truck. But it ain't that way at all.

I paid an undertaker to wash her body and put her in the coffin that I'd paid for out my own pocket. Before he nailed down the lid, I had a last look and took the necklace and the ring. Then me and the under-taker carried her outside and I saved a few dollars by digging the grave and burying her myself. I put her in the ground, put her jewelry in my pocket and brought Billy back here for Teddy and June to raise. When they asked after the jewels I told them the jewels was under-ground. In truth, I got Willa's diamond ring in my own pocket. The necklace of pearls she asked me to bury her with, I've been selling pearl by pearl to a fella in Dallas who don't ask no questions. The pearls are all sold but I still got the ring. My hole card. If the pigs fail again I'll have to sell it.

The luck of Dill Smiles ain't no luck at all, but compared to Teddy and June and Billy, it's like I step in shit every day.

JUNE FLOWERS BEEDE

Dear June and Roosevelt and Billy,

The past month has been what you could call very interesting. Even and me are on what Even calls "the up and up," and so I am going to surprise you this time by not asking for payment to keep up Willa Mae's grave.

If you have the time to read this letter you will soon discover what our new circumstances are all about. I hope you are not too busy. From your last letter it seemed like Texas was trying to beat Arizona as the hottest state. I hope your filling station has not run dry (ha ha) but I also hope that it has not run you ragged neither. I hope you have the time to read this because I have taken the time to write to you and it would be a shame to skip this good times letter after all the hard times letters I have sent your way.

Like so many things that come into your life, our present good luck came when we were just going about our daily business. We had not had any visitors in several days except an official from the bank in Tucson who came to inquire if we were interested in selling our land and motel. He left pretty fast when we told him no. But the banker from Tucson is hardly what I would call a visitor. The motel has been in a run-down condition for several years which is why I kept writing you all for payment. The payment would of helped. There were plenty of times that I thought I should write to my own flesh and blood, Dill Smiles, but you know as well as I do that Dill and her money are on a till death do us part basis.

On the day that turned out to be our lucky one, I was in the back working with Even who is becoming quite a horsewoman in her own right and if you ever manage to get out this way she and I will put on a show for you if Buster, that's Even's horse, is willing. We were out back working on her routines and up walks another white man in a dark suit. I thought he was another banker but, no, he was from The Rising Bird Development Corporation. They've got headquarters in Phoenix. They were hoping to build one of those big new shopping centers in the rear of our motel. It would give folks in that new housing development somewhere closer to shop. They wondered if I wanted to sell the land. There were several benefits to this. One was that our Pink Flamingo Motel would be in walking distance to a supermarket and that would be good for business. That is what came into my mind at first, the nearness of the supermarket, and then of course I thought of the money of the sale. I will not trouble you with the details of the sale but only say that we agreed to sell right away and the deal has gone through with very little trouble and I have received a fair amount of money for the sale of the five acres that was, before I sold it, the rear of our property. We still have enough yard for Buster and of course the Motel and swimming pool are untouched.

There is a matter that you might want to know about. The Rising Bird Corporation has plans to plow up and pave over what used to be my land. That is to say that they will be disturbing the place where Willa Mae is buried. It doesn't sit right with me and Even that this should happen. The little I know of Willa Mae, she was a nice person. We dare not rescue the body ourselves because of the threats against my person made by Dill Smiles. I have never wanted to mention this, but Dill Smiles told me at the time of Willa Mae's burial that if I so much as thought about disturbing Willa Mae and "stealing," as Dill put it, the jewels, that Dill would drive all the way out here and be very pleased to gun me down, her own mother.

I suggest that if you want to save Willa's remains from the fate I have mentioned above, please come out here and move her body. Even has made a lovely grave site here in the backyard, but it's time for Willa Mae to move on. Perhaps she would want to be reburied in Lincoln. If not, we have a nice cemetery in LaJunta that has welcomed John Henry Napoleon and would welcome Willa Mae Beede too.

I hope, June, that you and Roosevelt and Billy (and I am saying it like this because I know from your letters back that you, June, are reading this to the others), and so I hope, June, that you and Roosevelt and Billy do not think I have gone back on my promise by selling my land and thereby putting you all in this inconvenient situation. I hope instead that you all will be happy that I am no longer writing you asking you for upkeep money. I would send some of our recently acquired money your way but Even is still living at home and Buster, as you can imagine, is a very large mouth to keep fed.

I think you should consider resurrecting Willa Mae but of course the final decision is up to you. Again, they will begin plowing the first of the month. I hope that, because of the plowing up of the gravesite and my improved finances, that this won't be the end of our letter writing. I enjoy getting letters, especially from you all cause June uses such pretty words.

> Very Truly Yours,
> Candy and Even Napoleon

I get through reading the letter and, for a minute, nobody says nothing. Billy's standing there with her new dress held up and wanting us all to look.

"You was gonna shoot your mother?" Billy asks Dill.

"I never said nothing about shooting no one," Dill says.

Roosevelt and me are both looking at the letter. "Construction company's gonna go to work starting the first of the month and pave over her land and make a supermarket," Roosevelt says, repeating what I just read.

"We all heard the news," Dill says. "Nobody here's deaf."

I look to Billy, to see what she thinks. She's holding her dress up against herself with one hand and passing the other hand slow down over the fabric, like she's ironing out the wrinkles even though there ain't none.

"If we ever was thinking we should go get Willa Mae's body, we better go and get her now," I says. I make sure I say "body" and not "treasure."

"She's buried clear in LaJunta," Dill says.

"I know where LaJunta is," I says.

"It ain't like she's over in Fort Worth," Dill says. "LaJunta, Arizona, ain't no walking distance, now." Dill enjoys reminding us we don't got nothing but the eleven-bus, our own two feet, to get us around and she got that new-looking truck. The eleven-bus would, in my case, be the number one bus. Two feet make what looks like an eleven. One foot makes a one. When Dill came back from burying Willa Mae I went and got a map so I could see where LaJunta was.

"I know good and well where LaJunta is," I says.

"It's far," Dill says.

"We can't let Willa Mae get buried underneath some supermarket," I says.

"Arizona's near California," Roosevelt says, helping. "It may not be close like Forth Worth but LaJunta ain't the moon neither."

Dill stretches out her long legs, pushes her hat back on her head, then folds her arms across her front. "You start walking today you might get there by next year," Miss He-She-It says.

"I'ma put up my dress before it gets dirty," Billy says. She goes inside holding it up so it won't touch the floor, then places it gingerly back inside the box and slides the box underneath the counter with the rest of her things. When she comes back outside, she still got her new shoes on. They're too white to look at.

"What color are those shoes, girl?" Roosevelt asks squinting.

"White," Billy says.

"They so white they make my eyes hurt," Roosevelt says. Billy styles the shoes some, walking to and fro on the porch, holding her hand on her hip like she finally done joined the ranks of the Happenings. She sits up on the porch rail and swings her legs.

"Roosevelt's right," I says. "LaJunta ain't on the moon."

Dill stands up like she is ready to head home. "Traveling's high. It was high six years ago and it's more high now."

"We can pull some money together, can't we, Teddy?" I ask. I wait for him to tell me yes but he don't. He takes snuff and, standing, offers Dill some. Dill shakes her head and steps down a step. With Dill on the low step and Teddy on the porch they're standing eye to eye.

I want to stand up too, to make my point, but instead just plant the tip of my crutch on the porch, holding it upright with one hand, letting it help me speak the same way standing up would. "It's wrong to let Willa Mae's grave get paved over. Being in the ground is bad enough, now she gotta have a Piggly Wiggly or who knows what with all them people walking around and they shopping carts rolling around on top of her. It ain't fair is all I'm saying." I stomp my crutch, giving myself some emphasis.

"June's got a point," Teddy says.

Dill turns away from us to look at Billy. "You getting married Friday?" she asks her.

"That's right," Billy says.

"Maybe you and Snipes would like to go to LaJunta for yr honeymoon," Dill says.

"I ain't asking Snipes to go way the hell out there," Billy says.

"Watch your mouth," Roosevelt says.

"Willa Mae's getting paved over don't bother me none," Billy says.

"If you was my own child I'd slap your mouth for talking like that," I says.

"I ain't yr child," Billy says.

"I thank God you ain't," I says.

"Why you got to be so ugly?" Teddy asks her.

"I ain't being ugly," Billy says, "I'm just saying, if they gonna put a supermarket on top of her, I ain't wasting my honeymoon running out there trying to stop them."

Dill opens her mouth, running her tongue over the teeth she got left. "I guess that settles it," she says.

Me and Teddy thought, if we loved Billy the way our mothers and fathers had loved us, if we put food on the table for her and clothes on her back and took care of her when she was sick and told her to go to school and helped her as we could with her homework, that she would be ours. All ours. But she wasn't never ours no matter what we said or did. I was the first one who noticed she was pregnant. I looked at her one day. It was May. I asked her if her monthly was regular and she told me her monthly weren't none of my business. She had quit her job in March and had quit school the year before and then had the nerve to say her monthly weren't my business. Just as well she ain't my child, I guess.

Billy straightens both her legs out in front of her and points her feet, then she turns and looks me straight in the eye. "You sitting here talking about the body, but you only really interested in the treasure," she says.

"I'm talking about your own mother," I says.

Billy keeps on, not even listening to me. "I always said there weren't never no real treasure buried there nohow. It was all just a story she made up. I told you the truth of it but you stuck on believing the story," she says.

"Dill buried your mother with her jewels. The pearl necklace and the diamond ring," Roosevelt says.

"That stuff weren't no real jewels. They was fakes, wasn't they, Dill?" Billy asks.

"I ain't no expert on the subject," Dill says. "I just put it in the ground like she asked me to, I ain't no expert on its value."

"Hell, they was fakes, I'm telling you," Billy says.

"I said watch your mouth," Teddy says.

Billy closes her mouth and shuts her eyes. If she weren't pregnant she'd let loose of that porch rail she's balancing on and cover her ears with her hands. I seen her do it plenty of times. Like all Billy's got to say is cusses and she got to close up every place so the cusses won't come out. Me and Roosevelt and Dill look away. We hear Billy take a breath, but none of us look at her.

"This is Willa Mae Beede we talking about," Billy says. Then she gets down from the railing and goes inside. After a minute I can hear her rattling that tin money box she got.

"You two don't like the body getting paved over but Billy's made her peace with it," Dill says.

Billy comes to stand in the doorway. She's got a single pearl earring in her hand. It was Willa Mae's. "This is a jewel she had and it's a fake. She tolt me so when she gived it to me." She goes back inside. When she comes back out, the earring's put away and she has some money in her hand. Not much. "I could use help with my bus fare to Texhoma," she says.

Dill opens her billfold. It's made of pig leather. She made it herself. There ain't much money in it, but there's some. "I can only spare a single," Dill says. Billy takes it, but I can see by her face that she had hopes for more.

"A dollar's better than nothing," she says.

"Show yr manners," Roosevelt prompts.

Billy says thanks and Miss He-She-It tips her hat.

There was a time when Dill woulda gived Willa Mae and Billy the world. I guess that time's done passed.

ROOSEVELT BEEDE

If I had more money I'd take the time to hide it, but I don't.

"I got three quarters in my spot. They're yours if you want em," I tell Billy and she goes inside to get them. Through the filling station office, out the back door, over the two wood planks and underneath the yellow plastic tarping that makes a sort of covered bridge between the office and the house, a trailer, truth be told, going in there and squeezing past the fold-down sink to my bed. Shaking the pillow slip for a pouch. My spot.

We all see someone coming down the road.

"What's Laz doing walking down here?" Dill says.

"Maybe he wants some gas," June says.

"He better go back home and get his hearse," I says. And we all fall out laughing.

"It's good Billy's getting married," Dill says. "People were starting to talk."

"I ain't heard no one talking," June says.

Dill puts her hand in her pocket, fiddling with something. She's been fiddling in her pocket like that for years. Like a fella would touch hisself from time to time. Dill sees me watching her fiddle and stops, taking out her hand. I want to tell her that she can go head and fiddle all she wants to, it's her pocket and her privates.

"They was talking, believe me," Dill says.

Billy comes out on the porch jangling my money in her hand. It don't sound like three quarters, though.

"I found a silver dollar too," she says.

I look over at June who is looking at me. The dollar is the first and the last of June's leg money. "Let yr Uncle keep his old silver dollar for a little while longer," I tell Billy.

A smile passes over June's face before a new thought comes to her and she looks down at the floor. "We'll need that dollar for our own bus fare when we head up after you tomorrow," she says. And she's right.

Billy gives me the dollar. "I'ma pack," she says going inside. June clumps after her to help out.

Dill walks down the steps slow-like, taking one step at a time, placing one foot on the step then the other, standing still, then moving down the next step until she is standing flat on the ground.

"Guess you all won't be going to LaJunta then," Dill says.

"Don't look like it," I says.

"I shoulda brought Willa back here and buried her in the first place," Dill says, "then we wouldn't be worrying about her getting paved over."

"Water under the bridge," I says.

"Them diamonds and pearls woulda been nice."

"Whoever said you can't take it witchu didn't know my sister," I says.

"Willa Mae sure was something," Dill says, her voice going funny, sad or mad, I can't tell which.

I had plans that depended on someday getting the treasure my sister had left us. A new church maybe. But maybe not. Maybe just something easier, like a regular house instead of a trailer and land that we owned outright. I feel those plans move away from me, out of my reach. But there's something I wanted more than a house, something I didn't know I wanted more until now. My parents are buried in the colored section of the Butler County cemetery and my mind had planned, secretly, without me actually thinking about it, to lay Willa Mae alongside them. It woulda been nice, visiting them all at once.

If I was still preaching I would have something to say about the rightness of the Way and the roughness of the Road, but I just let out a heavy breath.

"How tall you, Dill?" I ask.

"Same as I was last time you wanted to know."

Dill is over six feet.

"You look like you growd."

"I'm too old to grow any taller," she says, hand in her pocket again, fiddling. "Only way I'm growing is out." But Dill is as tall as she is lean. Nothing ladylike on her at all.

"I'll tell you when the piglets get weaned," Dill says. "Then you can come by and pick one out."

"Sounds good to me," I says.

"Billy getting married'll shut a lot of folks' mouths," Dill says. She gets in her truck and goes, honking her horn at Laz as she passes him still coming down the road.

Laz shoulda been here by now. He musta stopped.

People been talking all right. June ain't heard nothing but I know better. They been talking in the beauty shop and in the barbershop, when they get they dry goods, and when they go over to Atchity's to order from Sears Roebuck. When they come by here to get gasoline, they catch a look if they're lucky, and tuck away what they seed to gnaw over together in public places, or in they own homes, after the dinner dishes have been cleared away. Old biddies talk. Men talk. Fathers and mothers talk. Billy Beede and her baby-belly and no husband. Billy Beede and Billy Beede's bad luck: father-she-ain't-never-knowd run off and dead probably; mother run wild and dead certainly; young bastard girl child tooked in by dirt-poor filling-station-running childless churchless minister Uncle and one-legged crutch-hopping Aunt. Girl growd almost to womanhood, also growd as big as a house with no ring on her finger and no man in sight. Old biddies talk and feel a ripple of delight coming from the satisfaction that they think they seed it coming. Men feel a ripple too. Snipes, Snopes, Snaps? They can't be sure but one of them seen Billy run across the road without looking for cars to jump into the fella's arms. None of them cept Laz never gived Billy the time of day but now they all rippling when they think of her and wish they gals and they wives would run across the road towards them like that. They've all seen Snipes' yellow car.

While the father and mother talk over dinner, their children, all born within the confines of marriage, hang around the doorjambs, standing just out of sight, listening. The good girls savor the details of Billy's business (her swole belly, the housedresses she wears these days that fit tight around the middle). The good boys strain to overhear and savor what, if I was in the pulpit, I would call the intimacies of unmarried intercourse. Those good boys overhear the details with pleasure but hope not to hear their own names mentioned among the lists of possible fathers. Being forced to marry a Beede, for the most part, is pretty bad.

I get an idea that June should ride with Billy tomorrow and I'll come up alone on Friday. I holler my plan into the house.

"Thanks, but Snipes wants just me to come tomorrow," Billy hollers back.

Laz has come up in the yard. He's laying between the two gas pumps with his hands acrosst his chest.

"Someone's gonna drive up and run over your head, Laz," I says.

He don't move for a minute then he gets up and comes to sit on the porch. Laz has a steady way about him. He don't walk too fast but he walks steady. Most days I wish he was the baby's daddy. Some days I'm glad he ain't.

"She gone yet?" he asks.

"She'll leave on the six A.M. bus."

He asks if he can tell her goodbye and walks inside, staying just a minute then coming back out.

"She's got a pearl earring around her neck on a string," he says.

"One of Willa Mae's fakes," I says.

"She says it'll match her wedding dress," Laz says.

"I guess it will," I says.

"I could give her a ride," Laz says. Texhoma is about four hundred miles to the north. Eight or nine hours drive.

"Billy," I says, turning my head to holler through the office and into the trailer where June's got her own hope chest open and is giving Billy things for her trip, "Laz says he'll give you a ride."

Me and Laz both sit there waiting for her to holler back.

"Good idea, Laz," I says. "I didn't want her showing up to Snipes' people, getting off a bus."

Billy hollers back, "I'd rather show up in a bus than in a hearse."

Laz leans against the porch rail. "I'll ask my father if I can drive the sedan," he says, getting up to walk back home and ask even though we both know Israel Jackson ain't gonna let Laz take the sedan nowheres.

A girl with a baby-belly and no husband makes folks sweat. Wives look sharp at they men, then, finding no fault related to the crime at hand, look even sharper at they sons. Men look at themselves and worry. They find relief in the facts of life: a lustful thought carries no spunk. Everybody looks in their doorways and nobody sees me standing there with my shotgun demanding justice. I wanted to know who I was after before I went shooting.

"Who the daddy?" I asked Billy. This was two months ago. If it had been Laz, he woulda taken responsibility already.

"No one you know," she said.

"I'll make him do right by you," I said.

"Let it alone," she said. "He loves me. It'll be all right if you just let it alone."

So I let it alone and I waited. Then I seen him come up in his yellow car and I seen her run across the road without looking.

I've always wondered what happens when you don't got a mother. Without a mother you don't get born. But after birth, what then? Over the past six years, watching Billy come up, I've had several different thoughts on the subject. Several things happen, and different people take them in different ways. Or maybe just one thing happens and it happens differently to each person it happens to. A mother helps a child learn the basics. Billy don't know the basics. Basic: *don't go opening yr legs for a man who ain't yr husband lest you wanna be called hot trash.*

People will talk. Let them talk. I can bear it. I am a Beede. I am a Beede so I can bear the people talking. I can bear pumping gas for Sanderson, I can bear losing my church. June Flowers is a Beede by marriage, not birth, so what June Flowers can bear is another story. I guess what Billy do or don't do, and what she get or don't get, is no more than just part of the Plan.

BILLY BEEDE

Lots of buses pass by Lincoln but most don't stop. Buses stop in Midland, two different ones at five A.M., one going east to Dallas and the other west all the way to Hollywood, California. An hour and a half after they go through, two more stop. One heading southeast towards Galveston and the other one, the one heading north, passes through Texhoma. The north one's the one I need to get. There's a old rattling bus that stops in front of Mr. Bub Atchity's at six every morning, except for Sunday. It'll get you to Midland in time for your connection. Miss that rattling bus and you gotta walk.

"Texhoma ain't much bigger than Lincoln," June says. She got one of her maps folded neatly to the spot.

Bub Atchity's standing in the doorway of his store wearing his nightshirt under the white doctor's coat that he puts on when he sells stuff like Scott's Emulsion. Laz says it ain't a doctor's coat but a dentist's, cause it has the buttons along the shoulder and it hangs just to his hip. Doctor or dentist's coat Mr. Atchity's wearing it over his nightshirt with his bare feet and legs poking out underneath. "I'm telling you it stops there," Atchity says.

"June's just making sure," Uncle Teddy says. I stand between them, not saying nothing.

"Come on in and buy a ticket, goddamnit," Atchity says, retreating inside to write it up.

I give Uncle Teddy my money so it'll look like he's treating.

"You be sweet up there with Snipes and his family," Uncle Teddy says, "so when yr aunt and me come up there tomorrow, we won't have to impress, we can, you know, just be ourselves." He looks at me like me being sweet will be hard, but I'm gonna be married so being sweet will come naturally.

"Tomorrow when you get there, head straight to the courthouse," I tell them. "Me and Mr. Snipes and everybody'll be waiting for you."

"That pearl earring looks nice how you're wearing it," Uncle Teddy tells me.

"We're proud of you, Billy," June says. She pets me on the shoulder and I smile. She's got a straw hat on, hiding her hair.

"I forgot to do yr hair," I says.

"I got a pretty scarf I can wear till you get to it," she says.

"You gonna buy a ticket or you gonna let me go back to bed?" Atchity hollers from inside.

"We'll take one to Texhoma. One-way, please," I say into the darkness of his store.

"I'm writing it up," Atchity yells.

"You want some candy or something?" Uncle Teddy asks me.

"I'm all right with the chicken," I say, holding up the sack, already a little greasy from the two chicken wings Aunt June fixed.

"Some candy'd go good with it," Uncle Teddy says and goes inside.

June and me stand there. June's leaning on her crutch. She lent me her own grip to put my things in. A small brown suitcase with the leather sides all cracked and sun-burned, but the clasps and handle still good. The one she had her everyday things in when her family was traveling to California. I got my own pocketbook. It's brown too.

"I'd like to get my grip back someday," Aunt June says.

"Clifton's gonna get me all new luggage for the honeymoon," I says.

"Where's he taking you?"

"It's a surprise," I says. I don't tell her he ain't mentioned the rings or the honeymoon. "He's been talking about going someplace exciting. Up to Chicago maybe," I says.

We stand there quiet, listening and watching for the bus.

"If this bus is late y'll miss yr connection," Aunt June says.

"It won't be late," I says.

The day is coming up, sunlight crawling up over Miz Montgomery's House of Style, where I had me a job once. The sun gets to the top of her place and splashes down main street, what on maps is called Sanderson Boulevard but I only ever heard one person call it that out loud. Main Bully, most people say. When Mr. Sanderson comes by every month to check up on how Uncle Teddy's pumping his gas, he says Sanderson Boulevard a lot. *We drove down Sanderson Boulevard to get here. We won't be taking Sanderson Boulevard home, though. Sanderson Boulevard used to be quite a street but now it needs repaving.* Like he's making up reasons why to say it. And Uncle Teddy nods at Mr. Sanderson and Aunt June looks blank and I want to tell Mr. Sanderson that him and his Sanderson Boulevard can go to hell but Uncle Teddy would just tell me to watch my mouth. Mother told me once that the street's named for Mr. Sanderson's father's father, Gustav Sanderson, who founded Lincoln. Mother said that Mr. Gustav coulda named the town after himself but he wanted to show how fair he was so he named his town after Abraham Lincoln instead. When me and Mother was living with Dill, we seen the younger Mr. Sanderson walking down the sidewalk. He expected us to get off the sidewalk for him and his wife but Mother told him to kiss her behind.

Aunt June shields her eyes from the sun so she can see Main Bully better, looking for the bus. From inside the store I can hear Uncle Teddy paying for my ticket and getting some candy. "Spot me a Baby Ruth," he says.

"Oh, hell," Bub Atchity goes.

"Me and June gonna buy two tickets from you tomorrow," Uncle Teddy says.

"Round-trip tickets too," June adds, turning her head to yell the news inside.

"Why don't you buy em right now?" Atchity goes.

"We ain't leaving until tomorrow morning," Teddy says.

June leans forward a little on one crutch, getting a better look down the street. The bus will come from the west, from where the night is headed, all bunched up like a dark-blue quilt.

"That bus is late," June says.

"We could go in and sit and wait," I says.

"If we inside when it comes it might not stop," June says.

I used to think that crutch under her arm hurt, but when she don't wear sleeves you can see she got a patch of skin ringing her armpit, darker than the rest. She says the dark patch is why the crutch don't hurt, even though she had the dark patch from since she was born and only lost her leg when she was my age. She says it was like something inside her knew she was gonna need that funny-looking skin.

"You leaving tomorrow you should buy yr ticket now," Atchity says. "Save yrself the inconvenience waking me up at five in the morning."

"You up anyhow," Uncle Teddy says and the two of them laugh. Mr. Atchity, he got eight children and Mrs. Atchity is still nice-looking.

When the bus pulls up, the Driver, a gangly white man with red-rimmed eyes, gets out. He stands at attention like he's in the army or something.

"Link-on!" the Driver barks. Where his shirt is open at the collar there's a sunburn. I give Aunt June a hug, surprising us both.

"Don't forget to eat," she says.

The Driver opens up the underside of the bus, like the belly of a big cow. Uncle Teddy takes my grip and slides it neatly underneath. I hold on to my dress box and food, letting Teddy give the Driver my ticket and help me get on. When I get up the bus steps and turn to wave goodbye Uncle Teddy's right behind me.

"Here go yr candy," he says, handing me the Baby Ruth he got.

He's standing on the steps and I'm standing at the Driver's seat. The Driver slams the belly-door and comes to get on but can't. Uncle Teddy's in his way.

I hold on tight to the dress box and the candy and the chicken.

Uncle Teddy turns toward the Driver, looking down on him from his steps-perch. He holds his pointer finger in the air like he's testing the wind direction or the Driver's worth.

"I don't want no Freedom Riders, now," the Driver says, looking past Uncle Teddy to get a better look at me.

"My niece is going to meet her husband up in Texhoma," Teddy says, establishing me.

The Driver's face relaxes. "All aboard!" he yells from his place in the dirt.

"Tomorrow me and my wife June'll be riding with you," Teddy says.

"Tomorrow ain't today," the Driver says, "I got a schedule to keep."

"You best sit towards the back," Uncle Teddy whispers to me.

"Yes, sir," I says.

He gives me a kiss on the forehead. Something he ain't never done. The kiss is wet. Not practiced. He gets out the bus, walking down the steps backwards. The Driver moves in quick, taking his seat. Outside, Uncle and Aunt stand together. She leans against him a little.

"Take your seat," the Driver says.

I walk back, past the empty seats up front, toward the back. Three other folks back there. All men. All sleeping.

There's an empty seat on the side of the bus that looks out over to the other side of the Main Bully, over at Miz Montgomery's side. I sit there, close to the window, looking across the double rows of seats, across the body of a sleeping man, his long legs unfolding out into the aisle, his head back and mouth open, but not snoring. Through his window I watch June and Teddy searching the windows for my face. The Driver cuts the engine on.

"This is a Mid-land-bound bus, now!" the Driver yells. No one wakes up. "Midland!" he yells again.

Uncle Teddy runs around the back of the bus, just reaching my side before we take off. He squints up his eyes, finding me through the window, and waves hard, hard enough for both him and June. I wave back at him, and as I look out across the aisle I see June, still looking for me on the other side, squinching up her eyes and leaning harder on her crutch, not seeing me but waving anyway.

We go.

East to Monahans then Odessa then Midland. In Midland the northbound bus is waiting for us. It's silver like a icebox, with the running dog painted on the side. I could try sitting in the front, where the view's better, but Uncle Teddy's right, that could cause trouble. Sitting in the back's easier and I don't mind. The driver says we gonna be in Texhoma by three. I got my dress in my lap, right where I can see it. The box is pretty and white with a red long-stemmed rose sculptured on the cover, such a nice-looking box someone might try to steal it. We head north. Stanton, Tarzan, Sparenberg, Patricia. Grandview, New Home, Lubbock, Slide. The bus fills with people. We cross the Brazos River. New Deal, Becton, Happy Union, Plainview. Mostly folks are quiet. There's a man two seats ahead, listening to country music from a yellow plastic transistor radio. *Yr cheating heart,* he sings. He's got a pretty good voice. I'm hungry. Mother tolt me that carrying a baby makes you sick all the time, but I ain't been sick yet. I think if I eat with the bus moving I might get sick so I wait until I'm too hungry to wait. Just before we hit Deaf Smith County I open the sack to just look at the chicken and end up gobbling both the wings and the Baby Ruth too, stuffing the bones and the candy wrapper in the paper sack and toeing it all under the seat in front of me. There's a little spot of grease from the sack on the top of the box and I wipe at it but it don't wipe off. Snipes ain't gonna be looking at the box. I feel underneath the lid. My dress is laying there quiet and soft. I'm lucky, cause inside, the grease didn't go through. When Snipes sees this dress he won't believe it. I bet lovemaking feels like lovemaking once yr married.

I got a seatmate, a church lady about my color, with a salt and pepper Betty Boop wig on that's pushed back on her scalp a little. She's sleeping and when we get near Wildarado she wakes up, opening her big patent leather pocketbook and looking inside.

"This yr first time on a bus?" she says to me, still looking into her pocketbook.

"No, ma'am," I says. "I rid the bus quite a few times."

"This is my first bus ride, old as I am," she says. She takes out some screaming-red lipstick and runs it across her mouth.

She sneaks a glance at my belly then tries to get a look at my left hand, to see if I got a ring or not, but I'm quick. I had my hand hiding underneath my leg from the second she woke up.

"Wildarado!" the Driver yells.

The church lady sits up straight, pulls her wig down hard on her head like it's a hat, snaps her pocketbook shut and gets off the bus without another word. Wildarado.

I got a seat to myself. I put my box onto it. It was in my lap all this time making me sweat. I fan my dress, no one sees nothing. No one's looking.

A man comes by. Looks at my empty seat. I cough, pretending I'm sick, and he moves on down a row or two.

We stop at Gomez. Not a town at all but just a small building of whitewashed cement with small windows and nothing around it but dirt and sky and sun. The sign hanging from the building has a cross on it. Must be a church. A lady gets on, big and white, coming down the aisle sideways. She's got a matching red flowered top and pants both made outa that stretch fabric, running tight acrosst her chest and behind. She's carrying a paper sack and a round red suitcase held to her wrist by a red loop. Her high-heeled gold slippers got red feathery pom-poms on them and the toes out. When she comes down the aisle the sleeping men wake up and look.

She eyes my seat and I cough. She coughs back, thinking she's funny.

"These yr things, right?" Miss Big and Flashy wants to know.

"Why would they be sitting on the seat next to me if they ain't mines?" I says.

The other people on the bus are done staring but the Driver is watching her in the rearview.

"Yr personals should be under yr seat or over yr head or in yr lap," she goes, reciting the bus rules. Mother used to say that the only thing worse than having to share a seat with someone is when you hate your seatmate before they sit down.

"Take your seats," the Driver says.

The Flashy Gal puts her hand on her hip and bigs her eyes at me. I big my eyes right back. She hands me her paper sack. The cans inside it cluddle together. She grabs up my dress box. "How bout you let Myrna put this up for you," she says.

"You already half done it," I says. My voice cuts the smile off her face but she disappears the box anyway, in the rack up top on the other side of the aisle where I can see it.

"You must have something nice in there," she says.

"A party dress," I says. "Me and my husband's going to a party."

"Myrna Carter," she says telling me her name and sticking her hand in my face. She got a row of gold bracelets halfway up to her elbows on each arm. Rings on each finger. I shake her hand but don't say nothing. She sits down. The bus takes off and we go down the road.

"Yr feet started swelling up yet?" she asks.

All anybody ever asked about in Lincoln was who's the daddy and when was I getting married. "They're a little swole," I says.

"When I was carrying Dale Junior my feet was so big I couldn't wear no kind of shoes," Myrna says, "And my chest got as big as—well it got pretty big, and it was pretty big already."

Snipes says my chest's growd some, but my brassieres still fit.

I hold my left hand out in front of me. She's looking at her chest but I wiggle my finger to get her attention. "I lost my wedding ring," I says.

"Wish I could lose mines," she says.

Billboards go by. Myrna calls out what they say as we pass.

"Stuckey's five miles! They got world-famous pecan rolls."

"I can read," I says.

"It's more fun to say it out loud, don't you think?" she asks.

I don't answer.

"Look! A place called the Double R Ranch where you can pick out yr own meat and and they'll cook it up for you."

She's like one of them tour books except she's talking. Mother used to do the same thing. I learned to read by her talking out billboards.

"Two miles off that road there's the only place in the state of Texas where you will get a fair deal on a used Cadillac," Myrna goes.

We pass more signs. She says them out loud but low under her breath. Then she nudges me hard. "Look," she says.

There's a billboard with a cowboy on it.

"I met my Dale at the rodeo," she says. Her voice goes lower, more private. "It was love but not true love. You know what I'm talking bout, dontcha?"

"Me and my husband, Clifton, we got true love," I says.

"Yr lucky," she says, "All me and Dale got is five kids."

"Five is luckier than none," I says, thinking of Teddy and June.

"Five is luckier than six," Myrna says. There's a meaning to what she's saying but I don't catch it. I'm looking out the window staring hard at the land going by and trying not to look at her big face in the reflection. She's talking to the back of my head.

"Want one?" she says. Something warm and metally touches my arm. She's pressing a beer at me. A freshly opened can of Pabst. "It's warm, but it tastes better warm," she says.

"No thanks," I says.

"If yr thinking it'll hurt yr baby, it won't," she says.

I shake my head no and she drinks it herself in long slow swigs. When she's through, half her lipstick's left on the rim.

"You gonna tell Myrna yr name?"

"Depends on whatchu gonna use it for," I says and she throws her head back and hoots.

"Keep yr voice down," a man riding towards the front says.

"Keep yr shirt on, honey," Myrna calls back. We giggle together.

"Billy Beede," I says.

"Got a nice ring to it. BB. Like a gun. Fast." She glances at my belly. "I didn't mean nothing by that," she murmurs.

"I got a husband," I says.

"Course you do. Pretty gal like you. Course you got a husband."

When we stop at Frankel City two little boys run down the street to meet the bus then stand there with they hands behind they backs just looking and grinning. When the bus takes off they throw rocks that ping ping against the sides and tires.

"If they break a window I'ma jump off this bus and whip them," Myrna says. They keep throwing rocks but they don't break nothing.

After Frankel City comes Truscott then Flagg. There ain't nothing out there but flat reddish-brown dirt and scrubby bushes and sky. And heat. There ain't no people. Some cows. No clouds. I wonder if my stomach's gonna get any bigger before tomorrow. Even if it do I'ma fit my dress. By hook or crook. I've decided but I gotta get the baby to decide too. *Don't grow no more today,* I says to it, making the words in my head then swallowing them and sending them down straight into the baby's head. *Don't grow no more today. Hold off yr growing until after the honeymoon then you can grow all you want.* The baby hears me. I can feel it hearing and listening to me, the mother, and saying yes. It's a good baby already.

"I wonder if this land round here was ever crowded," Myrna goes. "You know, if like, millions and millions of years ago this part of the world was a busy place. Sorta like Dallas, or New York City, you know. Bustling with Stone Age activities, Stone Age skyscrapers, cave people, you know, in they animal skins, hurrying hither and yon, shoulder to shoulder. You know there's a place in Mexico where they got evidence of the visits of spacemen."

"How about that," I says. Myrna's eyes are set wide apart. They're bright blue colored and she's got pasted-on lashes and lots of green eye shadow. The start of a sunburn on her cheeks. Lines from too much worrying around her mouth.

She finishes her beer, stands the empty out in the aisle and, easing off her slipper, brings the heel of her foot down on the can, making a little tin pancake. She puts the pancake in her department store shopping bag. Lots of other pancakes, red, white, and blue, in there.

She fiddles with the lever on her armrest, cocking her seat back once. Twice. A little boy in the seat behind her begins to cry.

"I'll tell you about me," she says. "It makes me feel good talking and the story's interesting so it won't hurt none." Myrna Carter's Hole is her mouth. She can talk to you or to herself. It don't matter. Some of her talking is nice, though, and she did ask about the baby.

"I can tell you the minute to the day my Dale quit loving me," she says. "I'd just had Daleen. Dale Junior, Dale-two, Dale-three, Dale-four, and Daleen. I'd just had her. And sure, I was big. I'd put on weight with each kid, so I was five times as big as I was when me and Dale locked eyes that first time. Dale ain't no Charles Atlas though, I mean, he ain't the boy who gets the sand kicked in his face, but he got a gut three times the size of mine. And there he was laughing."

She opens a beer, offering it to me. I shake my head no. She drinks.

"How come he was laughing at you?"

"Not at me. At a joke," she explains, swallowing her beer down fast and jiggling the near-empty in her hand. There's a quarter-size stain of beer on her blouse. "His brother Jimmy comes over and they're sitting around watching wrestling, you know, Saturday morning. I'm in the kitchen but I can hear what they're saying."

She got me listening to her now. Her big chest breathing smooth, her wide elastic three-snap belt coming unsnapped at the bottom. Her hair, the same red as the doodads on her shoes, is whipped high like cotton candy.

"Jimmy was telling a joke," she says, continuing, " 'How you f— a fat girl? Roll her in flour and look for the wet spot,' that was Jimmy's joke. Dale didn't have to laugh. And I'm fat and standing in the kitchen thinking, Dale, please don't laugh. And he didn't. Not right away. Then he like, leaned his chair back so he could see me watching him, fat in the kitchen and begging him with my eyes not to laugh and you know what he does?"

"He laughs," I says.

"Minute to the day, anything he felt for me was over and I knew it."

"That musta hurt," I says.

She looks me up and down. "No one ever called you fat, I'll bet," she says.

"They called me other stuff."

"I got the last laugh on Dale, though," Myrna says. Her voice turns low. Lower than when she was talking about the cowboy billboard. Like she's dragging her words behind her on a rope. "He thought he was gonna get me with kid number six. He knocked me up, but Myrna got the last laugh."

She takes two fresh cans out the bag, opening both and handing one to me. She touches her can to mines. "Cheers," she says and we drink.

"You in trouble?" she asks. Her voice is so low, so right-in-my-ear that I almost don't hear her. "If yr in trouble, I know someone who can help."

I turn to the window and sleep.

When I wake up we're stopped. There's a faded red wooden depot with a windmill water-pump in front. A small sign, plain and white with faded black letters:

Duck's Pass

Three Mexican cowboys, small and handsome in they clean just-bought duds, get on.

Myrna gives them a low whistle. She's peeling an orange with a Case knife. The skin comes off in one long spiral. She sees me looking at it and hands it to me.

"You good with dreams?" she asks and right away she starts in with the telling. "I had me a dream once that I was sleeping and my breasts fell off in the middle of the night. Both of them."

I fiddle the orange peel, squeezing the dimply skin, making it spray. She divides the orange, juice going everywhere, and gives me half.

"Had me another dream," Myrna goes on, "dreamt I made a phone call. A whole slew of numbers. Longer than just long distance. Phone rings and rings. Then the party picks up. On the other end guess who it was? It was *me*. I'd called my own self up. I knew it was me cause I could recognize my voice. But I couldn't understand what the f— I was saying, scuze my French, ha ha, it was like I was speaking in another language."

"Huh," I say.

"Got any idea what it all means?"

"Nope."

Sometimes I dream of Mother and me driving. She's got on her jewels and a fur coat. She asks me to read out the signs and I can't read none of them, or she's wearing a long evening dress, gets out the car and walks into a river. When she was living her voice was low and deep, like riding on a gravel road, but in my dreams when she talks her voice is high-pitch. I wonder if, when they pave the supermarket over, I'll still dream of her.

"I bet you got interesting dreams," Myrna says.

"I don't never dream of nothing," I says.

"Mostly I dream of my kids," Myrna says.

I eat my orange. When Laz heard I was pregnant, he got excited, like it was his even though he knew about Snipes and me. He showed me in one of his Encyclopaedias. A baby, just starting out, looks like the section of an orange. *I'm eating this orange but don't you grow none,* I says to the baby.

The bus rolls on fast. Myrna's got a slip of paper close to her chest, hiding the words from me.

"Me and Dale, we look across our kids at each other," she says. "We used to look at each other and there weren't nothing in between. Now we look at each other across our kids. Five kids. And each time we had one it was like this piece of Dale got born that I didn't even know was there." She sags back in her chair, handing me the piece of paper she's got.

"Doctor Parker, in Gomez," I says, reading.

"He's at where the bus stops. Where I got on, that's where his clinic's at," she says.

"He a friend of yours?"

"He can help you if yr in trouble," Myrna says. Her voice on the rope dragging in the dirt behind her. She tells me about how Doctor Parker is nice, how you have to spend the night, how it don't hurt, and other things.

"My husband and me ain't in trouble," I says. But she upends her last beer, not listening.

She sits straight ahead in her seat, putting both hands on her armrest and cocking herself slowly back, three times, until she's laying there almost horizontal. Her flattish belly, where her baby was once but ain't no longer cause she got the last laugh, stretches out long when she stretches out. The boy sitting behind her starts crying again.

We get to Royalty with its big gold shimmery sign right outside my window. Myrna gathers up her things quick.

"Stay sweet, Billy Beede," she says.

"You too," I says.

She walks down the aisle, fluffing herself like a Miss America would, walking down a runway. She gets off the bus and, after looking around, heads toward a taxicab.

Across from the depot there's a little piece of train trestle, rusted metal coming from nowheres and going to nowheres. The bus takes off again and the trestle disappears behind a car dealership. Mother tolt me once how when a person jumps off a bridge, on their way down, before they hit the dirt or the water or whatever, they got plenty of time to reconsider. I remember her telling me that. And I remember not believing her. Folks fall too fast.

WILLA MAE BEEDE

This song's called "Willa Mae's Blues."

My man, he loves me
He bought me a diamond ring.
My man, he loves me
He bought me a diamond ring.
Well, his wife, she found out, she says my
    pretty ring don't mean a thing.

My man, he loves me
He bought me a Cadillac car.
My man, he loves me
He bought me a Cadillac car.
Well, his wife, she seen us driving, and
    she saying we done gone too far.

She got the paper, she my man's ball and chain.
She got the paper, she my man's ball and chain.
She put her big foot down, bought me
    a ticket on the very next train.

ALBERTA SNIPES

I got Zekiel on my tit, Daniel on my knee and child number seven bout to bust out me any minute. Ruthie, Joshua, Adam and Eve, they with they daddy over in Lubbock, gone to spend money we don't got at the circus. Clifford wanted us all to go, he got real serious about it but I put my foot down cause here I am ready to drop this child. "You want me to drop this child in the middle of the circus?" I ast him, cause that's what I felt like would happen if I went. I would smell them elephants and, you know, the heavy smell they got would make me drop this child and there I'd be, having number seven not in a hospital. And after Clifford promised me seven would be born in a hospital too. "Can you hold that child inside another day?" Clifford ast me and I just had to laugh. This one ain't due till next month although you would think, looking at me, that it's overdue. If he a he, he gonna be Moses, if she a she, she gonna be Esther. "When you gonna start your work for Doctor Wells?" I ast him. There's a doctor in Midland who hired Clifford to make him a black doctor bag–style coffin and Clifford come home yesterday with a look of pride on his face that I only seen once before, when Ruthie was born. He worked all day and night, drawing and redrawing the pattern for the coffin and then this morning, all jumpy, talking about how it's Thursday and all of a sudden wanting to take us all to the circus. I tell him Thursday comes every week and the circus'll be back soon enough but Doctor Wells may drop dead tomorrow and if we don't got his coffin ready the Wells family will have to put their Doctor in a regular box. At least go pick out the wood for it or something, I tolt him, but all he wanted to do was take us all to the circus. I wasn't about to go. Not in this heat. We got a thermometer on the side of the house that says it's a hundred and two. But I let them all go on. Daniel cried at first but he can go next time. Clifford piling the children in the Ford and looking like he wanna tell me something before he goes, but just kissing me on the lips and saying how he's gonna bring me something pretty back.

It's like Zeke was born with a full set of teeth the way he pulls. Like he got fangs or something. And Moses-or-Esther always kicking.

It's around four in the afternoon when this gal, dark-skinned and on the narrow side, comes up into the yard. She just walks right through the gate towards the house. She's carrying a dirt-colored suitcase with the same color pocketbook swinging in the crook of her arm. She's carrying a big white box on her head. When she sees me on the porch she stops, setting down the suitcase and switching the box from her head to under her arm. She walks back to the gate, where we got the mailbox with the house number on it, then turns and heads at me again.

"How you doing?" I ask the girl. Esther-or-Moses kicks. Daniel shies his head away from the strange gal and Zeke bites down hard.

"I'm doing pretty good," the gal says smiling. She got a sweaty face from walking. She puts her pocketbook down next to the suitcase, and reaches her free arm up, swiping it across her temple, then licks the sweat off her upper lip with her lower one.

I figure she needs a coffin, but she don't look like she can afford one.

"You looking for Snipes?"

"Yes, ma'am."

"He ain't here right now."

"I'll wait," she says. She looks at the porch toward the long square of shade where I'm sitting. There's a rocker there, Clifford's chair, but something in me don't want her sitting in it.

"He's away all day," I tell her.

"Away doing whut?" she asks. Her hand tightens around her white box.

"You want a coffin you gonna have to come back tomorrow," I tell her. She narrow, like I said, but there's something fat about her. Something swole around her middle. I know what it is and don't want to know.

She stands on one foot, scratching her leg with the other. "Clifton tolt me to come Thursday," she says.

"His name ain't no Clifton, it's Clifford," I tell her. I switch Zeke to my other tit.

"I call him Snipes most of the time," she says.

"Call him what you want, I'm telling you he ain't here."

The gal holds her hand up to her forehead, taking the sun off her face. She got a wide nose and mouth, but pretty eyes.

"You his sister Alberta?" she asks.

I don't say nothing to that.

"He tolt me to come today," she says gently. She comes up toward the steps but I cut my eyes at her and she stops coming. Now there's a worry in her voice. "I'm getting married tomorrow," she says.

"Not to my husband you ain't," I says.

She don't move.

"Get yr narrow dusty hussy ass out my yard," I says.

She don't say nothing, but a look comes into her eyes. A look of—I'm not sure what. She walks away from the porch, with a bounce to her walking that she didn't have when she first came up here. When she gets to the gate she takes what looks like a wedding dress out that box, fishes around in her pocketbook and, before I know anything, she goes and lights the dress on fire, standing there, looking at the little flame it makes, watching it burn. Daniel moves to the edge of the porch to watch the fire too. Then, as quick as she starts it, like she done changed her mind, she stomps on the dress, putting the fire out and stuffing the dress back in the box. She yells something at me that I won't repeat and then she's gone.

Ruth, Joshua, Adam and Eve, Daniel, Ezekiel, and Esther-or-Moses. And me, Alberta, and him, Clifford. My husband is a good-looking man. What I mean is, this ain't the first time something like this has happened. I could mention it to him when he comes home, but me and him would just get to yelling and whatnot, so I ain't gonna say nothing. Hopefully he's gonna bring me home something nice, and something nice for Daniel too.

That gal had a funny look in her eye, and to burn up that dress— she's gotta be crazy.

Plus she never did say what her name was neither.

FAT JUNIOR LENOIR

She come in here about an hour ago, asking if she could use my restroom. Went in there wearing a green housedress and come out in this red-colored one. Waltzed out of here and down the street like she was going to a party. Now she's back, standing at my counter. Don't look like the party went so good.

"How much it cost to get to LaJunta?" she goes.

"You done visiting us in Texhoma?" I ask her.

"Just tell me how much it costs," she says. She looks square at me, trying to hurt me with her eyes. She got a white box with a rose on it, held tight under her arm, pocketbook and et cetera, plus a belly with a baby in it, I'd bet, and no ring on her finger neither. Looking at her makes me wanna scratch my itch.

I look through my book. "I don't got no listing for no LaJunta, Texas," I tell her.

"It's in Arizona, almost to California," she says.

I take out my other books, taking my time thumbing through the pages. I turn a page, look at her and smile. She pulls back the sides of her face, not really smiling, just aping me. She got the shape of mouth I like, nice and broad, plus a big gap tween her front teeth.

"You gonna have to go to Midland or Dallas and catch a bus going west—"

"How much?"

"Around nineteen dollars," I says.

"Shit," she says.

Alphonse Chumley, bent in two over the hard candy, stands up, looks her up and down, then bends back to the candy case.

The gal goes outside and sits in the sun.

"Whatchu want, Chumley?"

"I want a young gal who know how to cook," Chumley says.

"How bout a half pound of mints?" I says.

Me and Chumley watch the gal through the screen door. She got her face turned to the sun like a flower.

"Think she know how to cook?" Chumley says.

"Gal like that?" I says, "all a gal like that can do is burn."

"Gimme a pound of horehounds, fatso," Chumley says.

"You never get no pound of nothing," I says.

"Put it in two sacks," Chumley go. I sell him what he wants and he goes outside, making conversation with the gal, or trying to at least. He gives her the sack of cough drops but she don't give him the time of day. He walks off and she comes back inside.

"I wanna go to Gomez," she says.

"I feel sorry for LaJunta," I says. I laugh but she don't join in.

"How much to Gomez?"

"Gomez is fifty cents," I says.

"To Gomez ain't no fifty cents."

"You don't like me giving you a break?"

"Depends on what you want for it," she says.

"Gimme a smile," I says and she smiles, cheesing up her whole face, for real this time. "That'll be fifty cents to Gomez," I says writing up the ticket.

"Shit."

"Don't you got fifty cents?"

"I don't got shit," she says.

Like I said, she makes me wanna scratch my itch, so when she say she don't got the fare and only wants to go to Gomez, which ain't but an hour or so down highway 19, I tell her I'm on my way there anyhow and offer her a ride.

I got a 1958 Buick Roadmaster. It's a sky-blue four-door but the radio don't work. I'm a little on the large side so when she wants to sit in the back, I don't mind. I sing to her. I got a good voice.

"What kind of songs you like?" I ask.

"I like the radio," she says.

"I know all the hits by heart," I tell her. I sing "It's My Party" for her. When I get done with the song, I'm perspiring pretty steadily. I look in the rearview, hoping she likes me a little.

"Yr radio work?" she asks.

We ride in quiet the rest of the way.

There ain't nothing in Gomez. She tells me to pull up to this little white house with a cross on it. Like a church. She gets out my car taking her box and the rest of her things with her, and I wait even though she don't ask me to. About five minutes later she comes out. Carrying nothing but the box, just carrying it flat out in front of her like it's a white sheet cake. She gets back in the car and looks over her box at me.

"You wanna buy what's in this box?" she says.

"It's a little burnt-smelling," I says. Maybe she made a cake and cooked it too long.

"Something real nice is in it," she says, smiling, showing me her big teeth with the gap between them as wide as my little finger. I turn around in the seat as best as I can to get a better look at her. Her dress got one of them shoulder-to-shoulder necklines, and she got collarbones that poke out. Skinny. And a baby inside her and no ring.

"How much you want for yr box," I says smiling back.

"One hundred dollars."

I whistle.

"It's real nice inside," she says.

I had me a wife, Mozelle. She ran off with another fella. "One hundred dollars is about a hundred more dollars than I got, girl."

The gal is watching me. Her smile gets a little bigger. I put my hand in my lap to hide myself so she won't see nothing even though I got the feeling she knows all about what I'm thinking and all about Mozelle running out on me and all about me working in my store and eating more candy than I sell.

"You must got money," she says. "You got that nice store and you got this nice car."

I lift up and grab at my billfold, still looking at her the whole time.

"What's inside the box?" I says. I'm breathing pretty hard.

"For me to know and for you to find out," she says, smiling a little bigger. How she know I like her teeths, I don't know, but I do like them.

"I'll give you ten for the box," I says.

She holds her hand out for the money. A flat palm with long fingers and small fingernails. Dark on the skin side and light on the palm side. My hands is colored the same way but not so pronounced.

She gets out the car leaving the box on the backseat, and comes around to talk to me through my window, leaning down good and letting her dress gap a little so I can see her fronts.

"That's my husband who lives in there," she says. "You better go."

As she walks to the house I take off, watching her in the rearview as I head back home. I can't take no chances. Her fool husband who don't care enough about his pregnant wife to give her a ring might come out the house with a gun and the next thing I know, I'd be dead. I got too much to live for to be taking chances like that. Buying that box from her was chance enough. I pull over to look at what I bought and wouldn't you know it: there weren't nothing in there at all.

DR. PARKER

It's after five and my clinic's empty. Irene, who answers my phone and doubles as the nurse, has gone home. Throughout the day, my patients come in. Mexicans mostly, coming in here for vaccines and stitches. I'm the only doctor around who gives them service. I got three rows of books in my office full of their names. They pay me when they can and I'm pretty much well-liked because I treat them like people and I speak some Spanish. I'm eating my early dinner, a cheese sandwich, when the pregnant colored girl comes in.

She just stands there not saying anything. She's hasn't even closed the door. Finally she speaks.

"Myrna said you could help," she says.

I walk past her, looking out the open door. There's a light blue car waiting.

"Is that your boyfriend?"

"He's just a ride," she says.

I close the door. I try looking her in the eye but she looks around the waiting room, eyeing my shiny green cement walls and mint-color plastic chairs bolted in place to the matching floor.

"You gonna help me?" she says.

"I charge one hundred dollars," I tell her.

"I don't got nothing like that," she says.

"I'm sorry," I says, heading back to my dinner.

"Wait," she says. She takes what looks like a wedding dress out of a box, shoving the dress quickly into her suitcase then taking the empty box outside. In a minute she's back. It isn't until she's in my examining room, naked but covered to her neck with a sheet, that I got a look at how much money she had. Two fives.

"I can't help you," I tell her.

"Myrna Carter said—"

I glance at my degree on the wall. I graduated with honors. "I'm a certified medical doctor and you're five months gone," I say and leave the room.

She comes out, all dressed, a minute later. I'm sitting at my desk looking over some papers. She says she's sorry for asking me to work for cheap and puts one of her five dollar bills on my desk and has me write her a receipt. She says she will be back in a couple of days with the ninety-five.

She's got what looks like a pearl earring on a string around her neck.

"That's a nice pendant," I tell her.

"It's just a earring."

"Where's its twin?" I ask.

"Lost," she says.

Plenty of people come through my clinic needing help and short of payment. Over the years I've developed a pretty good eye for handsome jewelry.

"I'll give you ten dollars for the earring," I say.

"It ain't worth that much," she says, then she looks like she wants to kick herself, but it's too late so she goes ahead, speaking the rest of her mind. "It ain't no real pearl," she says.

"It looks real to me," I tell her. "It's worth about ten dollars."

She yanks at the string, giving me the pearl and stuffing the key that she was wearing with it into her pocketbook.

I write her out a receipt for fifteen dollars and tell her that she has to be back by the end of next week or else she'll be too far gone for me to help her. I do the best I can for people, but I'm not a baby-killer.

JUNE FLOWERS BEEDE

She left Thursday morning and by Thursday night she was back. She crept in here, not saying nothing. It was late. Me and Roosevelt was in bed.

"Someone or something's in the office," Teddy says. He whispers it to me. Most nights we sleep in our own beds. He got his bed on one side of the trailer and I got mines on the other. We both think it's more comfortable that way. Tonight I laid down in his bed. We ain't doing nothing except laying here but it's nice.

"It's a possum or a raccoon or a turtle," I says.

"That ain't no turtle. It's some fool looking for what he can steal."

"Let em steal," I says. "Don't put your life on the line for Mr. Sanderson."

We lay there breathing together. Each of our beds is underneath a window. I look out Teddy's window and see a half-slip of moon. It lights up the bed making us both look bluey.

"I'ma go see who the hell is in my store," Teddy says.

"They could have a gun and shoot you," I says. I take ahold of his hand. Pulling him back down into the bed as he goes to get up. He kisses me quick, right on the mouth, before I get a chance to close my eyes.

"You gonna miss me when I'm gone?" he asks.

"You ain't going nowheres."

"I'ma go see who the hell's in my store," he says, shaking loose of my hand and leaving the bed. He opens the trailer door yelling, scaring the robber and myself. I hurry to get up. He's already in the office with the light turned on.

"Who the hell is it?" I yell.

"It's Billy," he goes.

All I can see from the trailer is Teddy standing alone in the middle of the office. Him and Billy are talking low. Blood-to-blood talking.

"You hungry?" I yell to her.

She don't answer.

"I'm hungry," Teddy says.

"I ain't ast you, Teddy, I ast Billy."

It's quiet for a minute and then the light goes out in the office and Teddy comes back through the doorway, cross the planks and back up into the trailer.

"She's laying out her pallet," Teddy says.

"What happened?"

"She's gone to bed."

"We gonna go to Texhoma tomorrow?"

"I don't think so," Teddy says.

That was Thursday. Thursday night. Now it's Saturday morning and she's been laying on her pallet behind the counter for one whole day. Not saying nothing.

"Maybe he meant for you to come *next* Thursday," I tell her. But she turns away to look at the counter's underneath.

A customer comes inside and I stand at the cash register making change. It ain't easy. I gotta stand there and count money and be pleasant and pretend Billy ain't laying underneath the counter at my foot. When the customer's gone I talk to her.

"It ain't good for the baby you not eating and just laying there all day," I says. She don't say nothing to that, but she gives me a look that woulda cut my throat from end to end if her eyes was knives. Her Mother taught her to give looks like that, she sure didn't learn it from Teddy or me.

A car comes up. A Ford, by the sound of it. Billy hears its sound and lifts herself up to the level of the window to see what kind of Ford, maybe it's her Snipes or Snopes—we never did meet him—come to get her. It ain't. It's a dusty brown station wagon with the wooden sides and Roosevelt gives the fella full service, pumping the gas, cleaning the windows and checking the oil.

The pearl earring she had around her neck is gone.

"Where's yr pretty pearl?" I ask.

"I lost it," she says.

She lays back down on her pallet looking at the underside of the counter. When she was little and first come to live with us Willa Mae had taught her reading but not writing. If we'd put her in school right away she woulda been held back so I kept her at home for a year or so and taught her writing myself. First thing she did when she learnt to write her own name good was to cut it in the underside of the counter. She's laying on her pallet looking up at her name.

"What's sixty-three plus five plus ten?" she asks.

I'm not as quick with numbers as I am with words, so I take a minute. "Seventy-eight," I says at last.

"He'll do it for seventy-eight," she says.

"Do what?" I ask her.

She don't say.

She sits up and opens my grip, taking out that wedding dress she just bought. It's all balled up. She tucks it underneath her arm and walks straight out the office. Teddy, checking the Ford man's oil, stops to watch. When she pult the dress out it smelt funny. Like it was burnt.

MR. ISRAEL JACKSON

We got a strick policy regarding the return or refund of any merchandise we sell or rent out. Jackson's Formal and Jackson's Funeral both got strick policies. To get your money back or to get an ex-change, the merchandise in question has got to have our store tags still on it. Plus the merchandise in question can't have no signs of wear. We got policies as strick as stores in Dallas. Just because we're a business based in Lincoln, don't mean we ain't strick.

Billy Beede comes up in here and wants her money for her dress back. When the dress walked out it was a show dress, you know, one Mrs. Jackson had made for the express purpose of putting in the window and attracting business. We got all sorts of people passing through here and there's been a couple of times when Mrs. Jackson has gotten business off her show dress. Two years ago the Junior League of Amarillo was passing through on their way to Austin. They just happened to pass down Main and when one of them gals seen Mrs. Jackson's show dress, don't you know she stopped the bus and ordered herself a party gown from us. So the dress Billy Beede purchased weren't just no ordinary dress, it was a show dress and so its true value was worth much more than the price on the ticket.

I'm in the back doing the books when she comes in. She got the dress so balled up that I think she's carrying a rag or something with her. She plops it down on the counter like it was nothing. Mrs. Jackson is pressing Gloria North's baptismal outfit, so while she's surprised to see Billy, she don't think nothing of it at first.

"I need my money back," Billy go.

Mrs. Jackson comes over and spreads the dress out along the counter as best she can. Like I said, Billy'd balled it up pretty good.

"I got the shoes too," Billy says, plopping both of them down on top of the dress.

Mrs. Jackson takes the shoes off the dress, turning them upside down to look at the soles. "Shoes ain't been worn," she says softly.

"Course they ain't been worn," Billy says.

Mrs. Jackson keeps smoothing the dress out. It's a copy of the one she was wearing when her and me exchanged our vows. I peek out from the office. My younger son Laz says there is a lot of good in Billy Beede but I haven't ever seen much. He says she's got good deep down. Subterranean he calls it. Subterranean my foot. It's one of the few things Laz and me don't see eye to eye on. I got some evidence to support my point of view of her right now: Billy Beede's standing there with her arms crossed and there's a funny smell coming from the showroom, maybe it's her.

"The dress don't fit," Billy says.

Mrs. Jackson turns to look back at me, to see if I'm watching. I look down at the books. The money she logged in for the sale of that dress doesn't match what she's got in the cash register. I have to count up the figures again.

"You look so pretty in it," Mrs. Jackson says.

"I ain't gonna be needing the dress, Mrs. Jackson. I need—I need other things now," Billy says. She's talking so soft I have to listen hard to hear. She's telling my wife how that no-good Snipes didn't come through. And right then, I see a glimpse of what Laz is talking about. Billy's got that Beede luck, bless her heart. She worked for Ruthie Montgomery but they fell out and Ruthie let her go. Now she fell out with her no-good banana-coffin maker. Billy's got that Beede luck but, while I got sympathy for her, I ain't no softie like my wife.

Mrs. Jackson is looking at the sign Laz wrote out, stating our returns policy in big black lettering. The sign hangs behind the shop counter, so when she cranes her head around to reread it, she sees me watching her. I make a fist and sort of punch the air in front of me, hoping to punch the softness out of my wife.

Billy reads the sign aloud, a strong loud voice, proud of every word she reads. Then, "I ain't worn it and it's still got the tags on," she says.

"The dress looks like someone took a match to it," Mrs. Jackson mutters.

"I couldn't help it," Billy says. "You wondering what happened, ain'tcha? I'ma tell you," she says, raising her voice so I can hear without straining. "Snipes got a woman, not a wife, just some trashy thing that's crazy for him. She comed into the hotel where Snipes had got me a room and she tried to burn me up. All she got was the dress."

"Lord today," Mrs. Jackson says. I know my wife. When the good Lord comes into the conversation, my wife is seeing herself as a soldier of Jesus. She is thinking, in her mind, that if Jesus himself had run a dress shop, would he or would he not accept back into his flock the burned dress offering, which is to say that my wife is about to go soft.

I step through the doorway.

"We got a strick policy concerning returns," I says.

"I need my money back," Billy says.

"The dress is burnt," I says, standing behind Mrs. Jackson.

"I'll take half of what I paid," Billy says. She looks Mrs. Jackson in the eye and Mrs. Jackson looks down at the dress.

"I did you a good turn," Mrs. Jackson says to Billy. The two of them are quiet for a moment together. Now I know why the books aren't balancing right.

"His woman almost kilt me," Billy says softly. "Snipes wanted to marry me and his woman wanted me dead."

I look at Billy. She don't look away. She is telling a kind of truth. She is probably lying but in a crazy way she's telling a kind of truth. The crazy it-can-only-happen-to-a-Beede kind of truth. If such a thing had happened to me I woulda slunk home and not spoken about it, but here Billy is, blabbing a hard-to-believe version of her business, trying to get her money back so she can go on with her life. She needs money for the child, I guess. Still, our books ain't balancing out.

"We gotta draw the line somewheres, girl," I says.

And then, right on time, Mrs. Jackson chimes in. "We can't take back the dress, much as I want to, we can't," she says, pushing the dress towards Billy, who pushes it right back at her. My wife covers her mouth with her hands. I shove the dress at Billy who grabs it and wads it up tight, looking at us both as she's wadding it. The dress with all that lace and trim and train will only get so small. Billy stands there cramming it together with her hands, looking from me to my wife.

"Oh, goddamnit it to hell," Billy yells. Then she goes and throws the dress on the floor and walks out the store.

"I tried to help her out, " my wife says.

"She's a Beede and it can't be helped," I says.

DILL SMILES

I'm at Little Walter Little's barbershop. He can give me a good cut with his eyes closed and both hands behind his back. The kid he got working for him, Spider, gotta be watched out for.

"I don't want you cutting my hair, Spider," I says.

"I got my degree," Spider says. He yanks his neck back like it's on a rubberband, pointing the tip of his bullet head toward his diploma. "I got it framed and hanging on the wall," he says.

"And that's from The Negro Barber School of Midland, too," Little Walter says.

"It ain't like he wrote off and got it through the mail," Joe North adds.

"Whatchu know about nothing?" I says to North. North sells ladies underpants door to door. He's been this close to getting lynched more than once but he says he enjoys the work.

"You too particular wicha hair," North says.

"That's cause I got hair. If you had hair you'd be particular," I says and we all laugh.

Spider is still standing there with his towel opened out ready to swathe me up in it. He wiggles the towel, like him wiggling it at me is gonna make me get in his chair.

"I was near the head of my class," he says.

"First?" I ask.

"Three from the head," he says.

"He coulda stayed in Midland," Little Walter says. "He didn't have to come back home."

"I coulda wrote my own ticket," Spider says.

"He coulda gone to Dallas," Joe North says. Spider glances at North. Hearing his name mentioned in tandem with the city of Dallas, he stands a little straighter.

"Oh, hell," I says, going to sit in his chair and letting him swathe me.

He gets right to work and, watching him in the mirror, I'm impressed. He got the scissors snapping and the comb moving almost as good as Little Walter do.

Pastor Peoples comes in and sits in Little Walter's chair. "You going up to Warshington with us?" Little asks him but the Pastor don't say nothing. Washington, D.C., is a sore subject for Peoples.

"You got a good grade of hair, Dill," Spider says. "Sometimes good hair can trick ya."

I eye him in the mirror and he grins.

"In Midland we had all sorts of hair types to work with. All kinds of Negro hair. Mexican and white hair too," Spider says reassuring me.

"White folks sure is funny," Joe North says outa nowheres. Sometimes someone'll take him up on his favorite subject, but not today.

Little has covered the Pastor's face with a hot towel, and Pastor talks out from underneath it. "How many weeks it take you to get that diploma?" he asks.

"Weren't measured in weeks, it were measured in hours," Spider says. "Class hours, tests passed, heads trimmed, konks, plus shaving and manicures too. One hundred and fifty class hours."

"Sounds like they covered all the bases," Peoples says. His voice coming through the towel is thick with steam.

"Ain't that Billy Beede?" Little Walter says.

We all look. Billy's standing across the street, looking in the window of Ruthie Montgomery's place. *House of Style* Ruthie calls it, but it's just a beauty shop.

"Weren't she getting married?" Joe North asks me.

"Far as I know," I says.

"She don't look married to me," North says. "I can see a wedding ring at fifty yards and I don't see none on Billy Beede." The fellas all shake their heads and go quiet. Just the snapping of Spider's scissors.

Willa Mae Beede came to town on a Friday afternoon. I remember cause I was having me a particularly bad week and I was gonna celebrate by coming down here to Little Walter's and sitting in the back room with North and Walter and getting as drunk as I could on the thirty-eight cents I had. I wanted to get drunk and I wanted to look good doing it. I was gonna strut down Main Bully and then crawl back home. That was my plan anyhow. I only had one suit but I had me two ties. One was red with golden spots, the other one was a dark blue with sort of like a razzle-dazzle black strip running through it. I stood on my porch holding them both to the light. I couldn't decide which one would go best.

And there came Willa Mae Beede. No, not Willa Mae Beede yet, just a good-looking woman walking down the road. White woman, looked like. Wearing a red dress that showed off her shape. She was walking but she weren't walking like she was headed down an almost-dirt road that runs through a town that ain't on most maps, no, this woman was walking, more like what they call sashaying. Red dress, with her red purse to match just swinging on her arm, and red shoes to match all that, walking like she was walking down one of them fancy streets in the big city. Like she had someplace to go, or like she just came from someplace good, that's how she was walking. The way she was moving was something to see but what was following behind her was something else.

It wasn't just a car. It was a brand-new 1946 Bel Air. A bone-white with red, two-tone convertible, just crawling behind her. Two boys, Siam-Israel Jackson and Jimmy Montgomery, was pushing it. They had their shoulders behind the weight and they looked pleased to be straining. The woman looked like she was gonna walk all day. The boys looked like so long as she kept walking they'd keep pushing. I told myself I didn't know which I liked looking at more. All I had to my name was thirty-eight cents, but I was gonna get me that gal and her car both.

I walked through my front yard, not hurrying, choosing the red tie with the golden spots and getting it around my neck good by the time I reached the road. I let the other tie just fall in the dirt. They was like a parade and woulda passed me without stopping if I hadn't of spoke.

"Ain't nothing down that way," I says to the woman.

"There's a filling station that my brother runs," she says, smiling, turning, looking me up and down, liking what she's looking at, but not stopping her walking.

I was ready to push her car straight up into the air, all the way to the moon.

"I'll take it from here, boys," I said. And that was pretty much how we started.

Little Walter talks to the Pastor as his face steams. "You oughta go to Warshington with us, Pastor Peoples," he says. Next month there's supposed to be an organizing of some kind up there. Negroes and other Civil Rights folks will march around Washington and demand justice from President Kennedy. A few folks from here is going. Last time I heard Peoples talk about it he was sitting on the fence.

"I won't be going," Peoples says, his voice muffled by the towel.

"Dr. King's gonna be speaking," North says, but North ain't going neither.

"I done heard Dr. King speak," Peoples says.

"You just sour cause you ain't been asked to speak," Little says. Pastor says something to Little, something that sounds like "fuck you" but I can't be sure with the towel on his face.

"Suit yrself," Little says.

"I'ma head up there," Spider says.

"I'm not," I says. "Jez just had her piglets."

Little Walter takes the towel from Peoples' face and holds the mirror close. Everything about Peoples is thick. He got a thick chest and thick arms, he got a thick neck and pebbly skin from shaving. "We gotta find a way to cure me of these bumps," Peoples says, looking at his skin.

North is watching Billy out the window. "She ain't a bad girl," North says. "And Teddy and June's good people. They deserve better than what they got."

"I let Roosevelt in my pulpit once," Pastor says, pushing away the barber mirror. "Remember? I gave that Beede a chance to preach and he weren't nothing but tongue-tied."

"If you was Sanderson's grease monkey, you'd be tongue-tied too," Spider says.

"Teddy's through with preaching anyhow," I says.

"Still, Billy deserves better," North presses.

"Why don't you marry her?" Spider says.

"My ass is engaged," North says. "You marry her."

"Naw," Spider says, squinting his eyes and leaning in close as he clips around the right side of my head. "Billy Beede ain't my type."

"Teddy should take his gun and go visit that fool, Snoops," Little Walter tells me.

"Snipes," Spider says, correcting.

"Teddy don't got no gun," I says.

"You got a gun, Smiles," Peoples says.

"You gonna take a gun up to Warshington?" North asks Little.

"I'm putting my .32 under the seat," Little says.

"I could lend my gun to Teddy and he could go up there and visit Snoops," I says.

"Snipes," Spider says.

"You could go up there and visit that no-count yrself," North says.

"I ain't getting mixed up in no Beede business," I says. Then I say my next words before they can think them. "I've been mixed up with enough Beedes to last me my lifetime," I says.

Pastor Peoples thicks up his face. He will stand for me living in his town and sitting in this barbershop but that's about it.

"Willa Mae weren't constant in no kind of way," North says quietly.

"Except for being constantly wild," Little adds.

"If Willa Mae was my woman—" Spider starts to say, but Joe North looks at him and he shuts up.

We go quiet. Just the sounds of the scissors going around our heads.

Willa Mae went and visited Blackwell County where most of the Beede family stays at. There was wall-to-wall Beedes down there, she said. Not like up here where mentioning Beede will quickly turn into a conversation about Teddy or Willa Mae or Billy. There just ain't more Beedes to mention so the conversation don't got but so many places to go. And if the talk turns to Willa Mae and men are present then, if theys like Little or Peoples or North and actually heard Willa tell my business, or if they was like Spider, too young to be in on such things yet, they all know what was said. They all remember or remember being told how Willa Mae went and bellowed through the streets that I weren't no man. Probably because Dill Smiles didn't make enough money quick enough. Probably because Willa Mae was good-looking and hard to satisfy and Dill Smiles raised pigs. At first, it just came down to a woman's word against a man's word. Her word against mine. All the men in the world have been called non-men at some time or another by their woman. But, as time went on, I did get the looks and there were whispers. When I'd come into Little's for a haircut, men would notice that I never asked for a shave. They noticed I never went whoring with them and, even in the summer heat, I keep on my shirt. Over the years they all put two and two together. But it remains unspoken. North and me hunt together. I am the better shot. When two of Little's heifers got the hoof rot, it was me who cured them from it. For most of the people in Lincoln, the way I carry myself and the work I do and the clothes I got and the money I earn keeps their respect. I don't ask more from them than that.

"You Billy Beede's father figure," Joe North says to me. "You oughta go visit Snopes."

"Snipes," Little Walter says.

"Billy Beede ain't my child," I says, putting my face into a mask of frustration and regret, but behind the regrets I'm smiling, glad North is suggesting that I could father anything.

Across the street, Billy cups both hands to the beauty shop window.

"If I go to Snoops with my gun I'll shoot him," I says.

"We'd visit you in the jail," Spider says.

Joe North starts laughing. Cause if North went anywheres near the jail they'd put him in it. "Speak for yrself, Spider, I ain't visiting shit," he says.

"If I go shoot at Snipes, I'll kill him dead," I says. "He'll be shaking hands with the devil."

"Dill Smiles, you's a violent hell of a bitch," North laughs and Walter Little holds the razor away from the Pastor's neck so we can all laugh good and hard and the Pastor won't get his throat slit.

WILLA MAE BEEDE

Hey everybody, wontcha gather round
Roll up yr sidewalks
Lay yr red carpet down
Cause I'm here.
This gal is here.
This town, it's all mine,
I'm the gal with the shine, and I'm here.

Lie to yr woman, leave yr best girl
I'm dripping with diamonds, I'm studded with pearls
And I'm here.
This gal is here.
Get up, rise and shine, if yr ready now's the time
Look who's here.

If it's dry, it'll rain, if it's flooding, it'll stop.
We'll light up the dark, we'll drink till we drop.
The mountains'll move, we'll paint this town red,
And, if I'm feeling like it, I might even wake the dead
Cause I'm here.
This gal is here.
This town, it's all mine
Willa Mae's right on time
Yeah, I'm here.

MRS. RUTHIE MONTGOMERY

My hands are shaking pretty bad today. I hold on to the chair-back and they quiet down but when I raise them up over Miz Addie's head, they start shaking again.

"Yr doing fine," Addie says, seeing my shaking in the mirror.

"I got it pretty bad today," I says.

"Must be Jimmy's day or Spencer's," Addie says.

"Spencer's," I says. I can't meet Addie's eyes in the mirror when I speak my husband's name. I am lying and me and Addie both know it but she is my only customer and on a Saturday too, when my House of Style used to be thick with business. When my son Jimmy got kilt my hands started shaking and when Spencer died they shook more. But only on they birth or death days. Now my hands shake all the time. My only customer gives me an excuse and I take it. "Me and Spence woulda been married forty-two years today," I lie. Addie knows we was married at Christmas. She was my maid of honor, but she lets what I say stand.

"I'm gonna walk out of here looking like a million dollars, and I'm gonna take myself right over to Penelope Lincoln's and tell her she is wasting her good time and money going all the way to Midland to get her hair done," Addie says.

"I could use the business," I says. I hold my breath, slowly moving the comb through Addie's hair, parting it into sections that are almost even.

"Just a touch-up, Ruthie."

"I can see that."

"I was just saying."

"I ain't blind, Addie," I says.

She goes quiet and I get to work, lining a quick smear of grease around her forehead, ears, and nape. Tilda Gonzales, mumbling to herself and pushing a broom, passes behind us.

"Tilda ain't right in the head," I says, loud enough for Tilda to hear. Her husband hears too. He sits in the back spending his free Saturdays watching his wife work, making sure she don't cheat on him while she's cleaning for me.

"Tilda's a good worker," Addie says.

"Least she don't cost much," I says.

Addie sits up straight in her chair, watching closely as I run my finger over her new growth, the nappy part that needs relaxing.

"Yr hair grows fast," I says. I set my timer and start laying in the Dixie Peach.

"Walter is all excited about that trip to Warshington, but I don't know," Addie says.

"You all gonna make history," I says. I wish I was going but I don't got no car and Addie and Walter ain't invited me to ride with them. Penelope and Velma Lincoln are going too, but I wouldn't ride with them if they asked. Addie and Walter invited Pastor and Carla Peoples. If they don't go maybe I'll get asked. I set the timer and start in, smearing on a wide patch of Dixie Peach.

"Warshington, D.C., got all that humidity," Addie says.

"They shoulda took that into account when they planned the March," I says. "Seems to me, when they planned that March, they shoulda thought about how all that water was gonna be hanging in the air."

"They was thinking about marching to the Capitol," Addie says. "The Capitol's in Warshington."

"Then, when they thought about where they was putting the Capitol, they shoulda thought about the weather too," I says.

"It ain't until next month so I'll be able to get another touch-up before we go," Addie says.

Someone's looking in the window. My heart gets glad thinking it's a customer. It ain't.

"That's Billy Beede standing out there," Addie says.

"She can stand out there all she wants."

The bell hanging on the back of the door clinkles. Billy comes inside. Me and Addie and Tilda and Tilda's husband all look at her. She looks at us. She hovers up front, near the cash register while Tilda wipes it down.

"Hey, Tilda," she goes.

"Gutmarny," Tilda says speaking her Spanish-English.

"Tilda!" Mr. Gonzales calls at her, and Tilda hurries towards him with her broom and her rags, cleaning up back there even though she already cleaned it.

My hands start shaking again. I grab ahold of the big tub of relaxer, but they keep shaking.

"I ain't hiring," I says.

"I'm just standing here," Billy says.

My hands won't quiet. I only got a half hour to finish putting the relaxer on before I got to wash it out. My hands are worse than they was the last time Addie was in here. That time I burned her scalp.

Billy can see my hands shaking and the egg timer's hands moving and the relaxer already started. She crosses behind the cash register, taking her old smock off the nail where it's hanging and putting it on. When she quit working for me she threw the smock down and walked out. It stayed there on the floor for a whole week. I wasn't about to pick it up. I just let it lay there. Customers coming in had to step over it. Then the customers stopped coming cause Billy weren't here and they liked her, but they liked me too so they weren't about to go down to Sanderson's filling station and let Billy do they hair between the gas pumps. They went to Midland.

Tilda picked the smock up one day. I told her she could wear it but she didn't want to. It still had Billy's name on it then. Not no more.

Billy stands there buttoning the smock's top two buttons and leaves the rest open cause, as loose as it is, it won't close up over that fatherless baby she's carrying. She comes to stand next to me, taking over Addie's head without asking my permission. I go over to the cash register and sit down.

"I can't pay you no top dollar like you think you worth," I tell her.

"I'm just helping out," she says.

Addie is sitting back in her chair with her eyes closed, letting Billy work without worrying about how it'll come out.

"I can't pay you nothing," I says.

"I'll give you a good tip," Addie says smiling softly, "and I'll tell the ladies you're back."

"I ain't rehired her," I says.

"Don't look a gift horse in the mouth," Addie tells me.

Billy don't say nothing. She just keeps working, her hands moving quickly over Addie's head, putting on just the right amount of relaxer, her eyes, glancing at the timer, making sure everything's going right.

"Thought you was gone to get married," I says.

Billy don't take her eyes from her work. "I changed my mind," she says.

Tilda comes back up front, nodding and smiling at Billy as she passes her. She picks up her cleaning where she left off.

"You got a real talent for hair," Addie says to Billy. "You ought to go to beauty school."

"I might do that," Billy says.

Things between me and Billy was going good. Business was good too, until Miss Billy Beede thought she should be getting top dollar and maybe some day even have her name alongside of mines on my sign out front. She put her foot down and I tolt her to get stepping. And that was the end of that. But things used to be good. When she first came to work for me, after the first week, I went and bought a smock for her with my own money and I took the time myself to embroider her name on it like I got my name on mines. Swirl letters with gold thread. *"Billy."* When she quit I ripped the stitching out. Now she's standing up in here working her hair magic just like she used to do. But on her smock, where her name used to be, all that's left there now is a swirl pattern of little holes.

BILLY BEEDE

$$
\begin{array}{rl}
& 10 \text{ from selling the empty box} \\
- & 5 \text{ to Parker} \\
- & 5 \text{ bus home and dinner in Midland} \\
\hline
& 0 \\
+ & 5 \text{ deposit to Parker} \\
+ & 10 \text{ earring to Parker} \\
+ & 63 \text{ dress} \\
\hline
& 78
\end{array}
$$

He woulda done it for seventy-eight dollars. I coulda got a ride up there for free to save the bus fare. Dill coulda rode me or Laz even, in his nasty hearse, and I coulda got that doctor to do it for seventy-eight dollars. The five deposit and the ten from the earring plus the sixty-three back from the dress woulda made seventy-eight and I coulda begged him to do it for that much. Seventy-eight is on this side of a hundred, I woulda tolt him and he woulda done it and then I woulda been rid of goddamn Snipes and everything about him. And the next time Snipes come through here he would see me and my belly would be smooth without the baby and he would be like, where'd the baby go, and I would tell him and he would look sad and I would say, serves you right, you two-timing-married-already yellow-bitch's bastard, and you just put that in yr pipe and smoke it, you and yr fat red-drawers-wearing-bitch-wife both. Seventy-eight dollars woulda done it but could Miz

Jackson take her dress back? No. Hell, I wouldn't of took that dress back neither. I shoulda lit Snipes' house on fire instead of my dress. That woulda been smart.

"Whatchu thinking about, Billy?" Miz Addie asks me. She can see me in the mirror. I got my forehead frowned up.

"I'm thinking about beauty school," I says.

"There are some fine schools in Dallas you could attend," she says. "I could write you a recommendation."

"Schools in Dallas is high," I says.

Miz Addie cuts her eyes into the mirror, looking to see what Miz Ruthie is doing, if she should keep talking to me or if she should be quiet. We're all right, though. Miz Montgomery's got her nose deep in the latest *Jet*.

"I'll get Walter to write you a recommendation too," she says whispering. "Me and him could help you out with the tuition and maybe you could get a scholarship." She moves her head, full of her ideas for me, getting excited.

"Hold still," I tell her, "we're almost through." I got ten minutes left on the timer, then I'll let it work for a few, not leaving it on too long. If you leave it on too long the hair'll break. To wash it out, I'll walk her back to the sink.

"Think it over," Miz Addie says holding very still and whispering.

"Yes, ma'am," I tell her.

Miz Addie said she would give me a big tip. Maybe two dollars. If I tell her I've decided on beauty school and that I'm starting up a kind of bank account for it she may give me three or four dollars. Maybe even five. And then Miz Ruthie would have to pay me something, seeing as how I'm doing all this work. The relaxing and the washing, plus the set and the comb-out. She'll have to give me something for this. Miz Addie will tell her to give me something. Maybe a dollar or two or Miz Addie could just, when she's leaving the shop and goes to the cash register to pay, put the money straight into my hand, not giving it to Miz Ruthie at all, but just give the ten dollars it costs straight to me.

With that ten plus the five dollars' tip I would have fifteen. The fifteen with the five deposit along with the pearl money makes thirty. Maybe he would do it for thirty. Probably not.

"It would be nice if Miz Penelope and them knew I was working today," I says.

"I ain't hired you," Miz Ruthie says from her magazine.

"But here I am working," I says.

"I'll tell them tomorrow at church," Miz Addie says.

I reset the timer and step back watching her head, watching the relaxer work. You got to watch it close cause it works slow, underneath the pink crème, uncrinkling the hair and making it flat. My mother used to press her hair. She had her own pressing comb and would sit in the kitchen with the comb heating over the gas stove, pressing her hair herself. When I got old enough I helped. Then I would do it for her all by myself. The first time I seen relaxer, Dill did Mother's head in the backyard. Dill callt it a konk and it stunk. Mamma's hair came out so smooth I thought it was a wig at first then I thought it was magic.

I wash out Miz Addie's hair then set it. She likes the tiny rollers. I work slowly, reminding her how good I am at what I do, rolling her thin hair tight but not so tight it'll hurt, giving her a good head of thick curls that I'll comb out neat and ladylike, making her look as churchy as she is. If I do a good job she'll tell everybody come Sunday morning, but if I do a great job, making her hair so smooth and shiny that she won't believe it's her own, if I make her look that good, then she'll go home and get on the telephone or she could go to the phone that's by the cash register and call up Miz Penelope and Miz Velma and them right this very afternoon, and then, before she leaves the shop, all of them could be coming in here, standing in lines and crowding into the seats, pushing ladylike but pushing just the same for they chance to get they hair done by the one and only Billy Beede. Even Miz Ruthie, stingy as she is, says I got "hair magic." I'll be working on two or three heads at once. Miz Penelope got hair like an Indian so all she would want is a wash and set, but she don't like her gray showing so I would suggest a rinse and she would agree. That would be six or seven dollars plus the tip. Her sister Velma got hair like mines, but she's old-fashioned and still likes the pressing comb and I can get all the way down to the scalp without the head feeling it and she knows it, and that would be, with the tip, about nine dollars. I would get fifteen or sixteen dollars from the two of them, plus, with the money from Miz Addie: thirty-one. Put that with the twenty I already put down and that'd be fifty-one. I'd have fifty-one total. Then Marla Simms plus Miss Neetra Charles and Poochie Daniels and them, they like my bouffants and hell, even Mrs. Jackson, let bygones be gone by the wayside, I'd offer to do her hair for free and maybe then she'd take back the dress and I'd be set. Even if she don't take back the dress I could still get at least sixty by the end of the day and they'd look good for Sunday and I'd head straight up to Gomez. That doctor said be back within the week and I'd walk in there on Monday morning and lay my money down and he'd help me like he promised and then I'd be done with Snipes. Shit.

"Yr rolling me a little too tight, Billy," Miz Addie goes. Miz Ruthie cranes her neck to see.

"I was just thinking," I says, rolling gentler and smiling, "Church sure would be a more beautiful event tomorrow if Billy Beede could work her magic on the ladies today."

"I'll see what I can do," Miz Addie says, bending her chin to her chest and letting me curl up the back.

It's a whole hour since Miz Addie went. She paid the cost up front, putting what was really my ten dollars right into Miz Ruthie's hands. She got change for a five and gived me two. No one else is come in yet. Just me and Miz Ruthie sitting here. Tilda, finished cleaning everything, is mopping her way out the back door. Her husband's still sitting in the back room surrounded by the professional-size tubs of Dixie Peach no-lye relaxer. His hands is neatly folded in his lap, his small brown eyes watching his wife swish the mop back and forth across the white linoleum squares.

"Where please is your library?" Tilda mumbles to herself.

"We don't got no library," Miz Ruthie says.

"She's just practicing," I says. Tilda goes quiet and we sit there in the heat. Miz Ruthie got a big floor fan but it broke two days before I quit and she still ain't got it fixed.

"Everyone's going to Midland to get they hair done these days," Miz Ruthie says.

"They'll be in here in a minute," I says. "They'll come streaming in for business, just you wait."

"I ain't waiting all day."

"Miz Addie said she'd send them," I says. If she sends everybody she knows, I could make the money I need today and ride up to Gomez in a taxicab.

"Miz Addie didn't say she would send nobody," Miz Ruthie says. "All Addie said is that she would see what she could do."

"You and her is friends," I says.

"Addie probably went home and took a nap," Miz Ruthie says.

I watch Mr. Gonzales watch Tilda. Snipes never looked at me like that. There is a worry and a longing in Mr. Gonzales' eyes, like, if he was to stop looking at Tilda she would disappear and then turn up again in some other man's arms. Tilda and him got something. I thought I had something with Snipes. He stuck me with this baby, but I'ma get the last laugh on that. Shit. All that time I was calling him Clifton and his name was Clifford.

Tilda finishes mopping. She sets her cleaning things near the back screen door and her and him go through the alley and come around to the front where Miz Ruthie's got they money waiting. Tilda don't know much English but she knows not to walk across the floor once it's mopped and she knows how to get a man who she can have true love with.

Tilda and Gonzales go. A few folks walk by but no one comes in.

"I can't pay you today," Miz Ruthie tells me. "Next week, when I get ahead, I'll pay you then."

"Shit."

"That's the best I can do," she says. Her hands shake. She holds them together to stop them but they keep shaking. The floor dries. I walk through the shop, prop the back screen open with a cement block and sit in the doorway. There's a little alley back here, just unpaved dirt and nothing across the way but cans and boxes of trash from the beauty shop and the other stores. The air feels good. Today I made two dollars. I fish it out my smock, count it, put it back. I could get that doctor to help me for forty. Maybe thirty. His office smelled of bleach, like Miz Ruthie's floor smells now. His floors were green-fleck cement, like the floors at school only those was brown. A row of pale green plastic chairs, bolted to each other and to the floor, made a ring around the room. Myrna Carter said when Doctor Parker helps you, it don't hurt none and he lets you spend the night in a little room in the back and gives you chicken soup out of a can for dinner and your stomach would be flat and your worries would be over. When we was at Miz Candy Napoleon's, Mother went and tried to help herself. She said she could help herself and it wouldn't cost us nothing. She said she knew just what to do. She used a wire. She went into the toilet of the room we was staying in, Room 33, the one on the end, and she went in there and then come out and lay in the bed. I asked her where the baby went and she said it weren't gone yet but it would be soon. She said it didn't hurt at all and she'd be up and we'd be in California, picking fruit right off the trees in the morning. I asked her again if the baby was gone yet and she said she didn't know so I kept asking her. Miz Napoleon would come to check on us and Mother had the room door locked and would yell that we was OK and to let her rest. She didn't know what Mother was up to. Mother told me to go and ask Miz Napoleon to call Dill and have Dill come visit. Her voice was so light when she told me, that when I went and asked Miz Candy for what Mother wanted, I talked in the same light voice. Dill showed up and that was that.

What happened to Mother couldn't happen to me if I go to a doctor who's got a white jacket and a doctor-diploma and a green shiny floor smelling of bleach. And if that doctor took ten dollars for one pearl then he must think the pearl's real. He might take it to a jeweler so I gotta get the rest of the money together before he does. Or maybe the pearl is real. And if the earring pearl's real then the rest could be too. Ten dollars for one pearl. There was plenty of pearls on Mother's necklace. All I need is ten. Ten times ten gives a hundred. Anybody knows that.

Laz comes walking down the alley. He stops across the way and turns his back to me like he's looking at the piles of trash.

"What the hell you want?" I says.

"I heard you was back, I didn't believe it, though," he says. Something near his head flashes in my eyes. He's got a mirror, held up, and he's watching me without turning around to look me in the face.

"I didn't feel like getting married to no Snipes," I says.

"What you gonna do instead?"

"I dunno," I says. He puts the mirror in his pocket and turns around. Two years ago he asked me to ride with him in his hearse and I went. The whole time we rode, he didn't say nothing. I talked about this and that, how much I didn't care for school, how I was gonna move to California someday and get me a swimming pool, I was just talking, just saying words to fill up space. Laz stopped the hearse. We'd rode all the way to Lake Thomas.

"I would like to do it witchu," he said. He was looking at the water, not at me.

"I don't wanna do it witchu," I said. And he drove me home.

Laz crosses the alley to stand near me, stopping when my eyes tell him he's come too close. "Where's yr pearl?" he asks.

"I sold it for ten bucks," I says. Laz whistles.

"You ain't marrying Snipes?"

"I said I didn't feel like it."

"Who you gonna marry instead of Snipes?"

"I got better plans," I says. I give him a look that makes him quit eyeballing me.

"Like whut?" he asks.

"Whatchu think of Willa Mae getting buried with diamonds and pearls?" I ask him.

"For her to know and for you to find out, I guess," Laz says.

"I'm going to LaJunta," I says. "I'ma get the bus fare together and I'ma go get me Willa Mae's treasure."

"Want a ride?"

"Hells no."

Laz takes the mirror out his pocket, catching the sun with it, lighting up part of the beauty shop wall and then flicking the light in my face. "How come you don't call her 'Mother' is what I'd like to know," Laz says.

"That's just how we had it," I says. My words come out flat, like I'm talking about how hot it is. Laz stands there flicking his mirror and kicking dirt but I don't pay him no mind and after a little while he leaves.

Miz Ruthie comes out of the doorway to stand behind me.

"You got a job here if you want it," she says.

"I'll be back next Saturday," I says, getting up, walking down the alley towards home. I can see myself working next Saturday. I'll go get the treasure then head to Doctor Parker's and then, when I step off the bus back here from Gomez, I'll get right to work. Miz Ruthie will have my smock waiting for me. It'll have my name sewed back on it and the buttons'll all close up cause my belly will be smooth again. If they ask where the baby went I'll say I lost it, then I'll burst into tears. But I gotta go to LaJunta first. I'll get my bus fare together and head out tomorrow.

ROOSEVELT BEEDE

The sun comes up in back of our mobile home. If you want to see it, though, you got to go out in the yard cause we don't got no windows on that side. Sunset is different. The sun climbs up over the mobile home and over the filling station and then slides down along Main Bully, straight down it, like the road in the summertime was a canal, to set where the road ends, at the edge of Butler County. Me and June's sitting on the porch watching it. The sunset is so bright we don't see Billy walking up until she's almost on the porch.

"You ain't been over at Mrs. Jackson's all this time have you?" June asks.

"Nope."

"She took yr dress back?" I ask her.

"Nope."

June touches her hand to the scarf she's wearing cause Billy still ain't finished her hair.

"I'll get to it right now," Billy says. She goes in the back to turn on the stove.

"Where she been all this time?" June asks me.

"Dunno," I says.

We both turn, not wanting to miss the sun disappear down the road. Maybe cause Tryler, where we had the church, is west of here.

"Goodbye," June says, talking to the sun.

I hold my hand up, waving. Another day past. Another day spent working at Sanderson's. I can't complain too much, though. We got a roof over our heads and that's more than most got.

Billy turns the porch light on and comes back outside. The metal comb is hot. She stands behind June, taking the head rag off, parting her hair, and getting to work.

"I'm going to LaJunta," Billy says, her hands moving steady over June's hair.

Me and June both catch our breath. "What for?" June asks.

"Whatchu think for?"

"Don't get smart," I says.

Billy touches her hand to the comb. It's gone cold. She heads back to the stove to reheat it.

"I didn't hear her right," I says.

"Me neither," June says.

"I'll ask her again," I says.

"Let her finish my hair first," June says.

In two quick combs, Billy turns June's bangs to straight. She goes back to put the comb away and then comes out on the porch with us to sit.

"Yr gonna bring your mother back home?" June asks.

"Willa Mae can stay where she's at, all I'm gonna go get is the treasure she left me," Billy says.

Me and June trade looks.

Billy's sitting on the porch counting her money. Her head, neatly combed, is in my arm's reach. I hold out my hand and lay it on her hair, not petting her exactly, but not hitting her neither. She looks up at me.

"Miz Ruthie gave me my job back too," she says smiling.

"She better pay you top dollar cause you deserve it," June says.

"We gonna work it out," Billy says, turning back to her money. She's got what looks like about two dollars. June said Billy was talking about someone helping us for seventy-eight dollars. Maybe it was bus fare she was talking about.

"Bus fare'll be high, going all the way out to LaJunta," June says.

There's worry in her voice cause of the high price but there's a pleasure in her voice too: Billy is finally going to get that treasure. I'm not sure what to think. June takes Candy's letter out her apron pocket, squinting at the words in the fading light. I don't got to look at the letter. I remember what it read.

"Candy says they start cementing over the land on the first of the month. That's this coming Thursday," I says.

"I know that," Billy says, scraping her money together and putting it in her tin box. She don't ask for my silver dollar and I don't offer it. I wish she'd say something about bringing her mother home.

She goes inside, coming back out with her sweater on, and goes walking down the road without another word.

"I feel wrong about this," I says to June.

"Let her go," June says.

"You think she's headed there right now?" I ask.

"It's too far for even a Beede to walk," June says.

I feel wrong and then the wrong feeling presses up against the rock and the hard place that the rest of me is pressed against, and Billy's going to get the treasure and not Willa's body, like everything else, becomes bearable. There's lots of families I coulda been born into, families with more luck, or more money, but being a Beede means being able to bear the unbearable, so I guess I would rather be a Beede than be anybody else in all the world.

BILLY BEEDE

I'm standing on Dill's porch thinking of how I can get her to lend me my bus fare.

"Whatchu want?" Dill says.

"Just visiting," I says.

"What for?" Dill says.

"Can't I just say hello?"

"Yr Willa Mae's child," Dill goes, coming to the screen and standing there but not letting me in. "I better nail down the furniture and lock up the pigs."

I put my hands on my belly, hiding it. "I don't favor no Willa Mae," I says.

Dill don't speak.

"I got my job back at Miz Ruthie's," I says.

"You coulda gone into the pig business with me," Dill says, "I taught you everything I know, now look at you." Dill used to say she was a graduate of the Pig Institute of America which was just the day-to-day work of the breeding, buying, feeding and slaughtering of them. When me and Mother lived with Dill, Dill wanted me to have an honest trade, so she taught me the bacon-types from the lard-types, how to tell a Berkshire from a Chester White, why a Duroc is better than a Hampshire, that Yorkshires are the longest length and the most popular. Dill taught me how to build a good pen and how to check the fences every morning for holes and dig-outs. She taught me how to ring they noses, and why not to ring the boars cause they might hurt the females when they mate. Dill read to me from the Dictionary of Diseases. Abscesses, Anemia, Baby Pig Scours, Cholera, Dysentery, and Lice. Mange, Rickets, and Worms. I helped her with the slaughtering. I was getting pretty good at it.

"Jez farrow in her pen?" I asks.

"Her babies was born in the back room, same as you was," Dill says.

"I'd like to see them," I says.

Dill opens the screen door, leading me to where the pigs are. They're right in Dill's bed. Jezebel raises her head, eyeing us, while we stand in the doorway.

"It's just me, girl," Dill says softly and Jez lays her head back down.

We stand there, watching the piglets suckle. They stink more than I remember but I ain't gonna tell Dill that.

"Jez don't shit where she sleeps," Dill says proudly. "And she cleans up after her litter."

"I guess you didn't have the heart to move em out yr bed," I says.

"Heart, hell," Dill says. "You try touching them piglets Jez'll bite yr arm off."

The room is quiet, just the one bulb hanging overhead and the steady sucking. If my baby was gonna get born it would suck like the piglets do, but it's a Snipes and Snipes got to go.

"You was just like that," Dill says to me. "Yr mother used to say that you about sucked the life out of her."

"She seemed pretty alive to me," I says and we both laugh, longer than the joke calls for. I know when I stop laughing I'm gonna have to ask Dill for money and I ain't ready to get to that yet.

From my height, there ain't no looking Dill in the eye. I used to think, when I was real little, that I was gonna be tall like her. Then Mother sat me down and said how babies was made and how my daddy, Son Walker, was broad featured and short statured.

"You never come round here no more," Dill says.

"You said you don't like my company."

Dill shrugs her shoulders to that.

"Whatchu gonna name the piggies?" I ask her.

"You was the one who always named them, not me."

"It helped me tell them apart."

"I can tell the difference between the piglets without giving them names," Dill says. "Besides, these are all headed to market and I ain't never seen no use in naming something that's just gonna die."

She cocks her head toward me, taking a step out the doorway where we's both standing, to look me up and down. My hands naturally go to my belly again, like my hands can hide the baby-ness of it.

"You ain't named it have you?" she says.

"Nope."

"Yr gonna get rid of it?" Dill asks.

"That's right."

"Yr yr mother's daughter," Dill says.

"If I had the baby, I'd just be greasing Snipes' ass."

"And you figure you greased him enough already."

"That's right."

I lift my hands to fan away the heat of the hallway, even though there's a breeze blowing through. Dill's got a regular house with a bedroom, a hallway, and a indoor toilet. Windows at each end of the hall, so air can travel through on hot days and, should a tornado touch down, the house would stand some kind of a chance. But even with the breeze coming through, the pig smell makes my throat tight.

"I'm going to LaJunta," I says.

Dill's face goes blank like she don't know what LaJunta I'm talking bout or like she knows what LaJunta but she don't got no idea why I'd be saying I'ma go out there.

"I'ma get Willa Mae's treasure," I says. "I'ma go out there on the bus and dig up—you know, her remains and such, and get the treasure. She woulda wanted me to have it, seeing as how I'm in need. I'll use the money to get rid of this," I say fanning my hands around my belly, imagining my stomach smooth and empty again. I keep talking, telling Dill about Doctor Parker and his green cement floors and how he bought the earring and how ten times ten is a hundred. The air is hot. I fan my hands around my belly and then flap them a little under my arms and wipe my hand across my mouth and then underneath my chin.

"Hot," Dill says.

"You ain't sweating," I says.

"I ain't gone begging to Dill Smiles," she says.

"Anything you lend me I'll pay back," I says.

"I don't got nothing to lend."

"Yr doing well for yrself."

"You know how much my pigs cost me before they bring anything in?" she says. "You want me to show you my books?"

"I just need twenty dollars," I says.

"I'll show you my books," Dill says and we go down the hall to the sitting room where she got a desk with a roll-down top. She takes out her big ring of keys and unlocks one of the drawers.

"I just figured cause you got that new truck and all—"

"Look at these figures," she says, sticking the book in front of me. Rows and rows of numbers and names of sows, numbers of piglets per litter, prices of things bought and sold.

"I could make it if you lent me ten dollars," I says. "That would pay for the bus one way, the treasure would pay for my way back, and I'd carry a spade with me so I wouldn't have to buy one when I got there."

"I'll be selling the piglets in about six weeks," she says. "Some are already spoke for."

"They're gonna cement the ground on Thursday," I says.

"Course, I won't get as much money for them as I hoped," Dill says, thinking all about her pigs and not listening to me. "Yr uncle wants a piglet, and he can't pay. That's gonna cost me."

"Willa Mae wouldn't of wanted me to have this Snipes baby," I says.

"That's likely," Dill says.

"She woulda wanted to help me out."

"Who knows," Dill says, her face going blank.

"Me getting the treasure would help," I says.

"Ten times ten is a hundred," Dill says.

"That's the plan I'm thinking," I says.

Dill looks in her book, reading down the rows of figures and talks like the words she's saying is written down.

"If yr mother had wanted you to have her pearl necklace and her diamond ring she woulda gived them to you before she died," Dill says.

"She didn't know she was dying."

"She laid there breathing her last breaths and when she passed you clapped yr hands together and said 'good riddance.'" Dill says.

"I was talking about that baby she didn't want, not about her."

"That's what you say now, but I heard you with my own ears. You was thinking what I was thinking. And I was glad to see her go," Dill says. She turns the pages of her book like I'm not there. "You figure you just gonna waltz out there and dig her up and get rich."

"I need the money."

"She wanted to take her jewelry with her and it's bad luck to go against the wishes of the dead, ain't it?"

"Maybe not," I says.

I look at Dill who has looked up from her book to stare at me. She got a face shaped like a skull with skin, blacker than mine, stretched over it tight. Mother said that Dill, even though she weren't really a man, was the most handsome man she'd ever met. But Dill weren't never handsome to me.

Dill crosses the room and sits in her big yellow-covered recliner, flipping through the pages of her accounts book. I stand by her desk, not moving. She closes her book and closes her eyes, leaning her head back, her long body folded in half by the chair.

"I sleep here cause Jez got the bed," she says. "It ain't bad, sleeping in a chair."

Her ring of keys is on her desk. One of them keys is to her new truck.

"I can't loan you bus fare. You should stay here, have the Snipes baby and make the best of it," Dill says advising.

I cross the room as quiet as possible, opening the screen door and gulping in the night air. The air loosens up the pig smell.

"I'ma go to LaJunta and get that treasure," I says.

Dill don't say nothing for a minute. It's like she's looking at me through her closed eyelids. I go out on the porch, letting the screen door slam behind me.

"Suit yrself," Dill yells through the screen. "Suit yr goddamn knocked-up self."

DILL SMILES

I miss her. Willa Mae. Much as I hated her. Much as I was glad to see her dead. Much as every shovelful of dirt I dug up for her grave made me smile, much as I enjoyed that fool Nestor, the undertaker with his bundle of measuring strings, pulling a string from her head to her foot and glancing at his wife who would say "got it," then a string measuring her thickness, lingering a little too long around the body so that while I didn't say nothing, I didn't think it was my place to say nothing, I didn't think it was my place to say, "You undertaking fool, get your dirty string from round her breasts," his wife coughed and he eased the string off. Then folding her arms to her chest and a string to measure her hips.

"We got a coffin that'll fit her," Nestor goes.

"Praise God for that," his wife says. "On account of the heat," she adds. They had the coffin delivered by the end of the day. The wife washed the body and he watched. He drained the stomach and she watched. A plot at the cemetery cost more money than I had so Ma said it was OK for me to bury Willa right on her land. I dug the grave myself. I dug it myself and every shovelful of dirt made me smile. Willa Mae Beede was finally dead. And I was glad.

Folks in Lincoln heard I buried her and sorta stepped back from me after that. I became the one who had buried Willa Mae Beede. I became someone who had dug a grave and lowered their woman down into it. When a person do something like that, who knows what else they gonna do. Don't start nothing with Dill Smiles. Dill Smiles'll kill you with a look. Stuff like that, that's how the talk went for a while and I didn't mind. I mighta kilt her if she hadn't run off. I was gonna kill Son, but he ran off before I could get around to it.

His name was Son. Son Walker. Billy's daddy. The first man Willa ran around on me with but not the last. She met him in the jail in Lubbock and he drove her home to me then he stayed for a week. He had three trunks full of clothes. They'd go at it night and day. Then one day he drove off and she walked around the house like she was gonna die.

"Where you think he's at, Dill?" she would ask me.

"You got to put him out yr mind," I said.

"You think he loves me?" she asked. I didn't say nothing to that, I just leaned more over my calculations books. There was, as there'd been the year before, more loss than profits.

I'm sitting here in my chair. One lamp on in this room and another one down the hall where Jez and her piglets are. Billy walked out the house slamming the door just like Willa used to leave. Before Billy was born, she would leave by herself, going all the way to Brownsville and calling me to wire her money cause her car had four flats. I took the bus down, fixed the flats myself and we'd drive back together. Then she got put in the Lubbock jail for drinking and cursing. When she came home from Lubbock, she had a man called Son Walker driving her car. He drove the car, Willa, and me right into the ground.

In my mind Willa's standing in my front yard, wearing her tight red dress. She says her car's broke and I look under the hood then turn the key. It starts.

"You got a way with automobiles," she says.

"Yes, ma'am," I says. I don't tell that her car didn't have nothing wrong with it, that it was just overheated. We go driving. Driving all day long and in my bed at my house that night.

"You love me, Dill?" she wants to know.

"Hells no," I says.

I put her in the ground cause she asked me to. And she asked me to bury her with her favorite things. Her ring and necklace. But I didn't. I took them and I weren't wrong to take them. I took them and I sold the pearls one by one, for a hell of a lot more than ten dollars a piece, to keep myself afloat and I weren't wrong to sell them. And when I need to sell the ring, I'll sell it. Until then, I'll keep it in my pocket. And I'm not wrong to keep it in my pocket. Willa owed me the right to sell the necklace and she will owe me the right, when I need it, to cash in the ring. The bitch ran around on me and disrespected me in the street. The way I see it, me taking the fast-running, no-count, trifling bitch's goods is only fair. Still. I miss her.

LAZ JACKSON

I walk around at night cause I get my best thinking done when I'm walking in the dark. Also in the dark, there's people in they houses with they lights on and I walk by sometimes looking in, seeing what I can see. I see them eating dinner, or listening to the radio or watching the TV. Sometimes I see them at it. There's no one on the road most nights, except cars, going by fast, with they lights blaring in my face. Tonight, just past Dill's, there's someone.

"Halt, who goes there?" I says, trying to sound like Errol Flynn do in the pictures.

"It's me," Billy says. "You out peeping and creeping?"

"I'm just walking. People keep they lights on, it ain't my fault," I says.

Billy got something shiny and jingling in her hand. I hear it jingle and look towards it but she hides her hand behind her back before I can see.

"Whatchu doing out walking?" I ask her.

"I was over to see Dill. She got new piglets."

"Thought you was going to LaJunta."

"Tomorrow on the bus," she says.

"The bus don't run Sunday," I says.

"I know that," she says, but I can tell she'd forgot.

I look her straight in the eyes and she looks down at the ground. "Snipes weren't worth yr time," I says.

"I ain't studying no Snipes," she says. Her voice is just a little sad.

She looks down the road towards the filling station. There's one light on, the big sign that says Sanderson's Gas. She walks away from me backwards so I can't see what she got hidden behind her. I follow her and we walk down the side of the road like that. Her walking backwards and me walking forwards, in her face.

"If the moon wasn't out I wouldn't be able to even see you," she says.

"You as black as I am," I says.

"No I'm not," she says.

We keep walking.

"I'm twenty years old and I'll inherit my father's business," I says.

"So whut," she says.

"Let's you and me get married," I says. I wanted the words to come out sounding more debonair, but they didn't. I stand there, but she keeps walking, she don't stop. I ain't never asked nobody to marry me before and the words are hanging in the air like a clothesline between us. The line is getting longer and longer. I start walking again, kind of trotting to catch up.

"You hear what I said?" I go, not wanting to resay it.

"I heard you," she says. She turns her heel, almost tripping, then getting her balance back quick.

"I can be yr baby's daddy," I says.

"My baby don't need no daddy," she says. Her voice sounds mean but her face is smiling. I don't know how come she's smiling but I smile with her. She stops walking.

"You know what I need? I need me some money."

"You need a husband looks like to me."

"I need money."

"How much?"

"One hundred dollars," she says. She rests one hand on her belly and rocks back and forth on her heels.

"Thought you was gonna go get yr treasure," I says.

"I am but that'll take time. Gimme the hundred and I'll pay you back."

"Whatchu need a hundred dollars for?"

She's quiet, still rocking back and forth. The moon makes her face look like patent leather. "I can't tell what for," Billy says.

I take a step forward, towards her. Letting her breath get close to my breath, like she is breathing in the air that I'm breathing out.

"I give you the money what'll you give me?" I ask her. I fish in my pocket like I'm gonna pull out the cash.

She just laughs. "You scrounging in your pocket, hell Laz, you don't got no money on you."

"I do so."

"Yr folks won't let you carry money cause you eat it," she says.

Once some tough boys wanted my wallet. I ate a five instead of giving it up. I guess I'll never live that down. "I'm my own bank," I says.

She laughs and starts walking again. I don't walk. The line of words hanging between us gets longer and longer and sags.

"You marry me, I'll get the money for you," I say, yelling now.

"I got other plans," Billy says, laughing and walking away.

I stand there watching her go. Watching the light that says Sanderson's. Not turning to walk home until I figure she's safely reached the filling station, got inside the office, and taken out her pallet from underneath the counter. She tells herself the plan she's got is a good plan, and then she goes to bed.

JUNE FLOWERS BEEDE

Me and Teddy are sitting in the dark of the office when she comes in.

"I'm leaving in the morning," she says, taking out her pallet and fixing it.

"How much Dill give you?" Teddy asks.

"Plenty for bus fare," she says, laying down behind the counter so we, sitting in our two chairs, can't see her.

I poke Teddy in the side with my elbow, getting him to ask again.

"How much is bus fare?" he says.

"Dill gived me thirty dollars," Billy says.

"I stand corrected," I say.

"Yr Aunt June spent the evening cussing out Dill Smiles," Teddy laughs.

"I was calling her every name in the book. Now I stand corrected," I says. I would stand up, to truly be standing and corrected, but I figure they know what I'm talking about without me getting out of my chair.

"I'm leaving in the morning, and I'll be back by Wednesday," Billy says. It's like she's a haint, talking from her pallet underneath the counter where we can't see her, her voice rising up out of what looks like the cash register.

I give Teddy another poke in the side.

"I don't want you traveling alone," Teddy says.

"I'll be all right," she says.

"It's one thing for you to be going just to Texhoma. Going all the way to LaJunta, Arizona, is a whole nother story," I says.

"It's just a bus," Billy says.

"This is 1963," Teddy says. "It ain't safe you going all the way out there all by yrself."

"I'll be fine," Billy says. "Willa Mae and me used to go all over, just us two."

"It ain't safe," I says. "Especially with the baby."

"You don't want me going?" Billy says. Now she's raised herself up, just her head over the countertop.

"We're going with you," Teddy says. "Me and June both."

"We'll use the money Dill gived you for bus fare. One-way tickets all around. We'll cash in the treasure to pay our way back home," I says.

"You got it all worked out," Billy says.

"All sorts of things can happen these days to a young girl on the road," Teddy says. "Just the other day Aunt June read in the paper where that gal down in Corpus—"

"I'm heading out at four," Billy says.

"Bus don't leave on Sunday," I says.

"Be ready at four A.M.," Billy says and ducks her head back down underneath the counter and goes to bed.

Teddy and I call good night to her, but she don't answer. It's like her head hit the pallet and she went to sleep.

Teddy gets up and rubs his knees. "I'ma go tell Gonzales. They can watch the place until we get back," he says.

"Sanderson's coming on Wednesday for his inspection," I says, reminding Teddy of what he don't need to be reminded of. When Mr. Sanderson drives up once a month from Austin, everything is spit-polish and me and Teddy stand like army soldiers and Sanderson walks back and forth with his great granddaddy's riding crop underneath his arm and looks everything over. Then him and Teddy go over the month's receipts. Then Mr. Sanderson and Teddy go out onto the porch and Sanderson smokes one of his fancy cigars and Teddy dips his snuff and Billy goes to get some ice and I bring out tall glasses of lemonade. If everything's square, Sanderson gives us the privilege of pumping his gas for another month. He likes to go month to month. It keeps things at a certain level of responsibility, he says. Keeps me and Teddy walking on eggs, I say, though if Sanderson kicked us out, I don't know what we'd do or where we'd go.

"We'll be back in plenty of time for that Sanderson," Teddy says smiling. "It takes a day to get there and a day to get back and it ain't gonna take but a few hours to dig."

He goes out into the dark, a quarter of a mile down the road from us, to wake up Mr. Gonzales. Inside the filling station office it's dark, but outside it's darker. Inside there's something, although there ain't much. Outside there's nothing, or everything. Behind the counter Billy snores. Haw Hee Haw Hee Haw Hee Haw.

ROOSEVELT BEEDE

Me and June's standing on the porch in the morning dark. We got one suitcase, neatly packed, between us. A change of shirt for me, a clean dress for June. You leave town you never know who y'll meet. June got her big patent leather pocketbook, a gift I gived her when us two'd been married ten years, stuffed with peppermints and those heavy paper napkins she likes.

"I got my map of Texas and I got my map of New Mexico and I got my map of Arizona too," June says.

"Billy said be ready at four," I says squinting into the dark.

"It's four and we're ready," June says.

I turn around to look through the screen door at Gonzales and his wife and they three children, all washed and ironed, with wet hair neatly combed. Gonzales and the two older sons got on Sunday shirts buttoned to the collar. The wife and the little girl got on frilly dresses, like what you'd wear to a party and they hair's in braids with the ends tied with ribbons.

June watches me watching Gonzales. "We'll be back by Tuesday at the latest," she says. She reaches her free hand out and, finding my hand, gives it a squeeze.

"He wants to run this filling station," I says.

"We'll be back in plenty of time," she says. "Gonzales wanna run a filling station he gonna have to run one someplace else."

"Whatchu got underneath yr arm?"

"Just my crutch."

"Looks like a book," I says.

"It ain't nothing," June says.

"Looks like your map of the world," I says.

"You never know," she says.

"We only going to LaJunta," I says.

"You never know," she says. She turns a little bit so I can't see the book. Figuring if I can't see it no more, I won't think about it no more. My wife has brung her favorite thing and she is ashamed for bringing it. Cause she ain't brung it thinking we gonna travel the world, she has brung it thinking there's a chance we ain't coming back.

"Where the hell's Billy at?" she mutters.

"Maybe she left without us."

"Bus don't run Sunday."

"Maybe she's paying Laz to drive us," I says and we both laugh.

At least Billy won't be traveling alone. It ain't safe out there for a Negro gal. It's 1963 and a Negro life is cheap. The life of a Negro man is cheap. The life of a Negro woman is cheaper. The price of everything is always going up though, so could be that the price of a Negro life too will get high. Maybe the price'll rise to reach the value of the cost we brought in slavery times. Not this year though. Not the next. Maybe by nineteen hundred and seventy. Maybe by nineteen hundred and eighty or nineteen hundred and ninety the price will go up. Maybe by the year two thousand, but surely, the world will end by then.

The life of a Negro gal is cheap. The life of a Negro gal with a baby in her belly and no ring on her finger is cheaper. Standing here in the dark morning of the porch, looking down the road into the dark I can see the real reason why I want to accompany my niece. Her safety, yes, but something worse than her safety. Something in me tells me that my niece that I have clothed and fed for these six years might just go out there and find that treasure and she won't never come back. I am going for selfish reasons. June is selfish too, but she's also coming along cause she likes to ride.

"We'll be able to visit family along the way," I say. "Estelle, Big Walter, and they boy Homer; Blood and Precious, Cornelius and them wives he got."

"Family's nice," June says.

I look at my wife and she looks away from me, searching the darkness for Billy. Her family is in California. We don't got no kids between us. She is missing more than a leg, or I am missing more than a wife who is missing a leg. Sometimes I think June's full of children she's just keeping inside her and not letting them out. Sometimes she probably thinks the same of me.

Truck lights come bobbing up the road. Gonzales comes out figuring the truck wants gas.

"I'll fill this one," I says and he nods but stands beside me with his hands in his pockets like he owns the place. But the place ain't his yet and ain't never gonna be his.

The truck comes up fast, throwing dirt and gravel as it turns into the yard alongside the pumps.

The truck is Dill's. Billy's at the wheel.

She leans over and opens the passenger door.

"Get the hell in if yr coming," she yells. Her hair is a little wild, like she been fighting.

"Dill lent you her truck?" June asks, moving as quick as she can down the steps. I give her a boost helping her up, tossing our things in the back and getting in beside her.

Billy takes off, leaping back onto the road before I get the door closed good. On the porch, Gonzales and his family don't even got time to wave.

BILLY BEEDE

We're heading west. In a little while the sun's gonna come up right behind us. It'll rise that way till we get where we're headed, then it'll come up in our faces all the way back.

Aunt June sits in the middle and Uncle Teddy by the door. Both of them brought they spades. Uncle Teddy's long-handled one, throwed in the back with their suitcase and my things. Aunt June's got her little trowel, the one she works on her rosebush with, on her lap.

They both look out the window but they can't see nothing yet. Teddy glances at June's trowel. The digging point is turned towards her stomach. He takes it from her, turns the digging point towards the dashboard, then gives it back to her. She smiles.

"It's Sunday," I say. "We gonna be back by Tuesday. We'll have Tuesday night to get the place ready for Mr. Sanderson."

"We're gonna need help digging," Uncle Teddy says.

"We can dig it all by ourselves," I says.

"Candy and Even can help and I'll do what I can," Aunt June says, flicking the dirt from her trowel.

Behind us, the sky glows pink. Enough light to see by. June takes out one of her maps, holding it up close to her face, reading.

"Estelle and Big Walter stay in Pecos," Uncle Teddy says.

"That's on the way," June says. She takes out a pencil, licks the tip and draws the best circle she can around Pecos. The road is bumps so the circle she draws is bumpy too. I hold my arms straight out to keep the wheel steady.

"They got their son Homer. Maybe Big Walter and Homer can help us," Uncle Teddy says.

"They help they'll want some treasure," I says.

"You'll get the lion's share," Aunt June says.

"That's only fair," Uncle Teddy adds.

I start to think getting some help would be nice. We won't have much time to dig and the baby makes my back hurt.

"I ain't never met Cousin Homer and them," I says.

"They're very sophisticated," Uncle Teddy says and I imagine my father, Son Walker, and his sophisticated three trunks of clothes.

"Dill was real nice to give you her truck," Uncle Teddy says.

"She didn't give it," I says. "She only lent it."

"Dill ain't as tight as some of us think," Teddy says.

"I stand corrected," June says, pursing her mouth.

"That's twice in the span of one day," Teddy says, joking with her.

"Don't make me pop you with my pocketbook," June says.

"How far is Pecos?" I ask.

June looks at the map key then, inches her fingers along and mumbles to herself. "Looks like fifty miles," she says.

"Lemme see," Uncle Teddy says and June hands him the map. He looks it over, turning it this way and that, making the most sense he can of it without being able to read it, then hands it back to June. When she looks at it again he pats her leg.

"Find El Paso, that's where Blood stay at," Teddy says.

June finds El Paso, circles it, and calculates the miles.

"We'll get to Cousin Blood's tonight," Uncle Teddy says. "And we'll stay over."

"Sounds good to me," I says. We hit a bump and all bounce up and down. The baby bounces up and down too.

"Cornelius and them live where Palmer used to be," Uncle Teddy says.

June studies the map. "That's east of us."

"How far south is Harlingen? Libby and her family stay there," he says.

"Harlingen's a long way down," Aunt June says.

The pink sky behind us is yellowy now and white underneath that. I take little glances in the side mirror and watch the colors change. My arms are getting tired.

"Dill Smiles is awfully generous," Teddy says. "Lent you thirty dollars. Lent you this truck."

"I stole the truck," I says.

Aunt June grins. Uncle Teddy folds his arms over his chest.

"You planning on returning it today?" he asks.

"I'm planning on having it back by Tuesday night," I says.

We ride along in silence for a long while. Towns pass by. The space between my shoulders starts to hurt.

"I could drive some," Uncle Teddy says.

I pull over to the side of the road and we switch places.

He pulls back onto the road, making a wide arc and before I know it, we're heading back home.

"Oh, hell," I says.

"Teddy, please," Aunt June says.

"Treasure or no treasure I ain't no thief," Uncle Teddy says.

He drives hunched over the wheel. Hands holding the wheel tight, the brim of his hat pulled down against the sun.

I watch him. Aunt June lets out a heavy puff of air then looks down at her map. She's turned it so that now she's following our trip back eastwards. She lets out another puff of air. There's tears on her face. She wipes them away quick and don't say nothing.

I do what I seen my mother do once. There was some man driving her car and she wanted him to quit. I reach over, yanking out the keys. The truck coughs then stops.

"Dill weren't gonna help me atall," I says.

"She gived you thirty dollars."

"She didn't give me nothing," I says.

"You stealing the truck ain't right," Teddy says. "Dill's gonna come after us and there'll be hell to pay."

"Dill's standing in between me and what's mine," I says. We are yelling, me and Uncle Teddy both.

Then June speaks. "We've always wished we had more to give Billy," she says.

"Don't cross me," he yells at her.

"Hell, Teddy, it could help you and me out too," she yells back.

Teddy gets out of the truck, not speaking, and I take the driving again. We turn around and head back toward the west, toward the day that's just getting started.

JUNE FLOWERS BEEDE

We've parked in front of a big brick house in the middle of what looks to me like a white neighborhood. There's a fancy car in the carport. The house's got a wreath with a black-and-purple ribbon on the door.

"Here's where they stay at," Teddy says.

"Don't look like they home," I says.

"It's seven in the morning," Teddy says.

A little white boy rides by on his bike, throws a newspaper into they yard and rides on, without even looking at us.

"What's that wreath on the door for?" Billy asks.

"Mourning," Teddy says.

We sit there not knowing quite what to do. We wasn't expecting no wreath. All the yards are free of trash and the lawns are neatly trimmed. Billy looks back at they house then at the other ones on the block. I check the address I got against the numbers they got on the door.

"Big Uncle Walter must be doing pretty good," Billy says.

"I should change into my good dress?" I ask.

"We look fine," Teddy says. "Estelle is family. Sit tight, I'll go up and ring they bell." And he gets out the truck and goes up the walk, brushing down and straightening up his clothes.

He rings the bell and waits.

"I don't think no Beede lives there," I says.

"2112 Tierwater," Billy says. "We got the address right."

"Some white man's gonna come to the door with a shotgun," I says.

I feel something bad's about to happen. Like when I lost my leg. Fell in front of a plow. We was just playing. They said the only way to save my life was to take my leg.

The door opens. A young Negro man stands there talking to Teddy then, looking around Teddy, sees the truck and waves.

"That must be Homer," Billy says, waving back. Teddy and what-must-be-Homer go inside.

"How you feeling?" I ask Billy.

"I'm doing all right."

"Having children is a blessing," I says.

Billy rolls her eyes at me and looks away.

Across the street a man has come out his house in his bathrobe to look at us. A white man.

"I ain't having this baby," Billy says.

"Don't talk like that," I says.

She puts her hands on the steering wheel and looks straight ahead.

In the house across the street the man in the bathrobe is joined by his wife. They stand there, him stooping down to get they newspaper, her hugging her robe close to herself. She holds her hand above her forehead, cutting out the light, to get a better look at us. Billy rolls down her window.

"How you all doing?" Billy asks, her voice snarling.

"We're doing fine," the white folks say.

They stand there for a moment more then the husband nudges the wife and they turn and walk back up they sidewalk together.

"What the hell was they looking at," Billy says, not asking really cause she knows. Two Negro women in a truck and a Negro man walked in the nice house where the Negroes live.

"They think we moving in," I says and we both laugh.

"Snipes got a wife and children already," Billy says using the same voice to tell me that she just talked to the white folks with.

"So you don't want the baby."

Billy nods her head. "I don't owe him," she says.

We sit quiet.

"I could raise it," I says. "I wouldn't mind."

"I don't want it," she says firmly.

Three kids with they books walk past the truck on they way to school.

"I got a doctor up in Gomez," she says. "He got my name already in his book. All's I got to do is get the money together and show up."

"What the hell are you fixing to do?" I ask her.

She don't answer.

I reach my hand out to hit her. But I stop myself.

"You make that bed you gonna have to lie in it all yr life," I says.

"I made my mind up and I ain't changing it," she says.

And I don't got nothing to say to that.

I look towards the nice house. Roosevelt has always talked about Estelle but we never been out to visit her. We would make plans to come out this way, it ain't far, and then, at the last minute he would make excuses. Now here we are. We drove all the way here and he knocked on the wreathed door and a man came up and let him inside.

Funny how people meet. That's been my experience. The meeting of two people is everything. At least that's what I say. I met Roosevelt at the Brazos River. Me and my mother and dad and my four brothers and three sisters and dad's sister Aunt Clara. We was on our way to California, all piled into one beat-up Ford truck, with the wooden slats for sides and the tires as thin as hair ribbons, when we stopped to watch what my father called a "sanctified situation." A young preacher, wet from head to toe, baptizing people in the Brazos. We all got out to watch. I was only seventeen and had lost my leg the year before. Mother had said, God willing, my leg would grow back, like a lizard's tail. Daddy picked me up and carried me into the water on his shoulder. He stood there in the shallows. We was a little ways from the people, we didn't want to intrude, strangers that we was, and not having no plans to stay for more than supper if we was to be invited. Daddy standing in the shallows with me on his shoulder. Young Preacher Beede guided a woman out of the water and sent her back to shore. She was big and her white dress stuck to her body. Her hat had come off and floated downstream, the little cherry sprig in the brim making it spin crazily around. "God wants a miracle!" Young Preacher Beede yelled. He was looking straight at me. The water on his body could be sweat. He strode through the thick moving brown water to where I was, holding his hand out to where my leg used to be. Along the riverside, the people hurried down the bank following him. "God wants a miracle!" he sang. "Amen!" my daddy sang. The people started singing "Glory to Glory." When Young Preacher Beede reached out for me, I thought I could feel my leg growing. Before I knew it he had taken me off my father's shoulder and carried me to the shore and sat me down. My mother and brothers and sisters were on the far side of the river. My father still standing in the water. Young Preacher Beede walked back into the water to talk with my father and, after a minute of talking, they shook hands. Father turned and walked away, across the river, back to the family. Them on one bank and me another. The people surrounded me, asking me my name and how I lost my leg and all sorts of questions. I was just sitting on the bank and had to push aside the length of a woman's flowing dress to see my family, all getting in the truck and driving on.

At first I thought I had died. Then Preacher Beede came carrying two plates of food. Chicken, cornbread, mustard greens, red velvet cake. He wanted to know if I was gonna marry him. We got married the next day. I wanted to go to California. We didn't. And I still ain't got my leg back.

My husband and my father made a deal in the river. Once I asked Teddy what they'd said. He looked ashamed and answered by giving me a kiss on the cheek. I never asked again. I've had ideas, though. My daddy's talk musta been so shameful that it couldn't bear resaying. *She's a double burden on us being one-legged and a girl. She's one mouth to feed too many. We don't know you, Preacher, but, seems to me, she oughta feel lucky getting any sort of husband atall.*

Roosevelt is standing inches from my face, leaning through the car window.

"Let's eat," he says and opens the door for me, cradling my elbow like he always does, helping me out the truck and walking with me and Billy inside.

ESTELLE "STAR" BEEDE ROCHFOUCAULT

It's just like the Beede side of my family to show up unannounced. Not to call or send a note of some kind informing me of their desire to visit and then waiting patiently for an invitation. No. A Beede will just show up on your front doorstep smelling of sweat and saying they're "hongry."

Roosevelt is my cousin. His father and my father were brothers. My cousin is standing in my kitchen doorway while I do my best to prepare breakfast. Leftover smothered chicken, all the eggs we have in the house turned over easy, piles of grits. I've asked Billy to mix the biscuits. June looks to be the better cook but I cannot bring myself to ask that poor crippled woman to do anything but sit and rest.

"When's the last time I seen you, Star?" Roosevelt asks.

"You came to our wedding," I say. I look at Billy, unwed and rail-thin except for that hump at her waist. Either a baby or a tumor. If she were my child, it would be the latter. I add more grits to the boiling water.

"I seen you since that," Roosevelt says. "You and Big Walter and Homer was at my church."

I look him up and down. His black raggedy suit coat and work pants. His hat, looking like it just came out of the box, held in his hands. He had a country church years ago. He was making something of himself, then he stopped. When my Big Walter died last year I didn't invite them to the funeral.

"Every year you send us a Christmas card," Roosevelt says, "maybe that's how come I feel like we been visiting you all this time."

"Homer and I are so glad to see you," I say, not meaning it. Billy, over at the side counter, is a less competent cook than I thought. I take the bowl from her. The batter is over-stirred. "I'll take over from here," I say and she hangs her head.

"Ask your Aunt Star what else you can do," Roosevelt instructs.

"Set the table," I tell her before she can ask. She leaves the kitchen, head still hanging, to stand in the formal dining room, toeing the Persian carpet.

"She's a good girl," Roosevelt says.

"Of course she is," I reassure him. My son Homer is in the living room talking with June. "Homer," I call out, "show your cousin Billy to the silverware and plates, please." Homer excuses himself from June and shows Billy around. I watch my son. Both his eyes are on Billy's belly. Roosevelt watches them talk too.

"Homer's all growd up," he says. "He comed to the door, I thought he was his daddy."

"He takes after his father in every way."

"We woulda liked to come to Walter's funeral."

"He went so quickly."

"Earlier this year, was it?"

"Last summer. Over a year ago now," I say. Roosevelt eyes the black dress I'm wearing. I sewed my own mourning dresses but they look like they were purchased in Atlanta. My black stockings and black shoes are from Dallas. There are little speckles of flour on the dress skirt from where I'm cooking.

"Still wearing yr blacks," he says.

"Walter was the best of men," I say and he nods his head agreeing even though he knows my husband never did think much of Roosevelt or any Beede.

The breakfast is ready and we assemble at the table. Myself and my son sit on one side, and the three Beedes, with Billy in the center, sit on the other. The head of the table, my husband's place, stays empty. I invite Roosevelt, being the most senior man, to serve. He piles food on each plate, running out of eggs before everyone is served, so we have to adjust. "God is great," he mumbles into his folded hands. I wait in vain for something more eloquent. The Beedes begin to eat. Homer waits for my go-ahead.

"For the nourishment of our bodies we eat this food in Jesus' name," I say, allowing Homer and me to begin.

"Lovely house you got," June says.

"Walter worked hard all his life," I tell her. "I could have taught school, but we didn't need the income. Homer and I've never wanted for anything. Walter made sure of that."

Homer looks at me. He wonders if I will mention the bill collectors who call on us with admirable regularity. I will not.

"The china is from England, and the napkins are Italian," I say.

The Beedes look down at their plates.

"All this sure is nice," June says.

"I've risen above my Beedeism," I say.

The three of them smile, as if they understand what I have said, but that would be like having a pig understand that one day he will wake up from a dream to discover he's actually a man. June and Roosevelt and Billy will never rise above their Beedeism. They will always be Beedes, which is to say that they will always be grubbing in the dirt.

"Bet you got a good job," Roosevelt says to Homer.

"Homer is enrolled at Harper College," I say.

"It's just a junior college," Homer says.

"Morehouse accepted Homer, but Harper College is not but ten miles away. Especially after the passing of his father, I find my son's nearness a great blessing," I tell them. I reach out for my son's hand, giving him a gentle squeeze. When men from Levenson's Furniture visited, intending to reclaim the very table we're eating on, Homer willingly skipped a semester so we could make the payments.

We eat in silence. Billy shoveling her food, Roosevelt and June eating more slowly, Homer dabbing his grits with his biscuits. He has his elbow on the table. I look at him and he removes it.

"How'd the biscuits turn out?" Billy asks him.

Homer, with his mouth full, just smiles. But the biscuits are not good.

"Will you need to spend the night with us?" I ask.

"Oh, no," June says smiling, "we're—well, you could say we got things to do and places to go to."

I take a breath of relief. If they were to stay over they would smell up my rooms and spit in my sinks.

"Where are you all headed to?" Homer asks them.

I cough.

"To where are you traveling?" my son asks again.

The Beedes trade quick looks, then Roosevelt sits up very straight in his chair, puffing out his chest. "Willa Mae left us some treasure when she passed and we're on our way to collect it."

"Marvelous," I say.

"Is it in a bank?" Homer asks.

"Don't talk with yr mouth full, son."

Homer chews and swallows quickly. "Safety deposit box?"

"Willa didn't trust banks," Roosevelt says, puffing bigger and getting prouder. "My sister buried her treasure in the ground."

The air escapes my mouth so quickly that I find myself scoffing at them even though it isn't polite. Treasure in the ground. That's Beedeism for you.

DILL SMILES

White boys stole my truck.

I like to look at it first thing in the morning when I get up and here I am standing here looking at where it should be and I am standing here looking at nothing. White boys stole my goddamn truck.

Oh, they ain't gonna get away with this. I'll tell everybody I know. I'll wake up Joe North to get him to take me to Midland and we gonna tell the police. No. The white police ain't gonna do nothing about no nigger-lezzy's truck stolen by some white boys. White boys probably they sons or cousins. Or maybe they theirselves stole it. They got it halfway to Dallas by now, planning on repainting it and reselling it. Or they was drinking when they stole it, they stole it on one of them dares they always doing. White folks is crazy. They always getting drunk and then daring each other to do stuff. I knew a man, a nice man too, Brunson. Brunson was a good old boy, you know, a red neck with a red face to match. But he was fair. Went drinking with his friends one night and they got to doing them white dares and he jumped off the roof of the First National Bank in Midland. His head popped open like a goddamn cantaloupe. I heard his friends stood around laughing. That's how drunk they was. How's that joke go? *What's the most often last words of a redneck? Hey y'all watch this.*

White folks.

One of them probably riding in my truck right now, driving it too fast. Going from first to second, from second to third, his drunk white hands all over the wheel and the dashboard and the gearshift. His drunk white face and the goddamn faces of his drunk white friends, all crowded in the cab and some in the bed, just along for the fun. Admiring the ride. Hitting every hole in the road and laughing. Cause it ain't their expense. *It's just a nigger's truck. A nigger who's doing well for herself. A bulldagger nigger who got a sow with thirteen new nigger-sow piglets. Woulda stole the piggies but the nigger-lezzy Smiles, she sleeps with a shotgun. Oh, but you shoulda seen what nigger-lezzy Smiles used to sleep with. A white gal. Hells no. The lezzy didn't have no white gal. Sho. The nigger lezzy had yr sister. I'ma stop this truck and kill you. The lezzy's gal, she was colored. I heard her sing once. She looked white. So do you. Cut that out, that ain't funny now. I'm telling you the lezzy's gal looked white. Well she weren't. If she was white, the bulldagger woulda been hanging from every tree you can see. I never lynched no bulldagger. I ain't neither but I bet it's all right. Let's run this truck into a ditch. Let's run it into a tree and jump out fore we hit. Let's take it to Austin. I know a fella'll buy it off us for top dollar and no questions asked. He'll pay more if he knowd we stold it from a nigger. Wish I had a chance at that gal Smiles had. I had a chance at her. I had a chance at her too. You all lying. She woulda gived you a chance if youda asked. She was fast as this truck. Hell, she was faster than this truck, she was fast as lightning. She was white. She was colored, I'm telling you. She had a baby black as my shoe. Colored folks is funny. That's cause you ain't drunk enough. Pass the bottle.*

Somehow them white boys got my truck. They got in the house somehow—

Shit.

Billy Beede.

And right then I know it weren't no white boys stealing nothing. It was goddamn Billy stealing it. Stealing my ring of keys that I couldn't find this morning, then stealing my truck while I'm sleep. I stand right in the middle of the road where I'm walking to town and turn back, hurrying the other way towards Sanderson's. The living reminder that Willa Mae ran around on me has run off with my truck. Good. It's good Billy Beede stole my truck. Good, cause I'ma kill her for it and the law

will not severely punish a colored when a colored woman gets kilt.
Good, because if white boys had stole my truck they could be anywhere
with it, but Billy Beede stealing my truck has only gone one place. She
has gone to LaJunta and now all I got to do is go out there and kill her.
She will get to LaJunta before me. Ma will show her the grave. And she
will dig. She will come back this way and I'll be on the Monday bus
heading out there and she will be coming back here empty-handed and
sad and I'll see her in my truck and I'll stop the bus and shoot her as she
speeds on by. I'll kill her good and dead and the law will look the other
way.

WILLA MAE BEEDE

This song's about, well, I'll sing it to you, then you'll know. It's called
"Hatchet Tree Blues."

I buried my hatchet but it hatched out the ground and growd.
I buried my hatchet but it hatched out the ground and growd.
I laid it deep down in the dirt
And it come up like a bean along the row.

It growd leaves it growd branches, my hatchet tree's
   got a trunk four arms wide,
It growd leaves it growd branches, my hatchet tree's
   got a trunk four arms wide,
It got roots clear down to China, it gives shade to the
   whole countryside.

My hatchet tree's giving fruit, big old hatchets ripe
   and ready on the vine,
My hatchet tree's giving fruit, big old hatchets ripe
   and ready on the vine,
The one I loved, he cripple-crossed me
He gonna taste some of my hatchet this time.

HOMER BEEDE ROCHFOUCAULT

We could use the money.

Roosevelt is my uncle and Willa Mae was his sister. I am their nephew and so that makes the treasure my aunt's.

"How about I come along with you?" I ask.

Mamma tries to give me one of her looks but I keep both of my eyes on Uncle Teddy.

"We was gonna ask you the very same thing," Uncle Teddy says, looking pleased.

"We need help digging," Cousin Billy adds.

"Oh Good Lord," Mamma says.

"I hope I'd be entitled to a percentage of the profits," I say.

They get quiet. Aunt June narrows her eyes and Billy works her neck.

"We already decided Billy's getting the lion's share," Uncle Teddy says.

"How much are we talking about?" I ask. I've got a good head for figures. Professor Yardley wants me to get my degree in mathematics. He says I could work with the space program but I got my sights set on the Congress or the Senate.

"We don't know how much exactly," Billy says, "but you won't be wasting your time."

"My son does not need to be digging like some n——," my mamma says. She don't say "nigger," though, just the "n" part.

We all sit quiet. Aunt June traces the lace edge of her napkin. Billy eats another one of her rock biscuits. Uncle Teddy is smiling, trying to make peace.

"I didn't mean to say that," Mamma whispers into her plate.

"You stopped yrself just in time," Uncle Teddy says.

"I haven't been myself since I lost my husband," my mamma says.

I look out the living room window. My Mercury Park Lane is still in the driveway. I glance out there about a million times a day, and get up in the night to go look at it, expecting it not to be there. I had good grades—not straight A's but quite a few. My father talked his friends into giving him enough for the down payment and he surprised me with it a month before he died. I've had to work two jobs to keep it. It runs real good but I've never driven it any further than Harper College. "A treasure hunt sounds cool to me," I say.

"There is nothing cool about it," my mamma says.

"Yr right about the weather," Uncle Teddy says. "It'll be hot."

"That was not my meaning," Mamma says. She went to Spelman College. She graduated at the top of her class. My father was a More-house man.

"What we meaning is, we could really use Homer's help," Aunt June says.

"I'd like to be a part of what I see as an interesting prospect," I say.

"There is nothing interesting about going all the way out to some place in Arizona to dig who knows where in the dirt on a whim," my mamma says.

The Beedes are quiet. They eat and we eat. When they eat they make sounds. Mamma and I eat but we don't make sounds. I know what Mamma'll say when they've gone. She will say they eat like animals.

I take a good look at Billy. She's left-handed and she holds her fork in her left fist, like a yardman would hold it, and she don't got no wedding ring on and she got a need for a wedding ring. I wonder how many times she done it. I wonder if my cousin's one of them hot and wild gals. Over at Harper we got a gal like that. Cousin Billy sees me looking at her and puts her fork down. She puts both hands in her lap, hiding the no-ring. For a minute I think she will lean her head down into her plate and eat the rest of her breakfast like Chance, my daddy's dog, eats. But her right hand, the one with no ring that isn't supposed to have a ring, comes up. It picks up the fork slowly. The fork wobbles cause the right hand, the hand she isn't used to eating with, is guiding the food to her mouth. At the last minute the eggs fall and she makes a little snap motion with her neck, as the eggs miss her mouth. They fall into her lap. But that doesn't stop her. She picks the eggs gently up, returning them to her plate, then shovels at the eggs again and this time she gets it. Then she picks up a biscuit, chews hard, swallows, then speaks.

"Willa Mae Beede was buried with a long pearl necklace and a big diamond ring," she says.

"Where'd she get stuff like that?" I ask.

"Her—her husband. He gived them to her," she explains. She was about to say something other than "husband" but she said "husband." Professor Clarke over at college would of said Billy was about to make a Freudian's slip. But she caught herself just in time. Aunt June and Uncle Teddy are smiling pleasantly, letting Cousin Billy unfold the story, not contributing any information other than the silence. Me and Mamma lean in a little. Talking about "treasure" is one thing, talking specifics like diamonds and pearls is something else.

"Your mother got that jewelry from your father?" my mamma asks.

Billy smiles big. There's a little piece of grits on her lower lip. "Mr. Carmichael was her first husband," she says.

"I don't approve of divorce," my mamma says.

"Me neither," Uncle Teddy says.

"Willa Mae was married to Huston Carmichael the Third, he gave her the jewels, then he died. After years of mourning, she married my daddy. They had me, then he left her a widow," Cousin Billy explains.

My mamma touches her hand to her chest. "I know that kind of sadness," she says. She is talking about the sadness of having the man you planned to get old with walk out into the backyard one morning to look over the vegetables and falling down dead of a heart attack. And she is talking about the sadness that goes with that. Of thinking you were having one kind of life, the kind of life with no worries and plenty of money and a son on his way to his father's alma mater college, and then, overnight, your life turning into bill collectors visiting you and marks on the carpet where certain prize pieces of furniture used to sit, and a son in junior college and not even really being able to afford that.

"If your dear husband, by some mistake, had been put into his grave with a treasure that he meant for you to have, me and Uncle Teddy and Aunt June would do what we could to help you get it," Cousin Billy says.

"She was buried with the treasure by mistake?" I ask.

The Beedes stay quiet.

Billy goes into her pocketbook, taking out a photograph and passing it across the table to us. I lean in to look. There's a white woman, or what looks like a white woman, standing in the middle of the desert right next to one of them big prickly man-shaped cactuses. In the picture, there's also the shadow of the man taking the picture.

"She's beautiful," my mamma says, the words jumped out of her mouth like she didn't want to say it.

"She's got on the necklace and the diamond ring," I says. You can see them in the picture plain as day.

"And she and your stepfather meant for you to have them?" Mamma asks.

"That's right," Billy says.

Uncle Roosevelt coughs. Aunt June moves her food around on her plate. Mamma told me a few things about Willa Mae Beede, but she didn't mention her jewelry or her looks.

Billy reaches to take the picture back. By instinct, she reaches with her left hand. No ring. Mamma raises her eyebrows.

"My dear husband, Mr. Clifford Snipes," Billy explains quickly, "he refuses to buy me a ring until he can afford the best. From the looks of your house, Aunt Star, I bet Big Uncle Walter treated you just like that too."

"Big Walter Rochfoucault was a Morehouse man," Mamma says.

"So you know what I'm taking about," Billy says.

Uncle Teddy looks at our grandfather clock. They've been here for two hours. "We could use your help, Homer. We need to get out there quick and dig quick," he says.

I look at Mamma. When she couldn't pay the bills and took me out of school I was ashamed. Mamma gives me her nod of approval.

"All right, then," I says, getting up to pack my things.

"I'll fix some food for you to take along," Mamma says, "and you better call me right when you get there, too," she adds and it's all settled.

ROOSEVELT BEEDE

Homer's got a fancy car.

"Plenty of automobiles come by our filling station on any given day but I ain't never seen one as nice as this one here," I tell him. We've turned off his street and onto the main road that will lead us back to the highway. West west more west then we'll be there. Homer turns around, taking his eyes off the road, and giving another flurry of waves goodbye to Star, who has gone around the side of the house to catch a last glimpse of us. We go down the main road and she vanishes behind a low concrete garage, but Homer keeps waving anyway.

"It sure was good of her to let you come," I says.

"I enjoy knowing that I can help my family," he says. He turns around in his seat, watching the road again.

"She don't like you far from home," I says.

Homer makes a face. "She figures this is the lesser of two evils," he says.

"Nothing evil about what we doing," I says. I'm glad he's coming to help but I don't exactly approve of all the lies Billy told to his mother.

I lean back, getting comfortable in the bright white leather seat. Star said the NAACP of Pecos got together and bought the car for him. When he went away to college they gave him a big send-off, even though Harper's just ten miles to the south.

We turn onto the highway. I look behind and see June and Billy following us in the truck.

"This model's called a Park Lane," he says. "You can tell by the chroming on the sides."

"All right," I says reminding myself to look at the chrome once we've stopped.

"Now I'll show you what this baby can do," Homer says, stepping on the gas pedal. We got the top down so the wind whips at us pretty good. I hold my hat on with one hand and hold on to the middle arm-rest with the other. We go fast. Then faster. Homer looks at me and smiles. I smile back.

"I sure do like a fast ride," I says. I got to yell so he can hear me.

"Mamma hates me going over forty," he says. He looks at my hand on the armrest. I move it to touch the paneling, pretending like I'm feeling the quality of the dashboard materials.

"A man's got to open it up once and awhile, else he ain't a man," I yell. Homer nods in agreement. I sneak a look at the speedometer. We're going seventy-five. I take my hat off, before it flies off. If it flies off I'll want to stop for it and Homer ain't stopping. I crunch it down between my legs. Young men go fast. When I was Homer's age I went fast. I didn't have no car but I had a cart that we used to tote wood and groceries and what-have-you. There was this hill out by where we stayed at and on Sunday afternoons me and Willa Mae would go up there and ride down in the cart. Both us together, screaming all the way down the hill. Once we got this barrel, it smelled like pickles. Willa got inside it and rolled down the hill. No one else had ever rolled down the hill in no barrel. Kids, boys mostly, would come and watch her do it. She was braver than any of us. Boys would watch her and girls would watch her. Girls with admiration that became jealousy. Boys with admiration that became lust. She got the idea to have folks pay. And kids would bring they pennies or they favorite things, playing cards, odd-colored marbles, chewing gum and peppermint candy, as payment for her performance. Then one day she announced her retirement. She said the rolling made her stomach feel funny. She asked three older boys to drive the barrel down to the South Concho Draw and we all watched it float away. I thought that was the end of fast Willa Mae.

"We left them in the dust," Homer says. I turn to look. The road points out behind us, tight and straight, the hot tar of it almost singing in the heat. Sure enough, we have left the truck far behind.

"Blood and Precious stay in El Paso. June and Billy don't got the address," I says. I got the trip pretty well planned-out. Breakfast with Star in Pecos, dinner with Blood and stay the night there. Get up early and hit LaJunta in the morning. Maybe Star'll put us up for the night when we return, dripping with the pearls and diamonds and whatnot.

"We'll stop at a filling station in a little bit," Homer says, "the ladies can catch us then."

We whip down the road. Everything standing still looks like it's moving. A steer raises its head, big long horns pointing east and west, looking at us.

"You studying to be a doctor, then?"

"I'm studying law," Homer says. "Mamma wants me to follow in Daddy's footsteps but my professor at school, Professor Clarke, he says I got a natural talent for public speaking and such."

"Gonna be a lawyer?"

"Professor Clarke says I could be a congressman or senator one day." Homer smiles and sits up straighter thinking of himself behind a big desk. Congressman or Senator Homer Beede Rochfoucault. Then he adds, "I would like to be placed in a position where I can do the most good for my constituents."

"Your constituents," I says, repeating, and nodding my head. But I'm not sure what the word means.

"The people need good men," Homer says smiling at me. And I know then that he will make a good politician, not a preacher, cause he ain't been called, but a politician, one who ain't been called but, through the force of his own personality, calls others to him. That's largely the difference. A man of God is called by God. A man of the people calls the people. Some men are called by God to lead the people. But that's rare. A man of the people thinks the people are calling him but it's just his own voice, overly loud, shouting his own name and hearing it echo back to him through the open mouths of the people, mouths open in awe and wonder watching a man shout his own name loud. A man of God has his mouth shut until God opens it, forces it open sometimes. And sometimes forces it closed. When I took June from her family the first night she cried. So I promised her that we would go to California too. We got in a borrowed car and went. But after a day of riding I got brittle. It was her happiness or mines and when we reached the Texas border, I told her I was as far west as I could go. So I turned around. We headed back eastward, passed through Tryler, seen that piece of land for rent, stopped right there and built the church, and things, for a while anyway, was going pretty good.

Homer looks at me. I look at the speedometer. We're doing eighty.

"How much you think the jewels are worth?" he asks.

"Hundreds," I say. I see the disappointment working into his face, like a drought coming, but not there yet. "Thousands," I says, correcting myself. "Several thousand dollars."

He smiles then hefts up his lower lip, considering. "Cousin Billy isn't married is she?" he asks carefully.

"Sure she is," I says quick. Too quick.

"We're two men riding in a car," Homer says. "We can be honest with each other. Maybe Billy could be my wife."

"That would be a good thing," I says. How he knew Billy weren't married I don't know. He goes to college so I guess he's pretty smart.

"Billy's situation will just stay *entre nous*. That's French for secret," he says smiling. Billy's business will stay secret. A secret shared between two men going eighty miles per hour with the top down.

A siren comes up out of nowheres. The police with they single red turning light and they thin wailing siren charging down the road behind us. Homer looks in the rearview mirror but doesn't slow down.

"We can outrun them," he says. His voice is flat and hard.

"I ain't packing for no shoot-out," I says, trying to make my voice sound like a cowboy.

"I don't got no gun either," he says and, slowing down, pulls over to the side of the road.

LAZ JACKSON

I comed over to look at Dill's new piglets. Last time there was a runt, Dill culled it. This time I'm ready to take the runt home. I got a pasteboard box with me. Dill is sitting on her porch. I come up through the gate and just stand there watching her. She's looking at me but not looking at me.

"How you doing, Dill?"

"Whatchu want?"

"Jez had any runts?"

"Nope."

"None smaller than the rest?"

"Nope."

"You sure?"

"I'm sure," she says.

I stand there looking into the empty space of my box. There was gonna be a runt in there and I was gonna carry it home. It woulda lived in the box. It woulda growd out the box. Got big and bigger and bigger. And I woulda rode my pig around in my hearse and maybe even won a ribbon, at least third place, in the Butler County Fair. Least that was my plan. Shit. I asked Billy to marry me and she said no. Now there ain't no runts. Double Shit. I let go the box and kick it. It flies a few feet then scuttles along the ground. Dill turns from looking at me to look at the box. She looks at it like it's something worth looking at, so I look at it too.

"You can have it if you want it," I says.

She don't say nothing.

Then I notice the box is in a place where Dill's truck's usually parked. And the truck ain't there no more. It ain't where it usually is and it ain't nowheres else. Well, it must be somewhere but it ain't in Dill's yard.

"Where's your truck?"

"Stolen."

"Tripple Shit," I says.

"Billy Beede stole it," Dill says. "She stole it and she's gone to LaJunta in it."

"Shit Shit Shit Shit," I says.

Dill turns from looking at the box to looking at me. I turn my head away. The feeling I got for Billy is strong but, with Dill looking at me, it shrinks.

"I gotta go get my truck," she says.

"You getting North to take you?"

"I ain't mixing North up in this," Dill says.

"Billy shouldn't be stealing from you," I says.

"I'ma kill the bitch," Dill says, "I'ma be on the morning bus tomorrow and get out there and I'ma kill the bitch."

I know she don't mean it. She do want her truck back, though, that's sure. It'd be nice to go to LaJunta. Billy'll be there.

"How bout I take you?" I says.

"No thanks."

"We could leave today. Hell, we could leave right now."

"I ain't riding no place in no hearse."

Mother and Dad don't let me drive the sedan we got.

"The hearse rides good," I says. "Plus I just cleaned the vents so the air oughta come in nice."

Dill spits hard at the box and hits it dead on.

"What the hell you standing in my yard for?" she says. "Go get yr goddamn hearse."

I run down the road all the way home. I got the keys in my pocket and I tell my folks I'm going on an errand with Dill and that I'll be back in a couple of days. I tell them she's paying me for my time. Then I'm gone.

I don't bring nothing but the clothes on my back. Dill brings a cloth bag with brass closures. Something in it looks heavy. She don't bring nothing else. No food or water. I hope she's got money for gas.

The hearse is dove-gray inside, outside it's black-faded-to-green. My father's second-best hearse. His new one, a 1962 Cadillac, is white on white in white. We got the fly windows open plus the vents so the air's coming in good.

We drive slow.

Outside of Fort Stockton we pass a chain gang.

"Look, there's your brother," Dill says joking, but I don't look cause I done already looked, a quick glance into the faces and profiles of each man. None of them's Siam-Iz, and besides, he's in Huntsville and that's way east of here.

We ride for a whole three hours in silence.

"I remember Willa Mae," I says.

"She's hard to forget," Dill says.

I think I'm talking in my head but when Dill answers I realize that I'm talking out loud.

"When folks talk about her all they tell is stories about her flash and whatnot," I says. Dill's face frowns up and she looks at her cloth bag. "But I don't think of Willa Mae like that atall," I add quickly.

"She was something," Dill says.

"She was always singing," I says. "Always making up songs and singing them." Dill nods. We ride in silence. Town signs pass.

Something else comes into my head. I wait for a lot of miles before I say it, then I figure what the hell. "What's it like, being a man?" I ask Dill.

She looks at me, her eyes like two slow snakes. Dill is more of a man than I am. She's had Willa Mae and she's had herself. That's two women more than I've had.

"Don't you know what it's like?"

"Not yet."

"How old are you?" she wants to know. I tell her.

"Yr twenty years old and you still ain't had no woman?" she says.

"Not for lack of trying," I says.

"You should talk to Poochie Daniels," Dill says. "She's friendly enough and I could put in a good word for you."

"I already done talked to Poochie," I says. "Goddamn Poochie turned me down."

WILLA MAE BEEDE

Ain't the long road long
Ain't the big load heavy
Ain't my old soul weary
Ain't that so.

Ain't the way you treat me
Just a mistreat-treating
Ain't I out that door
Ain't I gone.

Ain't I gone
Ain't I gone
Long gone longer than yr arms is long
Ain't I gone
Ain't I gone
Long gone longer than yr legs is long
Ain't the way you treat me
Just a mistreat-treating
All that's left is this here song.

BILLY BEEDE

Mother said that the stretch of highway from Pecos to El Paso was probably the most boring road in the world, and she had been on a lot of roads. She said there was more interesting country but it was someplace else. When me and her would drive, if the scenery weren't much, she'd liven up the view by telling me about the better places she'd seen. When we came out this way that last time she was talking about how we was gonna drive all the way to California. She'd meet Mr. Right in Hollywood and she was gonna get married again, this time for good, and we was gonna drive up California, from Hollywood all the way to Oakland where she knew some people. There's a road running right up the coast and you can see the ocean the whole way. That's a road worth driving, she said. We was gonna get her new husband to get us a brand-new convertible and she would drive, and I would ride shotgun like I liked to and we'd let the new husband sit in the back. We would drive along the water and have picnics whenever we wanted.

Aunt June looks up from her map. "Where's Teddy and Homer?" she asks.

"I guess they took off," I says.

"Teddy'll make Homer slow down. He knows we ain't sure where Blood stays at," Aunt June says. She looks out the window, watching the grass clumps and red dirt go by. We're only going forty. There's a bush of a white puffy flower every ten feet. "That's Queen Anne's lace," Aunt June says.

"Who's Queen Anne?"

"Dunno. It'd go nice next to my rosebush. How bout we stop, I'd like to pull some up."

I press the gas pedal down a little harder. We go forty-five. "If we stop we ain't never gonna get there," I says.

"It'd only be for a minute. You could jump out for me, rip a clump up by the roots, and then we'd get back on the road." Her voice is pleading, like a child.

"We'll stop on the way back," I says. She pats the flat part of her dress where her leg used to be. She looks let down but I ain't stopping right now.

"Devil's claw, wild weed, Holy Ghost, Rosy Everlasting," she says, pointing out and naming the flowers as we pass.

"They got nice names," I says. "On the way back we'll stop lots, you'll see."

We ride in silence.

Mother and me would go for these long drives but always come back. We was living at Dill's house then. Some days, usually when the weather was hot and Mother said she could smell the pigs, we would get in the car and drive. She would tell Dill we was just going around the block. We would stay out all day, heading for someplace she thought sounded good. Lampasas, Zephyr, Crystal City, Navasota. She drove fast like we was running late, the sky just whipping by and her taking little sips from a bottle that she held between her legs. Sipping as she drove. Sometimes getting drunk. She had a ritual before she turned on the engine. She would take her diamond ring and her pearls off and thread them into the lining of her skirt. For safekeeping. Her "real stuff" as she called it would be kept safe and she wore the fakes while she drove. Just in case, she would mention, but just in case of what she never did say. Once she forgot where she put her pearls and cussed me out for stealing em, then remembering, she pulled em from the hem of her skirt like a magic trick. Once we was in a jail in Galveston and she got the sheriff to bring her some Lucky Strikes. Mostly we'd just drive. We'd get to one of them good-sounding places, creeping down the dirt road main street, the folks on porches desperate from the heat, the kids and dogs all lolling in the shade. Nobody doing nothing.

"I heard this town was where the Happenings was at," she would say. There'd be anger in her voice. The town's bright name had let her down.

We'd stop and I'd sit in the car or near it while she went to talk to people. Various people. In juke joints if there was a piano, she would let me come in and she would sing. Mostly I'd just sit in the car and wait for her to come back.

We hardly never stayed out late. Just sometimes. It'd always get cooler in the evening and Mother would feel the cold air and say she could stand the place now, and I knew she meant the pig smell and we would head back. A few times we was out late though. We'd come home in the middle of the next afternoon.

"Where you been?" Dill wanted to know one time. Her face was all twisted from no sleep and too much worry.

"I been to London to see the Queen," Mother said.

Dill hit her, knocking her to the floor, then went outside to do the chores. I watched her laying there thinking she was dead. She lay on the floor for the rest of the day and I started thinking I guess I was gonna be a pig farmer for sure now, and maybe that wouldn't be so bad, and then I heard her snoring, laying there snoring. She'd fallen asleep.

Aunt June is looking at me driving and looking at my belly.

"I guess you won't be naming your baby Snipes," Aunt June says.

"I ain't naming it nothing."

Every time we hit a bump, my belly almost touches the steering wheel.

"Maybe it'll be a boy," Aunt June says brightly.

"It ain't gonna be at all," I says.

She's looking at my belly, but I look evil at her, making her look at something else. She studies her map then glances out the window.

"Claret cup cactus," she announces, seeing some.

"Willa Mae and me was headed out here to meet her new husband-to-be," I say. "They had the wedding all planned and then she died."

"Is that so," Aunt June says.

I can tell she don't believe me. I decide to do what Mother called "ice the cake"—when you put a finish on something and it don't matter what the person watching thinks. "I was at her bedside when she died," I says. "I was holding her one hand and her husband-to-be, the richest man I ever seen, he was holding her other hand. You shoulda seen him cry when she passed."

"Is that so," Aunt June says again.

"Believe whatchu please," I says, steering towards a big hole and hitting it hard and watching the shock on Aunt June's face. "Believe what you please, but I'm telling you the truth."

OFFICER MASTERSON

I just pulled over a late-model red Mercury convertible going over eighty miles an hour. It's got two Negroes in it. I can hear the people up in New York and Chicago and Warshington and Hollywood. I can hear all them talking. Calling me a white supremacist cause I done pulled over two speeding Negroes in what looks like a brand-new car.

There's a young one driving and an older one riding with him. I told them to both get out the car and stand with they hands on the hood and they legs spread. I radioed for assistance, but Sheriff Jim Baylor's taking his day off, fishing.

"I'ma have to look at your license," I say to the young one.

He don't say nothing. The older one looks at him and then the young one speaks. "It's in my billfold," he says.

He's got on tight brown pants. His back pocket's got a bump in it. I touch the bump with my baton.

"That your wallet there?"

"Whatchu think?"

The older one, his hands cupped on the car hood to save his palms from the heat, turns his head a little and looks at the younger one again. "That your billfold?" he asks him.

"Yes, sir," the younger says, answering the older Negro, not me.

"Go take it outcha pants," the old one tells him and he does what he's told, taking out his wallet and holding it in his hand with his arm out straight from his body. Usually a fella with his hand out like that under these circumstances would have his hand shaking. The young fella's hand is firm. Almost like he's resting his arm on something. On his innocence, or his crime.

"I got a billfold too," the old one says.

"Where's it at?"

"In my coat pocket."

"Go head and get it then."

He reaches in slow, removing the wallet, paper-thin black leather, placing it a few inches away from his hand on the car hood.

"Homer," I says. The license's got his whole name but I can't make head or tail of the last one. Sheriff says all niggers should be named Joe Washington. Says we oughta pass a law to make it so. Negroes and Negras both. All Joe Washington. I had the stupidity to ask how then would we know one from the other and Sheriff said we can't tell them apart now anyway so what's the difference. He laughed and I laughed.

"Stand here while I radio in your information," I says. I tell Shirley back at the station what I caught and she checks through the postings but there ain't no one looking for what I got.

They stand with their hands still on the hood. Their heads are down. I could let them go. Give them a ticket for going too fast and let them go. I pride myself in being fair. I could just let them on their way with a speeding ticket. But Sheriff wouldn't never let me hear the end of it. If I was to let them go there'd be plenty of laughs and talkings behind my back. I might even stop getting the days off I put in for. Things like that happen.

"This your car, Beady?" I says, looking at the older man. Him and his son was out driving fast, and I'll put money on them being father and son, even though they don't got the same name.

"Bead," the older says.

It's got an "e" on the end, but I guess you don't say it. "This yr car, Bead?"

"No, sir."

"Is it stolen?"

"I am not no thief."

The old man is looking up at me, the light from the hood of the car makes his face glow. He got a way about him, like he's somebody or used to be somebody and he even looks familiar, but Negroes got a way of looking familiar when you don't know them, especially when they've done something wrong.

The younger fella looks up and smiles. "There's a twenty in my bill-fold. It's yours if you want it," he says.

I open the wallet and pocket the twenty. "I'm gonna have to take you both in," I says. And they both hang they heads. I feel a little jolt, of pleasure, maybe. The hanging heads of men, any men, and the power of the law.

Problem is I only got one set of handcuffs. I cuff one to the other and lead them both to my squad car, opening the back door and letting them get in.

"That's my car," the young one says struggling a little.

"Don't you worry about it," I says.

A pickup truck drives up. Two Negras in it.

"Teddy!" the woman yells.

"I'm taking them in," I says. Then I remember I'm a fair man and add, "If you like you can follow us."

A younger gal leans over the older one, narrowing her eyes at me. Damn if she don't look familiar too. "Whatchu gonna do with Homer's car?" she asks.

"We'll just leave it here," I says. "Won't no one take it."

I get in my car and head toward town. In the back they sit quiet like they're made of stone. "We gonna have you spend the night courtesy of the town of Tryler, Texas," I says.

"Tryler? That's what this town's called?" the older one asks.

"That's right," I says.

We pass the sign that says the name of the town.

Something about the town of Tryler makes the older Negro start laughing. The younger one looks mad but the older one, I'm watching him in my rearview, the older one's laughing to hisself. Then he's crying. Tears coming down his cheeks but a shake like laughing still jolting his body. Like I said before, Negroes is funny.

HOMER BEEDE
ROCHFOUCAULT

His boss comes in all excited. Two caught niggers. Him with his cap full of fishing lures on his head and his big stomach hanging well over his belt. His subordinate, the one who caught us and cuffed us and hauled us in here, took just my pictures and fingerprints but put us both in the cell.

"Where's the stuff on the old nigger?" the Sheriff wants to know.

"He ain't done nothing," the Deputy says. "It was the young fella that was driving."

The Sheriff leans against the bars. His belly squeezes through the metal slats. "The old nigger's an accessory," he says.

"Oh, hell, Jim," the Deputy goes.

"He's an accessory to the crime," the Sheriff says again. His lips are wet and his eyes, round and pale-colored, look Uncle Roosevelt up and down. Uncle Roosevelt stands up. He's a head taller than the Sheriff but he stoops a little. On the way into town he was crying. Maybe he's got a record or something, maybe he's scared they'll find out he robbed a bank or shot somebody once.

"Take his goddamn picture and prints or I'ma take your goddamn badge," the Sheriff screams. The lures rattle on his head. His voice is high.

The Deputy takes Uncle Teddy out and walks him down the little hallway. I sit there, letting the Sheriff look at me.

"We put out what you call an All Points Bulletin," he says, lifting his fat hand up and fingering one of his lures. "We got you good and caught, now we just gotta find out whatchu done."

I want to kill him right now. I want to stand up and reach my hands quick through the bars and bring his fat lure-topped head into the cell with me and leave the rest of his cracker ass just standing there. But I don't move. I sit. My elbows on my knees, my eyes on his.

"You look like Martin Luther Coon," he says.

"My name is Homer Rochfoucault."

"I wish to God you was Luther Coon. That'd be a good-looking feather in my cap."

I want to kill him right now but I don't move. He might want to kill me too but he don't move either. The Negro-College-Going Youth eye-balling the White-Just-Back-From-Fishing Sheriff. If we was in a play those would be our parts. There's plenty of times a man has, in situations just like this, forgot himself and just played his part. In the middle of the quadrangle at school there's a little stone plaque dedicated to the memory of Randall Clay. I used to think it would be a fine thing to tell men like this Sheriff here just what I think of them and then end up killed and honored by a plaque with my name on it. Until now.

"I haven't been given my phone call," I say.

"What phone call?"

"I'm allowed a phone call."

"We don't got no phone," he says smiling.

The Deputy comes back to the cell and leads in Uncle Roosevelt. We sit together. Neither of us saying nothing. Both of us looking at the floor. His picture took, his fingertips, like mine, black and inky-smelling.

The day passes. The Sheriff and the Deputy get tired of just standing there looking at us. They are waiting for the phone to ring, news of some white gal we done raped or some money we stole or some white man we shot or something. The phone don't ring with shit.

They both take up chairs across from the cell. The Sheriff not taking his eyes off us and the Deputy looking like we looking, down at the floor.

"I seen them somewheres before," the Sheriff says.

"That's what I thought too," the Deputy says.

"Especially the old nigger."

"He don't got no record though."

"Maybe he got a brother who's on the run," the Sheriff says. "Old nigger, you got a brother?" he asks Uncle Roosevelt.

Uncle Roosevelt looks up but don't answer.

"Answer me, goddamnit!" the Sheriff screeches.

"He don't got no brother, Jim," the Deputy says.

"I wanna hear it from him!"

"Mr. Beady," the Deputy goes, saying the name wrong again but at least he's saying it.

"Bead," Uncle Roosevelt says softly, "you say it Bead."

"It's got uh 'e' on the end," the Sheriff says.

"You say it Bead," Uncle Teddy says even more softly.

"Mr. Bead," the Deputy says.

"He ain't no mister," the Sheriff says.

"I don't got no brother," Uncle Teddy says. "I'm pretty much the last Beede in my line."

We all fall silent. I'm the last one in my line and maybe the two crackers are the last ones in their lines too. And all of a sudden I'm thinking of Cousin Billy. I'm locked up in a Texas jail with crackers with guns trying to hang some crime on me and here I am thinking of how nice it would be to get with my cousin. I should be thinking of other things. More respectable things like getting my law degree or at least digging up the treasure and paying off my mother's bills with my percentage of it or I should be thinking how one day I'll become president and pass laws for fairness. But I'm just thinking of getting with Billy behind her nonexistent husband's back.

"Any word, Shirley?" the Sheriff yells.

"You been here, you hear the phone ring?" Shirley yells back.

They sit there a moment longer. They took my wristwatch when they took my picture. My daddy gave me that watch. If they don't give it back I will kill them.

There is a piece of sunlight coming through the cell window slantwise. It's thin and yellowy, like watery soup. My father went out into the yard to check on the garden. My mother had the table laid for breakfast. We sat there waiting for him to come in and eat and he had fallen down dead in the mustard greens.

"It's time for my dinner," the Sheriff says standing. The Deputy stands up too.

"What should I do with the prisoners?" the Deputy asks.

"Don't do nothing with them," the Sheriff says leaving.

The Deputy stands there against the wall, watching his boss leave the jail and drive off.

"Shirley, go get the prisoners some sandwiches," he says.

"You want to feed them, you go get them sandwiches," she says back. When we came in I got a quick look at her. A big woman with a big tumbleweed of brass-yellow hair, arms like hams, tits like twin footballs. "It's Sunday and I shouldn't of even come to work today in the first place," she says. I can hear her packing up her things to go.

"I'm gone," she says. The screen door slams behind her.

"I guess I'll get the sandwiches," the Deputy says. He leaves the room then, coming back, grabs ahold of the cell door, shaking it, making sure we're locked up good and tight, then goes out.

Me and Uncle Roosevelt sit there awhile.

"You ever been locked up?" I ask him.

"No," he says.

"Me neither," I says.

"I got a feeling about that Sheriff, you know the fat one," he says.

My stomach sinks. I think of the plaque in the quadrangle at school. "What kind of feeling?" I ask.

My Uncle's voice is flat. "I got a feeling that fat cracker ain't seed his own dick in many a year," he says.

We both laugh at that.

There's someone standing at the window of the cell. Standing on her tiptoes, barely able to see in. Cousin Billy.

"You wanna bust out?" she says. "I could bust you out."

"The Deputy's gone for sandwiches," Uncle says.

"You got a gun?" I says.

"I got a razor-file," she says. "It could cut the bars."

"We grown men, girl," Uncle says. "If the bars was cut, no way in hell we could slip through this little window."

"It was an idea," she says.

"How's June?"

"Aunt June's fine."

"I got a feeling we'll be out in the morning," Uncle Roosevelt says. "Go back and tell your Aunt June to sit tight."

Billy turns and goes across the road where they got the truck parked in the shade.

"She had a good idea," I says. My hot and wild cousin.

"I tolt you she was a good woman," Uncle Roosevelt says. "A good family-minded woman. Can't never go wrong with a woman like that."

JUNE FLOWERS BEEDE

We can see the window of where they locked up. It ain't easy sleeping sitting in the seats so we laying in the truck bed now. Lucky it ain't raining is all I got to say. Nothing we could do about the police. Billy is laying on her side. First one side then the other. I done quit talking about the baby she got. I'm pretending she don't got no baby inside. She's getting rid of it. The Bible says *Thou shalt not kill,* but by the look on Billy's face, if me or Teddy was to try and thwart her, she'd most likely kill us too. She's made her mind up so I gotta make my mind up too, remake it away from having a baby in the house to just being me and Teddy and her in the house like it already is.

"Excuse me," someone says. A white man, sounds like.

Billy sits up quick and I sit up slow. The white policeman, the one who took Teddy and Homer in, is standing there at the tailgate with a package in his hand.

"I brought your men sandwiches," he says. "It took longer than I thought to get them. I had to make them myself. I made some for you all too." He lifts the bag towards us. We don't move.

"We ain't hungry," Billy says.

I look at my hand. It's reached out automatically for the food. I drop my arm, pretending like I was flicking the offer away. "Thanks just the same," I says, trying to make my voice sound hard like Billy's do. We're in Tryler. I can only make my voice sound so hard.

"We don't got no colored ho-tel in Tryler," the policeman says.

"We fine right here," Billy says. Her voice has a thick strangling sound that loops around the voice of the policeman, his voice trying to be kind, and the sandwiches in his hand, strangling the kindness out of them both. This policeman don't know how lucky he is. He got a one-legged Negro woman who ain't saying much and a two-legged knocked-up Negro gal who is only being disagreeable. The white policeman's lucky that Billy ain't doing a Willa Mae right now. She'd be cussing him out and telling him to go south.

He leans on the side of the truck. Billy gives him one of her looks but he don't back off. "We got two extra beds in the jail. You two gals are welcome to them," he says.

"No thank you," Billy says almost before the offer clears the policeman's mouth.

"Ma'am?" he says, asking me directly.

I look at Billy. When you got one leg you feel like you deserve other things. Like an extra piece of pie or a real mattress on a real bed instead of sleeping in a truck. Billy's face is telling me blood is more important than comfort. But Billy ain't my blood. Roosevelt ain't my blood neither. Here I am, with my Flowers' blood still in me, in deep with these Beedes. Instead of being lifted up over the Brazos River and carried across to the young and good-talking traveling preacher and being enveloped in his promises of better things and being nestled in the bosom of the folks he had listening to his every word, I feel like I done fell into the river of Beedes and got swept along in they thick brown water. The first months of our marriage, I swam against the Beedes. I told Roosevelt I wanted to go to northern California where my family was at. He coulda preached there. We borrowed a car and went west for about a day then he turned around. He weren't interested in no California. He was the husband, after all. It came down to me or him. He bought me a hardcover map of the world and he built his church. It seemed all right for a while, then somehow there weren't no God in it no more and he knew it and I knew it too. But I couldn't just leave. I was too far downstream to just get out. Beede is more my blood now, I guess. Like I got me one of them transfusions.

"I'm good right where I'm at," I tell the policeman.

He pushes against the side of the truck as he leaves. "If you change yr mind, I'll be right there in the office all night. And don't you worry about yr men folk. It don't look to me like they done nothing but speeding. They'll be out first thing in the morning," he says.

"It'd be nice if they could get out now," I says.

"I gotta do my job ma'am," he says. He stands there, several feet away from the truck, looking up and down the length of it, then sighs and turns to walk back into the jailhouse.

"If you want to take one of them beds, I'll be all right out here by myself," Billy says. "Willa Mae got me locked up more than once, that's how come I ain't too partial to them, you know."

I wanna tell her that a bed would be good for her baby, but she don't got no baby, she and me have agreed on that much. "When me and my family was on our way to California we used to sleep outside all the time," I says.

We sit there in the quiet. It gets dark. There are stars out. My Daddy knowd the names of some of them. Venus. Orion. Big Dipper. North Star.

"You miss your family?" Billy asks.

"Yes and no," I says.

"I know whatchu mean," she says. "Sometimes I miss Willa Mae. Sometimes I don't. I mean I miss that she ain't alive but I don't wish she was here. If she was here, me and her'd be in the jailhouse and I'd be listening to her either cuss that Deputy out or sweet-talk him into bringing her some Lucky Strikes. She got a Sheriff to bring her a bottle of champagne once."

It's dark. No moon. She can't see my face and I can't see hers.

"How come you call her Willa Mae?" I says.

"That's her name," Billy says.

"Don't be smart with your Aunt June, now."

Billy lets a heavy breath out. "She liked being called her name," she says.

"You liked it too, I guess," I says.

"Look at all them stars," she says.

"Big Dipper's right there," I says pointing, but I can't tell if she's looking or not.

"I callt her 'Mother' in my head, but not out loud," Billy says. "That was the way she wanted it."

I can't hear Billy breathe or move or nothing. I let out a long sigh but she stays quiet. I move toward her, sliding slow across the ridges of the truck bed. If I move too fast she may run off. I get close enough and put my arm on her shoulder. She lets it stay there for a minute then shrugs it away.

"This town is Tryler," I says. "It's a hard town."

"Every town's hard," Billy says.

BILLY BEEDE

We was in the jailhouse in Abilene. We was in the jailhouse in French-burg. We was in the jailhouse in Sweetwater. We was in the jailhouse in Wildarado. The Galveston jailhouse caught Mother, not me. I stayed in the car hiding underneath the seat for a whole day. Brownsville jail-house. The jailhouse in Santa Anna. A jailhouse in a place called Alice. Others I can't remember. I think it was Greenville where Dill came to get us out. They got Mother's fingerprints on file all over. She said she was running out of places to go. The beds all smelt like bad luck and piss and sweat. We was locked up once and Mother did something with a man and he turned the key. She didn't think I knew what she did, but I knew.

We was in Santa Anna. She told me she'd been locked up for steal-ing, but the way the men was looking at her, I knew she'd done some-thing else. They locked me up too cause I was crying outside wanting my mother. The lady who worked at the desk looked at Mother sleep-ing in the jail then looked at me. "She your real mother?" the lady wanted to know. "Whatchu mean?" I asked the lady. "Your mother's the one you came out of, silly," the lady said, laughing, thinking I didn't know that much. I just let her laugh. "I ain't come out of nobody," I told her and that made her shut up. *I been in the jail from Abilene to Galveston.* Mother would sing that. I can't recall how it went exactly. *I been in the jailhouse from Abilene to Galveston. I seen the Gulf of Mexico, through the jailhouse walls.* It went something like that.

WILLA MAE BEEDE

I been in jail.
From Abilene way down to Galveston.
I seen the Gulf of Mexico through the jailhouse wall.
I wore my chain gang stripes digging ditches by the road
But I swear to you I never did much wrong.

They locked me up,
They thrown away the key.
They tell me that I'm never going home.
They got me wearing stripes and digging ditches by the road
The bad they do's worse than the bad I done.

I went begging to the Sheriff
I went pleading to the Judge
I swore on a stack of Bibles miles high
Still they put me on the chain gang
Still they threw away the key
Guess I'll live in this great prison till I die.

ROOSEVELT BEEDE

The Deputy comes to my cell just before the light comes up. He's got his keys in his hand.

"You can go now," he says, unlocking the bars.

"The boy's still sleep," I says, looking at Homer.

"I'll unlock the cell anyways," he says letting the door yawn open. "Leave when you like."

"The Sheriff wants to keep us," I says.

"I'll take care of the Sheriff," he says. "You all go on your way."

"I'd like to take a walk around the town," I says. He nods, giving me the OK, and I cross the threshold and walk down the steps. I've heard men say that free air smells and feels different from the air of bondage. It's true. There is a lightness to it and a crispness and a willingness of the air. In the cell the air is hard like the cell is hard. The first breaths They breathed when They was set Free, back in the day, that musta felt different too.

If it's where I remember it to be it'll be standing just around that bend there, past the cluster of thin pines. The pines are thicker than they was when we was here. I used to be able to see my church in between them as I walked up but I don't see nothing now. I will see it soon though, it's just around the turn.

And then I get there, standing where it used to be. Used to be. Standing where it is. No. It ain't there no more. There is a space of land. A clearing. And a sign, with seven letters spelling out some writing, posted in the lot. Nothing else. Not even the markings on the ground showing something used to stand here. The dirt-clumped grass is green, it ain't even flattened or worn. I stand there slapping my hand against the side of my leg, thinking if I slap myself hard enough or suck my teeth long enough I will suck and slap my church back into sight.

A fella comes up walking to work with his lunch pail. I can see him out the corner of my eye. A white fella. He stands a few feet behind just watching me look at the blank space on the land and not saying nothing.

"That land's FOR SALE," he says. "You buying it?"

"No," I says.

"You lost?" he asks.

Yes. That's it. I am lost.

I talk without turning around to look at him. "There is a church here," I says. I can't say "was" because my church is still in my head.

"It was tore down," he says.

"It was tore down," I says repeating.

"It makes an interesting story," he says kindly. "A crop duster hit it by accident. No one, not even the pilot, was hurt. After Best crashed into it, funny enough, that was the crop-dusting fella's name, colored fella too, you know, just trying to make his way, so Best, who I guess weren't the best of pilots, crashes down. Nothing suffered but the old raggedy church."

"The old raggedy church," I says.

"You musta seen it when it was up," the white fella says. "It was all bowed wood. We used to bet money on when it was gonna come crashing down. It was whatchu call an eyesore."

"It was a church," I says.

"I don't mean no disrespect," he says, "but it were an eyesore, I'm telling you."

"An eyesore," I says repeating.

"And after it got crashed into, well, the fella who owned the land at that point, I forget his name, some bigshot from Dallas, he had the damn thing—"

"The damn thing," I says repeating. "The goddamn thing."

"He had it tore down."

The fella finishes his story and stands there, looking from me to the empty land and back again.

"You ain't from around here," he says.

"No."

"You maybe went to that church once," he says, "that was, at least on one Sunday in your life, your place of worship, and here I am calling it a eyesore and whatnot," he says.

"Call it what you want," I says.

"I go to First Baptist," he says. "My church ain't much to look at neither. My wife is wanting to convert, you know, she wants to be a Catholic like that President Kennedy. But what do I want with some I-talian pope fella all the way over in Italy telling me when to sit and stand and whatnot, I tell her."

I close my eyes and open them. My church is still gone.

"All right then," the man says going. He walks down the road with his lunch bucket creaking as he swings it.

I keep standing there. It weren't just a church. It was my church. I made it myself out of slats of pine wood. I rented and cleared the land. I was going to preach in a church like I'd done for years along the rivers. Me and June showed up here. God had been quiet from the moment I turned our borrowed car around, from the moment I put my foot down and reminded June that I was the husband, and the wife would bend to the husband's will because I'm my own man which means I didn't want to go to California and live under her daddy's thumb. *I just turned around,* I told God, *it ain't like I ditched my wife in some ditch by the road.* But God stayed quiet and I stayed turned around and we showed up here. Pastors wanted us to join their churches. Not build a new one. They guarded their congregations like money. And God was silent in my ear, but June didn't know that, she just thought building a church made me tired. She didn't know my calling had gone and I thought, if I could just build a church, my own church with my own hands, then my God would come back into my ear like he had been since I was small. A man gived me a good deal on the wood and I remember kneeling down with them pine boards and the smell of the pine and thanking God for making it possible for me to rent the land and buy the wood outright and I didn't need help from nobody. I could make it on my own all right in Tryler. I set the boards flush. Tongue and groove. It was as tight as a boat. No light shone through except in the spaces I had left for the windows. Me and June painted the church together. We painted it white. And it was ready. I would preach every day of the week. Loudly. There was a few people who liked what I had to say and folks who knew me from my river days would make a trip to hear me. But my calling—. And then it turned out that the pine boards was green. They hadn't been cured and, after a year or so, they buckled and bowed. Eyesore, the fella called it. I guess it was.

When I say I lost my church I let folks think I'm talking just about the structure. I talk about how the bank came and kicked us off the land cause, try as we might, we couldn't pay the rent. That version of the story's easier to tell. I tell how the bank took my church. I don't tell about God leaving my ear. All and all, I still expected the church to be standing. Maybe weathered and worse for wear, but if not standing, then at least a pile of tumbled-down slats and crushed windows, cause we did put windows in, one on each side made of blue- and yellow- and red-colored glass. I expected to walk up here and see the church or the remains of the church or at least, at the very least, the place where my church had trampled down the ground.

I move a little to the left. The worst is coming. I can feel it coming. The path that led down from the church steps is growd over too. And worse than losing my calling, worse than losing my church, worse than seeing the grass green and not brown and trampled down, worse than all that, is that I can't recall *exactly* where it stood. Where, say, the front porch started. If I walked right now into the empty field, and spanned my arms out, I wouldn't know, *for certain,* where the door or windows was. The land has forgot it and I've forgot it too.

There is nothing to look at no more. I go back to the jail. I got my silver dollar in my pocket. It'll go towards breakfast.

June is there, awake earlier than all the others and a little sleepy-looking from laying all night in the truck. She's sitting on the front stoop, rubbing her one knee like she do when she's feeling her artharitis.

"You gone to visit your church," she says. Not asking cause she knows where I've been.

"That's right," I say and I smile. "It looks better than it did when we left it."

"How bout that," she says, smiling with me.

"Someone fixed it up. It don't bow no more."

"Maybe it'll be yours again someday," she says.

I look at her square in the face. "Let's hit the road," I says.

BILLY BEEDE

I'm riding with Cousin Homer in his car. About twenty miles west of Tryler. Teddy and June are up ahead in the truck. We're letting them take the lead. I got the directions to Uncle Blood's writ out, but we ain't gonna get nowhere near there for a while yet. We lost a whole day on account of that jail.

"Uncle Roosevelt says you going to keep me from going too fast," Homer says.

"I can't keep you from doing nothing," I say.

"You ever go fast?" he asks.

"I'm a married woman," I tell him and he just sticks his bottom lip out and nods his head. I can tell he don't believe me.

We ride along looking at the road. I got a scarf on my head to keep my hair down.

"What you need are some sunglasses," Homer says, "then you'd look like a movie star, heading towards Hollywood in her convertible." We both smile at that and before I know it I start singing one of Mother's songs. I say it loud, not really singing more like yelling. Homer laughs.

You may not want me, riding in your car
You may not want me, while you smoking yr cigar
But I'm your jewel, Daddy, I'm your most precious jewel.

"You planning on being a singer?"

"I don't got the talent."

"Singers make good money."

"I got a talent for hair."

"You got more going for you than that," Homer smiles.

He puts his hand on my thigh. I don't move it. It feels warm. His hand is smaller than Snipes', but heavier.

"Maybe you could be my woman," he says.

"I don't know about that," I says.

He keeps his hand there, moving it inch by inch up my leg and when he gets to my crotch he shovels his hand in between my legs and right up against my thing. The baby don't seem to mind.

We ride without talking. We pass a little house right on the side of the road. A man and his wife sit in lawn chairs in the front yard watching the cars pass. They got an oil pump in the back.

"How come you're named Billy with a 'y'?" Homer asks. He's still got his hand down there.

"It's after Billie Holiday."

"Her name has an 'ie' not a 'y.' "

"Willa Mae had her own way of doing everything," I says.

"My mamma told me about your mamma," Homer says. "What she told me is pretty remarkable."

"She loved to sing," I says. "Even though she's passed, I feel like she *still* wants to be a singer."

Homer hears that and takes his hand away. He looks at me, lifting up his eyebrows. "That's an interesting theory, but it doesn't hold water," he says.

"It's just something I feel," I says.

"I've got a whole year of college under my belt," Homer says smiling. "First thing you learn in college is what holds water and what doesn't hold water. Yr ideas about yr mother being passed and still wanting to be singing, they're nice ideas, but they don't hold water," he says.

"I knew her pretty good," I says.

"I'm just saying," he says.

There's a Texaco up ahead. The red star with the big green T.

"Now, that treasure she's got waiting for you, *that* holds water," Homer says. He takes my hand, lifts it to his lips. Kisses it. His kiss feels better than Snipes's. Smarter maybe.

He lets go of my hand and pets my titty. It feels good.

"You're a hot and wild mamma," he says.

"No I ain't."

"You and me and that treasure could have some hot and wild fun," he says.

I shrug my shoulders and he moves his hand off. He looks mad.

"Let's stop and get gas," I says.

WILLA MAE BEEDE

Lucky day,
Oh lucky, lucky day
All day long the day that I met you.
Sunshine and roses
And Valentine-proposes
Lucky, lucky-ducky-lucky day.

My hey-day
Hey, this is my hey-day
How long is such a good day gonna last?
You turned my head this evening
Wore my bed all out, then you set me dreaming.
I woke up alone, I guess my lucky day's done passed.

BILLY BEEDE

This filling station here is better than what we got. The bright Texaco sign, the big clean office with a garage next door to it and, across the road, a place to eat.

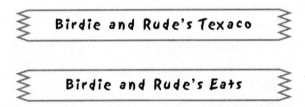

Birdie and Rude's Texaco

Birdie and Rude's Eats

A skinny white gal comes out. She's got on a Texaco uniform that fits her close and long yellow hair swinging free. She looks us both over then gives a sly look at the restaurant across the road.

"We'd like some gas," Homer says.

"Yes, sir," she says.

Homer holds out a five-dollar bill. I see it's the last bill in his wallet, but the yellow-haired gal ain't seed it. He takes it out slow and confident like there's plenty more bills where that comed from.

"This yr place?" Homer asks.

"You betcha," she says.

I wanna ask who Rude is, but I don't say nothing.

She takes Homer's money. Her and him look each other in the eyes, then her eyes slide down his body, looking him all over.

"We'll take two dollars' worth and you can keep the change," Homer says. His voice sounds nervous.

"I thank you," the gal says.

I cough and she looks at me quick. She don't see no wedding ring, so she looks back at Homer.

"Nice car you got," she says.

"It's a Park Lane," he says. Her and him smile at each other.

"How bout that gas?" I says.

"My cousin and I are out for a ride today," Homer says, his voice sounding deeper now, deeper than it did when he was talking to me. The white gal peels herself off the car, going to pump the gas and clean the windows. Homer watches her as she works.

"Our place is bigger than this," I tell Homer.

"They've got a restaurant," Homer says.

"We got a restaurant too," I says.

"I'll come visit sometime, little cousin," Homer says, patting me on the head. Patting me on the head like he ain't felt my crotch and kissed my hand a mile ago.

I get out the car. "I'ma go get some sandwiches," I says.

The gal pipes up quick, "Rude don't serve—well you know, you'd best be getting food someplace else."

I head across the road anyhow. The diner's got a sign in the window saying

We don't serve NO niggers

I peek through the screen and don't see no one. There's a radio playing Elvis. I turn back to see what Homer's doing and a truck is passing. When the truck clears I see Homer sitting on the top edge of his seat talking to the gal while she checks his oil.

Inside the diner is quiet. No one around. A list of the specials on the back wall above the grill. Three tables, all of them empty except for salt and pepper shakers and bottles of hot sauce and menus. Out back, sitting in the sun, there's a lean white man, wearing shiny black lizard-

skin boots and a white apron and a paper cook's hat. He's reading a
newspaper out loud.

"Jesus has been spotted in Dallas!" he says.

There are two pies on the counter, both covered with glass cases.

"Legless woman gives birth to twins!" he says.

One pie is pumpkin. The other cherry. I take the cherry pie, the
whole thing, and head back out front, hiding it behind my back. Homer
ain't at his car. Probably went to the restroom. I'm making a shovel with
my fingers and scooping the pie right out the tin plate. It's still warm.
One of them, probably the man in the white apron, cooked it. I got five
slices left and I leave them on the front seat of the car to go look for the
restroom, around the side of the building where the sign points to. They
got one for ladies and one for gentlemens with a "Whites Only" sign
that's been crossed out, rewrote, and crossed out again. The ladies room
got yellow tile on the floor and a yellow-colored toilet and a yellow-
colored face bowl with a tap for the hot and a tap for the cold and a slim,
almost-used-up yellow-and-white bar of soap. I take my time in there,
using the toilet then washing my hands and patting my face and neck
with water and fixing my hair. I lift up my dress and look at my belly. It
looks bigger than it did last week. Maybe Homer touching me made it
grow. I don't know what to say to the baby so I don't say nothing. I
think of it with Snipes' face and that makes it easy to hate.

I look in the office. It's neat and clean, twice the size of ours. They
don't got no pallet under the cash register like we got, just a desk and a
chair and a cash register and pictures of tires and a calendar with a pin-
up gal on it.

Through the back of the office door, where we got our trailer at,
they got heaps of junk. Anything you could want. Seats from a movie
theater, the purple velvet fabric gone blue-gray in the sun. A tricycle. A
baby buggy with big wheels. Three or four rusted-out cars with they
broken windows and they hoods up and no engines and no seats. A row
of plastic dwarfs riding reindeers, the kind of decorations people like
Mr. and Mrs. Jackson put in they yards at Christmas. Piles and piles of

old tires. A sign that says "Mobil Gas" with the red flying horse. A shed with a door with a cut-out crescent moon on it, the old outhouse. The door's closed. I'm about to go back to the car when I hear the moaning sounds. More like whimpering, like a dog caught in a raccoon trap.

I look through the slats of the shed. There's plenty of sunlight coming through so I can see them. Homer's leaning up against the wall and the gal is kneeling in front of him. She got his thing in her mouth.

Back in the car I sit on the top of the seat back like I seen Homer do. I eat as many pieces of pie that I can. Three more pieces then I'm full. Homer comes striding through the office with a grin on his face.

"They got a good-looking restroom," he says.

"How so?" I says, but he don't say. His zipper is opened and he sees me noticing it and turns around and zips up.

The gal comes out of the office and, after looking over at the restaurant and spitting, leans her tight pants in the doorway, trying to look bored.

"Come see us again sometime, hear?" she says.

"Will do," Homer says.

When we're out of sight of the filling station, he takes up my hand again and gives me another kiss. I don't say nothing. He stretches and yawns and falls asleep and I keep my eyes on the road.

DILL SMILES

Me and Laz are almost to El Paso. He drives good and steady. I told him we gonna try to get all the way there without hardly stopping and he don't mind that.

"There's a good-looking car," Laz says. We pass a Texaco belonging to Birdie and R-something. A red convertible parked out front with nobody in it.

"That car ain't for me," I says.

"What kind is it?" he asks.

"How the hell I know," I says. Willa Mae had a Bel Air.

"That's the car for me," Laz says. He watches it in his rearview and then pulls his eyes back to the road. "I'ma get a car one of these days. My own car."

"With what money?"

"I'm my daddy's right-hand man," he says. "What kind of car you think would best suit me?"

"Lemme think on it," I says.

I look him over. His black smooth skin. High cheekbones and pointy chin. His wool cap, sitting on the back of his head. Head forward, concentrating. Plaid shirt, black suit, clip-on tie, hands not gripping the wheel but pressing hard against it, working hard at doing just a little bit of work. A slow wit but not lazy with his eyes on the road.

"Whassit like?" he asks.

"What's what like?"

"Women," he asks. He looks steady but sounds a little jumpy.

"You got to find that out on yr own," I says and that quiets him, leaving me free to think.

Willa Mae. She went and told whoever would listen, North and Little and them, that I weren't a man. She didn't mean to. Son Walker had her under his thumb. When he showed up and told me he was staying, I told Willa she could do whatever she wanted with him but she was gonna have to do it in my house and in my bed and I weren't sleeping on no floor. So they would do it right there while I read the newspaper. I didn't like it but at least I could keep my eye on her. Someone heard about Son and Dill Smiles in bed with Willa Mae and called Son sissified and cut him in the street. He couldn't hold his head up. Wanted to leave town. That's how come Willa started talking. Cause if Son was in bed with Willa, and Dill weren't no man, then Son weren't no sissy. Shit. He left her anyway.

Me and Willa Mae. We started up quick and we ended just as quick. That's how we went. Quick.

"I gotta take a piss," Laz says. And I nod cause I do too and he pulls over to the side of the road. The sign, "Welcome to El Paso," is just ahead. He stands there, with his back to the road, taking his thing out. I walk a distance, so I can have my privacy.

LAZ JACKSON

She pees standing up.

UNCLE BLOOD BEEDE

I ain't got much of a place but at least it's mines. Blood's Bucket, established in 1943. Me and Precious been running it since then and we gonna run it until we die. We do all right. We could do better if we sold a variety of drinks and a full-course dinner, but all we sell is my Block and Tackle. Could do better, but we do all right.

They come in about an hour ago. Cousin Teddy and June first, then little Billy and Homer, Estelle's son. The first thing I get them to do is stand up against the wall so I can mark they heights. Teddy and June ain't been here in twenty years and they're a little shorter. Billy, all growd up's taller than she was in 1957. I ain't never met Homer so his mark is fresh. I show them my best table, the one furthest from the front door and closest to the back exit. They pull up the chairs and, the four of them, all hunched over, count they money. Me and Precious stand behind the bar, giving them they privacy. They count and recount a pile of coins.

"You shouldnta gived that policeman that twenty," Teddy says to Homer.

"I was trying to get us out of a scrape."

"And it only got us into one."

"He was trying to help," June says. She looks over at another table where she got four different kinds of flowers, pulled up off the side of the road by the roots and brought in from the sun.

"How much we got?" Billy asks.

"Twenty-four cents," Teddy says, and they all lean away from the table. The little pile of money looks lonesome.

Precious comes out from behind the counter with a pitcher of ice water and four jars. She stands there serving them and Billy looks at her ring. A big fake bunch of rubies.

"Uncle Blood gave me this ring when him and me got married," Precious says.

"I don't remember it," Billy says. She was small when her and Willa Mae stopped here on their way to Hollywood.

"I need more than water," Teddy says.

"I was waiting for you to ask," I says. I go underneath the bar and come out with a big jar full of my famous brew. Drink this, walk a block, and tackle anybody.

"We don't got enough money for gas," Billy says. She looks from me to Precious while she says it.

"I'd give you what I got cept I don't got nothing," I says. And it's true.

"Maybe some customers'll come in tonight," Homer says.

"It's the end of the month and the beginning of the week," Precious says, coming back to the counter as I go over to the table to pour drinks for Teddy and Homer.

I stand there watching the men drink. Teddy swallows his and smiles. Homer throws his back and stands up hollering.

"I got one of my two Josephs working for me," I says, "I could ask them for a loan on your behalf."

"We only need about ten dollars or so," Teddy says.

"Ask him for more if he can spare it," Billy adds, "just in case."

"I'll see how much he's got," I says.

"And tell him," Billy adds, "tell him we're only borrowing it till we dig up that treasure. We'll pay him back by Wednesday at the latest."

I go on outside.

Directly in back of my juke is a cement windowless shed where I keep my Brew. When I found that the heat in the summer had a way of turning the taste I took to leaving the door open then had to hire the two Josephs to guard the place on account of spies and thieves. A man named Joseph and another man, not his brother, who also goes by Joseph. They look Mexican but they say they are Indians. First Joseph says he is Comanche, second Joseph says he is Seminole. The two men, while not claiming to be related, look a lot alike.

"Inspection?" Joseph asks. He stands up straight, making himself as tall as he can, even though he only comes up to my shoulder. I would not cross him, though, small as he is.

"Let's take a look," I says.

Inside the shed the hard red-dirt floor is clean with all the jars neatly stacked. There's a little place in the center of the room. Long enough for a man to lie down.

Outside the door Joseph stands like a soldier on watch, his shotgun, with the butt in the ground, next to his foot and the barrel slanting out.

"How's it looking tonight, Mr. Joseph?" I ask him.

"Looking A-OK, Mr. Blood Beede."

"Seminole Joseph, am I right?" I says, guessing.

"Comanche Joseph," he says.

"It's the light," I says, making an excuse.

"You got customers tonight? That's fortunate."

"Not customers."

"I heard two vehicles. A truck. A Chevy truck and a new car that my ear can't place."

"They's family. Come to visit."

"Family is fortune, Mr. Blood Beede."

I stand there, agreeing with him without saying nothing. I stare at the back of my juke joint. I can see through the back door. They're hunched again over the table. Still and quiet like an oils painting. Joseph is looking in the same direction that I am looking but I can't tell what he's looking at.

"They need money and I ain't got none to give them. End of the month beginning of the week," I says.

"My pockets are empty too, Mr. Beede. Last night the wife made dirt soup," he says and we laugh.

"Thanks for letting me ask you, Mr. Joseph."

"I am always willing to entertain the possibility of anything," he says. The other Joseph told me that between them, they'd had seven years of college.

I walk inside, standing in the doorway.

Inside Billy turns from looking at the money pile, knowing all them looking at it won't make it grow. She takes Precious by the hand, looking at the ruby ring, turning it this way and that, watching the flash of the fake stones in the dim light of the room.

Family is fortune.

PRECIOUS BEEDE

Billy's looking at my wedding ring. I let her look as long as she likes. June's at a table by herself with her flowers. Blood, Teddy, and Homer are at the bar. Blood closes one jar bringing out another, older one. He gives them each a spoonful. They sip it like medicine.

"We don't got enough gas money but I bet the cars could run on this," Teddy says and the men laugh.

"Yr ring's got nice rubies," Billy says.

"They just glass," I says.

"I'll call my mamma to wire us some money," Homer says getting up.

"That's an idea," Blood says.

"I don't want Estelle lending us nothing else," Teddy says and Homer sits back down.

Billy is looking at my face, searching it, feature by feature. I know what she's thinking. I'm light. Lighter than her mother.

"You could pass, couldn't you?" she asks me.

I tell her how me and Blood was in town the other year and there was this Klan rally marching through like they do, marching in they white robes and waving they flags. They was handing out handbills and they handed out one to me, wanting me and other good white women like me to join them. Me and Blood laughed over that for about a year. "I guess I could pass," I says. "I ain't never felt the need, though."

Billy looks at my ring again. "We could try something," she says. The way she says it makes everybody look at her. She looks around the juke at all of us, then takes a glance at the door, making sure no one else can hear. Her eyes got a kind of fire in them. We all see it. "Willa Mae and me used to pull what's called a ring trick," she says.

"What's a ring trick?" Homer asks.

"We'll need yr ring," Billy says.

I twinkle my rubies and I look at Blood. He gives his OK so I slip off the ring, laying it on the table. It sets there between me and Billy. She don't touch it.

"I'ma need something different to wear and something like a hat and some sunglasses. We're gonna pull it at that filling station where me and Homer was before and they can't know me," Billy says. We all nod, like we know what she's talking about but we don't. None of us ain't never done no ring trick before.

"Is it a scam of some kind?" Homer asks. His voice is higher than usual.

Billy don't say nothing. June looks at Roosevelt who looks like he's gonna cancel Billy's plan but he don't say nothing neither.

"I got things you can wear," I says.

Billy picks up my ring, holding it to the light.

The day me and Blood got married, when he gave me that ring, his chest was puffed way out and he was grinning. It was a perfect fit without me ever telling him my size. The red of the ring matched the color that his hair used to be. His hair's gray now.

"Hold it up to your eye and it's like rose-colored glasses," Blood tells Billy.

Billy does like he says, holding the ring to the light. "We might not get this back," she says.

WILLA MAE BEEDE

To pull the ring trick right, you gotta pick the right Place. That's the most important part. If you don't pick the right Place, then yr just wasting yr time. It can be a filling station or a restaurant or a store. Of course, it's gotta have a cash register with some kind of money in it, but most important is that it's gotta be run by a man who got a Hole in his pocket. He makes decent wages, he may own the Place hisself or he may work it for a richer man. He makes his pay on Friday but on Friday night he's down at the track, or around a card table or he got dice in his hands, using his little bit of money to get hisself some more. He is the kind of man who would steal outright, if he had the guts to steal. This is the kind of man you want running the Place. Someone who looks himself in the mirror each morning while he shaves his face, who looks at his wife and tells himself and her too that he is the most honest hardworking man in the whole world and what is the world coming to with all these robbers and thieves about. But, of course, he would cheat and lie and steal if he only had the guts. You pick a Place run by a man like that and you got your ring trick pretty much done for you.

Son Walker taught me this trick. We would pull it together. When Billy came along and got old enough, Son was long gone but me and Billy would pull it together with whatever man we could find cause you need at least three people to do it. Dill ain't never pulled it with us cause she believes too much in hard honest work.

Like I was saying you need three folks, not counting the man who runs the filling station. You need a lady, a man, and a third person. The lady plays the Rich Lady, the man plays the Driver, and the third person plays what's callt the Finder. The Rich Lady's gotta be played by a gal who's got the airs of sophistication about her. She gotta look like money, even though she don't got a dime. It's best if she's flat broke cause that'll put the fire in her belly and makes her the best Rich Lady she could be. I would always play the Rich Lady. Now the Finder can be a man or a woman or a child. They got to be real honest looking. The Finder was always Billy's part. Getting a man to play the Driver wasn't never too hard. There's plenty of men who can drive a car.

After you pick your Place and get yr three people, next you need a Ring. Use one that looks real but ain't.

Then you need a Car.

The Car's gotta be good-looking. If you don't got one that belongs to you, go head and "borrow" one for the purpose. You only gonna be using it for a quick minute. It's worth it.

So you got your three people and you got yr Ring and yr Car and you got your Place all picked out. Say yr planning to pull yr ring trick at a filling station. We call the man working the filling station the Grease, short for Grease Monkey. OK. So the Rich Lady gets in the backseat, and her Driver, he's wearing some kind of suit or something and a cap, he drives her up to that filling station. He stands by the car and he waits. The Rich Lady goes to the restroom or the water pump or what-have-you, saying she got to freshen up. Make sure the Grease sees her go to freshen up. Make sure the Grease sees her go back to her car. The Rich Lady sashays away, and when she comes back to the car she's all flustered. Make sure the Grease sees all that. She tells the Grease she done lost her diamond ring in the restroom or by the water pump. Her and her Driver look around for it. She looks flustered and her Driver looks more flustered than she do. The Grease might help look he might not. The Rich Lady tells the Grease that, should he find her ring, she gonna give him a five-hundred-dollar reward. If yr playing the Rich Lady make sure you looking right at the Grease when you say "five hundred dollars." Say the money like there was more where that comed from. Say it slow. Make sure he hears you. Look him right in the face when you speak. Look right into the Hole you know he got in his pocket. Say "five hundred dollars" like it ain't nothing to you. You might have to practice this bit before you get it right. Say "five hundred dollars" and try to sound bored. Don't suck in your breath or suck your teeth when you say the money. Breathe the green of them greenbacks out to the Grease. Make him feel like that money is already in his own pocket. Then you write down your phone number for him. I always tolt them Hollywood, California, or New York City or Chicago. You gotta learn the exchanges of these places by heart. Write the number on a slip of paper and remind him that, if he should find the ring, there will be a five-hundred-dollar reward. Then you hit the road.

When yr pulling out, turn around and watch him. He should be looking around for the ring as you go.

Next thing that happens you don't see but you know how it happens cause you planned it. Your Finder comes up to the filling station. She just a poor scrawny thing walking up out of nowheres looking down at the ground as she walks.

Lo and Behold.

The Finder done found the ring. Now of course that ring wasn't never lost cause the Rich Lady only just pretended to have it and to lose it and the Finder done pretended to find it but had it with her all along, you know. So the Finder done found the ring. And she makes a big deal of it. Maybe she got to holler cause the Grease is most likely as not in the toilet scrounging every inch of the place for that very ring, so your Finder got to holler and jump around and make a scene. Make sure yr Finder ain't shy and quiet. So the Finder hollers and the Grease comes out and he works like a mule to get the Finder to give him that ring. He's thinking of that five-hundred-dollar reward money in his pocket, the things he can buy with it, the stories he gonna tell his friends, maybe he already in his mind done quit his job pumping gas, maybe he already in his mind is on his way to the Big City and is in the middle of a long and satisfying five-hundred-dollar reward-money drinking-and-whoring spree complete with cards and dice and a young gal who's the spitting image of Jean Harlow. Your Finder's holding up a ring she just found, holding it up to the sunlight and saying something bout the twinkling of the diamonds and your Finder's got the Grease's whoring-and-drinking spree twinkling in her hand. And he gotta get that ring, see. And them guts that he never had to steal and that Hole in his pocket work together and push an idea up into his head.

The Grease tells the Finder that he gonna give her money for the ring. No he ain't gonna split the reward money with her, he don't even mention no Rich Lady's reward. He just goes to his filling station cash register and opens it up and gives the poor dumb-looking Finder all the money he got in it. He ain't thinking of what his boss or his wife gonna say when they find the till empty. He's hearing them dice and them whores talking. He got a Hole in his pocket that needs filling. He cleans out his own till, giving it all to the Finder in exchange for that ring. What the hell. The Rich Lady will send him his reward. He knows it. The Finder grins big, real happy to get the maybe thirty or forty dollars out the cash register, and the Grease is laughing cause he got real money coming his way. The Finder takes the money, gives the Grease the ring and heads off. Now the Grease got the ring. He calls the Rich Lady's house. He don't expect her to be there yet but he figures he gonna talk to one of her servants. The phone number don't go through. The Rich Lady don't exist at all. The Finder is long gone and meets up with the Rich Lady and the Driver in they agreed-on meeting place and there they are, for the cost of a costume jewelry ring, thirty or forty dollars the richer.

Like I was saying. Me and Billy used to pull that one together quite a bit. We never got caught once. Well, we got caught once or twice but it was worth it. My Billy's got promise. She was the best Finder I ever seen. She's got what you call a Natural Way, and if she moves to a big city like Chicago or New York she could do pretty good for herself.

DILL SMILES

We pass an old sign.

> **Pink Flamingo Auto Court. 5 miles.**
> **Take a dip in our pool.**

Two sign painters are up there, crawling on the sign like ants, sprucing the lettering up.

"We almost there?" Laz asks. I nod yes.

A minute later we get to LaJunta.

> **Welcome to LaJunta, pop. 30.**

There's five buildings crouched along the edge of the highway.

"LaJunta," Laz says. He's looking at me now. I nod my head. He drove real good. I thought he was gonna fall asleep and steer the hearse into a ditch or a tree or something but he drove as good as I woulda.

Laz slows the hearse as we pass through the town, squinting at the little buildings. All of them cement, all of them sand-colored. A building with a flag out front. The law and post office combined.

"You grew up here?"

"Hells no."

"It's smaller than Lincoln," he says.

This early in the morning there's just a few people on the street. All of them whites. No Mexicans. None of us. They stare as we go by. Some of the men take off they hats.

"They don't know the difference between a funeral and a hearse that's just driving around," Laz says. He rolls down the window, looking at a man as we pass. A rancher-fella with an unshaved face and a sagging mouth and his hat across his heart, looking like he is about to weep. "No one died," Laz says to the man, but the man don't seem to hear. Laz slows down even more.

"I don't want to miss the motel."

"They got a big sign out front, you won't miss it," I says and we pick up speed again, leaving the little crowd behind us.

About a mile beyond town proper we see the big pink flamingo, standing on one leg and framed in neon. When Laz sees it his mouth opens up and it stays open until we've pulled up in front. Four little pink buildings with windows like patch pockets. All arranged in a half circle around the parking lot and the empty swimming pool. The building on the end's got a sign saying "Office," the others got numbers on them 11, 22, and 33. Each one got a new coat of pink paint.

"They know we're coming?" Laz asks.

"They will in a minute," I says.

I knock on the office but there ain't no answer. The door is freshly pink-painted plywood with a little doorknob, brass metal under a thin layer of pink paint. I stand there knocking for a good while. The thin screen is hot, the door behind it warm to the touch. After a while I kick the base of the door with my boot. But I don't kick too hard. Behind me, Laz, out of the hearse, stands in place, stretching his back, his arms, his sides.

The first time Willa Mae was here, I brought her. It was Christmas and she'd been living with me for three whole months. I wanted to show off the gal I was planning to marry.

There's a screeching sound as the screen from number 33 opens. A tiny walnut-colored woman wearing cowboy gear stands in the doorway. Her arms piled high with dirty sheets. She pats a space down in the middle of the pile, getting a good look at me.

"Hey, Ma," I says.

BIRDIE

Co-inky-dinky. I read about it in my *National Geographic*. A car pulls up. Fancy. Same kind that was here before but not. That's whatcha call a co-inky-dinky.

Rude is standing at the pumps crying about how his cherry pie got stolt and did I see anybody come up and steal it and I don't say nothing cause I did what I did with that Negro boy. He couldn't of stole it. And his wife he was with or his cousin or whoever the hell he said she was, she was pregnant and honest-looking and she didn't steal it. So Rude is standing there going on and on about how he's gonna get another gun to protect us and I ain't saying nothing cause something in my head thinks he's gonna get another gun so he can shoot me with it cause he knows what I did with that Negro boy. He is trying to smoke me out by talking about his cherry pie, but I ain't falling for it. I was crazy enough to marry Rude and I was crazy enough to put his name on the sign up there with mine and I'm crazy enough to cheat on him but I ain't crazy enough to tell him what I do.

I ain't the only one who cheats. I only started cheating cause Rude started cheating. Rude's short for Rudolph. The reindeer not the movie star. But none of that don't got nothing to do with the car that pulled up while he was going on and on about his pie.

A fancy car. And the same model and color like the one them colored cousins was driving or my name ain't Birdie. Only this one ain't theirs. It couldn't be. This one's got different folks in it. A white lady.

Rich as the day is long and her Driver. They just glide off the road and up to the pumps like they's riding on air.

"Get the hell across the street," Rude says to me in his do-what-I-says-or-I'ma-hit-you voice. I head across the road to the diner. We both know that, by the look of the Rich Lady, she gonna give him a big tip if he does a good job and he wants me to go cut out so he can get the whole tip for himself. I go across to the diner all right and I sit at the counter reading my *National Geographic*. They got a story in there about the Indians of India and how when they die they get cremated.

Across the street I watch them. Rude giving them full service and the Driver opening up a black umbrella so the Rich Lady can get protection from the heat. That's what you call living. The Rich Lady's living while Rude's scurrying around, pumping they gas and checking and double-checking they oil, double-washing they windshield. I can see his arms pointing and waving and his mouth going as he talks to the Rich Lady. I can't hear what he's saying but I can see how he's saying it. Stooping his back and working and running his fingers through his hair, making sure it's neat, probably using his gimme-a-big-tip voice. He polishes her headlights. We been married two whole years. This was my daddy's filling station and diner until he got too sick to run it so I ran it and when me and Rude got married I let Rude put his name up there with mines and that kilt my daddy pretty much. "Birdie and Rude's Texaco, Birdie and Rude's Eats," even though my daddy told me I was crazy. We been married two whole years and I ain't never seen Rude polish nobody's headlights. We don't see eye to eye, but that don't mean I like watching him beg. He's over there begging for a big tip and I would rather read about the Indians of India.

Getting cremated must hurt on some level but if you ever done anything you regret, I think it's the only way to go. Cremating's gonna be the way I choose. It would burn up all the evidence of what could be called my indiscretions. Talk about burning yr bridges. My body tracked-over with all the fingerprints of other men other than Rude. Those fingerprints will turn to smoke as my body burns.

I like reading *National Geographic* cause when I'm reading about faraway places time passes faster than when I'm reading about familiar things. When I look up from my magazine over a half an hour has gone by like it was nothing. Rude is in the office, from where I'm at it looks like he's on the phone. The fancy car's gone and what looks like a gal, in a big straw hat, is walking away fast down the road.

CANDY NAPOLEON

I don't run no Taj Mahal but I can say that, through hard times and good times, I've kept this Pink Flamingo running.

"You got the manners of a gentleman," I says to Mr. Laz Jackson. We're sitting out at the picnic table in front of Room 11. He's eating my baked chicken and is working fast through his third helping of my legendary cornbread dressing.

"It's kind of you to feed me," he says.

"You got manners enough to eat what's in front of you," I says.

"I'm hungry for sure," he says. "Dill wouldn't let me stop except for when it was necessary." He pulls his knit cap down on his head low, covering his eyes and thick eyeglasses, but he keeps eating.

"Dill's been funny all her life," I says.

"You oughta know, you being her mother and all," Laz says.

Dill, my own flesh and blood, don't want nothing but coffee. She's sitting out there on the grave with her gun. I got another daughter, Even, my only child with Big John Napoleon, the King of the Cowboys. Why do I call her "Even"? I didn't really want her but the good Lord got even with me. She turned out good, though. Still lives at home.

"You all come out here to dig up Willa Mae?" I ask him.

"I think we come out here not to dig, ma'am," he says.

"Ain't you hot in that wool cap?"

"No, ma'am," he says.

When he finishes his dinner I take him to see the rooms. They're all the same and the outside color scheme is continued indoors. Pink bedspreads and curtains. Pink end-tables with matching pink lampshaded lamps.

"How long you gonna be visiting?" I ask Laz.

"That's up to Dill," he says.

The way he says Dill's name makes it sound like they got a bond of some kind but I know enough about Dill to know Laz ain't her sweetheart. I offer him Room 11 to sleep in. He pets the bedspread then lays down, looking at the ceiling then at the walls. There's a photograph of me riding Trigger, one of John Henry's horses. It was the first rodeo where I showed off my standing-in-the-saddle act. Laz gets up from the bed to take a closer look.

"That you?"

"A long time ago."

"Standing up and riding in the saddle," he says. He looks from the photograph to me. I had style then. Now I got more style. My mail-order wig with my hair cascading down to my shoulders. My straw cowgal hat. My hot green western shirt with the silver fringe. My pressed dungarees and red snakeskin boots. I got a gold necklace in the shape of a horseshoe. Turned to the side the horseshoe makes a C. John Henry gave it to me. Horseshoe for luck and C for Candy. I smile at Laz showing him my two front teeth, gold like my good luck charm.

"I could ride bareback too," I says.

"I'd like to see that," he says.

Each room's got windows in the front and back. I part the curtains on the back. We see Dill, looking at the grave site with her head hung down. I open the front curtains. "In the morning you can wake up and look at the pool," I tell Laz.

"There ain't no water in it," he says, as politely as he can.

"Lemme show you our horse," I says and we go around back.

The crickets hiss at each other. A baby rabbit wallows in the cool dirt underneath a little soaptree yucca. "Feels like we walking around in a oven," Laz says.

"Radio says it'll be a hundred and ten degrees today," I tell him and he looks impressed.

Buster's got goat-milk-colored skin and eyes green as spinach and a swayback. We tether him up to the clothesline. He can run back and forth as much as he likes and a clothesline's cheaper than a fence. Laz pets Buster then fans his hand slow in front of Buster's face, moving the flies away. I look over at Dill. She's moved away from the grave and walked to the far edge of the field. She stands there looking at the single tractor, property of Rising Bird Development. The tractor's tires are right on the edge of my already-sold property line, ready to start plowing the land and making that supermarket come Thursday.

"The grave's over there," I says to Laz and we leave Buster to go look.

Dill sees us walking and leaves the tractor, crossing the field in her long-legged strides, beating us there. At the head of the grave there's a mound of stones, chalk-red but white-painted, in a low pile. A sprig of cudweed, with its round papery-white flowerheads and its nice lemony smell, is wedged in the middle of the rocks.

Dill snorts. "You put in them rocks?" she asks me.

"Even done it," I says. "She gathered and painted the rocks and puts a new flower there when the old one wilts." Even was eighteen when Willa Mae and Billy comed through. She seen her sister Dill kissing a dying and bloody woman on the lips.

Laz stands at the foot of the grave, looking at it. He takes off his cap and bows his head. His hair is pressed down and uncombed and a little long for my taste. "It's a nice headstone," he says.

"Cept the head's at the other end," Dill says.

I fight back the need to slap my daughter. Last time I hit her she was eight or nine. She was taller than me already and she hit me back.

LAZ JACKSON

I wonder when Billy and them will get here. Maybe she's changed her mind and won't come at all.

Dill shows me what's in her cloth bag. A pistol. She took my hearse into town and came back with a newspaper for Miz Candy, some peppermints for Even, and two boxes of bullets. Now we're both at the grave, walking around it and looking from the grave to the office and the motel rooms.

"Billy and them could come around either corner," Dill says.

"You gonna shoot them?"

"I ain't letting them dig," Dill says. "You be my lookout. When they come you tell me."

I don't want to be no lookout for Dill. She's got a gun.

"They probably ain't gonna get here before the tractors start," I says.

"Line up them cans and bottles," Dill tells me, pointing to a cement half-wall on the far side of Room 33. I line them up and she stands astride the grave and shoots. She hits them all but one.

"Line them up again," she says and I line them up again. She shoots them all down this time.

Miz Candy comes outside to sit on the back porch and read her newspaper.

"How come you shooting?" she asks.

"Just passing time," Dill says.

After a while of Dill's shooting and me resetting, Miz Candy goes in and gets a chair so Dill can sit while she practices her gun. Dill sits there, in a fold-down chair, right next to the grave. Me and Miz Candy sit in the shade.

"Dill's a good shot," Miz Candy says. "If a man was sitting in that tractor, Dill could shoot his eye out from where she's sitting right now."

The tractor's at the edge of the already-sold five acres. From where I'm sitting it could all fit in my hand. Shit. "Dill's planning a shoot-out," I says.

"She better not," Miz Candy says.

"I'm just saying what she said to me."

Miz Candy waves at Dill, catching her attention. "You kill Billy and them, you'll get the electric chair," she yells.

"I'll take my chances," Dill yells back.

Miz Candy stands up and puts her hands on her hips. Dill quits shooting. When she sits back down Dill starts up shooting again.

"Dill and me don't favor," Miz Candy says frowning up her face at Dill like she knows they mother and daughter but ain't sure how it happened.

"She wants to kill someone," I says.

"She can want all she wants but she ain't killing nothing," Miz Candy says. Her mouth is set in a hard line. I relax a little bit, but just a little. "If you ever have children make sure you have more than one," she says.

"How come?"

"You might not get it right the first time."

"That's good advice."

"I got a second daughter, Even, she's following in my footsteps. Not like Dill. Even's a horsewoman, like me."

"I'd like to meet her."

"She don't get up till after noon," Miz Candy says.

"More cans!" Dill commands me, and I reset the cans again on the cement wall. She shoots them down and I reset them, getting new empties from the trash when the ones getting shot get too full of holes. The bullets move faster than you can see them. You can hear the ringing sounds when they hit. You can see the cans jump up, surprised.

"That bit of cement wall's the start of Room 44," Miz Candy says.

Dill shoots. Buster, the horse they got, stamps back and forth.

"I guess there ain't gonna be no digging," I says.

"Billy ain't had her say, yet."

"They might not get here," I says.

"They'll get here," Candy says.

After a while, Dill quits shooting. She relaxes in her chair with her straw hat pulled down over her face. "When they get here, you tell me," she says, going to sleep in the sun. Miz Candy's nodding over her newspaper, falling asleep too.

I go look around, peeking into the rooms from their windows that face the back. I peek in the window of the office. There's some papers on the desk. There's a kitchen with pots on the stove, and the sack of mints Dill bought when she bought her bullets sitting on the table. There's a bedroom. One bed neatly made and in the other bed there's a big gal sleeping. She's about the size of two of me. A fan on the ceiling moving slow. Pictures of horses on the walls.

Out front's the pool. It's painted blue so, from a distance, you would think it had water in it. If you passed the Pink Flamingo quick without stopping, you would, maybe in the heat of the desert, kick yrself for not stopping to take a dip. But there ain't no water in this pool. There's just a wooden diving board that looks full of splinters, sticking out like a dried-up tongue over the big blue-painted cement hole. I always thought the water made a pool blue, not the paint.

The big gal comes out of the office to stand beside me. She got on a white dress and white sneakers with no laces or socks. She's eating the mints.

"Only guests can use the pool," she says.

"They got to bring they own water, too," I says. She laughs and I like the way her body shakes.

I tell her I come here with Dill Smiles and she runs, pretty fast too, around the house to see. After a minute she comes back to me, walking.

"You my sister Dill's friend?" the gal asks.

"Kind of," I says, and we tell each other our names.

"You taking Willa Mae home in yr hearse?"

"Dunno yet," I says.

Even takes a red-and-white peppermint out of the sack, holding it between her finger and thumb, letting the color melt off a little before putting it in her mouth and crunching down. The mint smell coming from her mouth makes the hot air smell good.

"I'm bored looking at this pool," she says. She goes around back again and this time I follow her. We stand there looking at the horse.

She jerks some grass from the ground and holds a clump out. "Buster," she says to the horse. He comes over. She holds the clump flat on her hand. "You gotta feed him like this or he'll bite you," she says.

Buster mumbles the clump into his mouth. Stands there chewing.

"My mom's training me to ride bareback like she do."

"You gonna be in the rodeo?"

"They're coming to town in October. I'ma try out," she says. She keeps feeding the horse.

Buster stands very still, eating, pricking up his ears and turning them backwards and forwards listening to Dill sleeping and Candy sleeping and the tractors plowing the land even though they ain't started plowing yet. But they will be. Come Thursday, first of the month. Maybe they're making a sound right now that only Buster can hear. He pricks his ears east. If Billy and them are coming down the road the horse might hear them coming. He can hear Billy's baby being born too, I'll bet, even though that's farther down the road than Billy and them getting here. I'ma ask Billy to marry me again. Maybe the horse can hear that too.

Dill, stretched out in her chair, baking in the sun, draws a long line with herself.

"Yr sister sure is tall," I says.

"Mister Dill," Even says laughing. "But she ain't no real man."

Yr sister's more of a man than I am, I say in my head, not out loud.

Buster's skin shivers and he takes off, running back and forth.

"He's gonna break free and run off," I says.

"We're getting a fence put up when the tractors start," Even says.

"If I was Buster I would break free and run off just for fun," I says.

"Where to?"

"I would just run, you know, around," I says. I take off my glasses wiping them clean on my shirt. The horse makes a nice white blur then I put my glasses on again. I see Even looking me up and down and I tuck my shirttail in and smooth down my cap.

"Guess how old I am," Even asks. I look her over and guess eighteen.

"I turned twenty-four in May," she says, cocking her head and looking womanish.

"I'm twenty," I says.

She walks over to Buster and unclips his chain.

"He's gonna run off," I says.

She ain't looking at Buster. She's looking at Laz.

"You was watching me sleep," she says. She takes my hand. Her hands are nice and big and cool to the touch. I wanna get with her, but I don't know how to ask.

"Tell me something," I says.

"Tit for tat," she says.

"How much do a horse like that cost?" I ask instead of what I wanted to really ask.

"Ma won him throwing dice," she says.

I asked first. I had tit. Now I got to tat.

"How come they call you Laz?" she asks.

"I was born not breathing," I says. "Laz is for Lazarus."

"You wanna watch me sleep some more?" she says. I don't say nothing and she leads me by the hand back into the office.

We do it. I ain't never done it before except in my mind thinking of

Billy mostly and sometimes looking at a dirty picture. Even's done it before and she knows what to do. She takes off her dress and lays on the bed. She's got on a white brassiere and white underpants. Then she takes them off too. Her body is mountainy and warmish-cool and reddish-brown like the dirt. I take off all my clothes and my glasses and my wool cap too and I do what she tells me, getting on top of her soft warmish coolness and putting my thing in her and she don't got to tell me how to move it cause somehow I know that so I'm moving it around while she says *Lazarus* over and over in my ear. Even is rocking me in her arms and I'm loving her with my eyes open, but when I close my eyes I can see Billy Beede with her wide smile. After we're through, I close up my pants and she pulls her clothes back on. I've taken advantage of her, now I got to assume my responsibilities.

"I guess we gotta get married," I says.

"I like you but I don't like you like that," she says.

"I'm trying to assume my responsibilities," I says.

Even throws back her head and laughs. "We had some fun, but you don't got to go to town with it," she says. She sits up in bed and I sit up with her. We watch the horse out the back window. Loose from his chain he's halfway across the field, almost to the tractors.

"One day I'ma stand on his back and ride him. Maybe today," Even says.

"Want me to catch him?" I says.

She lays her hand on my leg, to keep me from moving, then she whistles, putting two of her fingers in her mouth and blowing hard. That horse hears her calling and comes trotting back toward the clothesline just like a dog would.

WILLA MAE BEEDE

Deep down in this hole
I got to thinking
About the promises I made but ain't been keeping.
Deep down in this hole
I got to drinking
I got drunk and I done cried myself to sleep.
Deep down in this hole
It's a cold cold lonesome hole
I made my bed
Now I'm laying in it all alone.

BILLY BEEDE

We're about two hundred miles from LaJunta. Four more hours then a few hours to dig. I'll ride with them back to Lincoln and take the bus up to Gomez from there. Aunt Precious and Uncle Blood sent us on our way with three jars of Uncle Blood's Block and Tackle to give as presents to Miz Candy and celebrate with a sip when we get the treasure. When we get rich they'd like to get rich too. Not more than they deserve. Just enough to get side-by-side burial plots, matching headstones, and white Cadillacs to take them to their graves. And maybe a marching band. I tolt them there'd be enough for everybody, but I don't know. I don't like spending it all before we even get it.

Uncle Teddy and Aunt June are following behind in Homer's car. I'm driving the truck with Homer riding shotgun.

"Yr mad at me," Homer goes.

"No I ain't," I says.

"Yr mad cause I was looking at that filling station gal."

"You was doing more than looking," I says.

West of El Paso there's groves of pecan trees with their slim brown trunks planted in perfect lines along either side of the road and rolling like a thousand-spoke wheel as we pass by.

I drive along, reading the road signs. Vado and Chaparral. Through Las Cruces and across the Rio Grande where it cuts up through Mexico and Texas heading north. When I came out here with Mother I could read some of the signs but not all of them. Now I can read them all.

Homer's got a piece of paper folded on his lap. He unfolds it, studies it, then folds it neatly back up. "I have a strong feeling for you," he says. "You turned me down so I got mad."

"And then you went with that gal," I says.

"I was just trying to get you jealous," he says. "Are you jealous?"

"I'm driving," I says.

"You're driving me wild," he says smiling. I smile too. I can't help it.

He unfolds his paper, holding it up to the dashboard and pressing it to the inside of the windshield so I can see the figures he got written down without taking my eyes off the road. "Here's the amount the jewelry will bring," he says. He points to a figure on the paper and I glance a look.

"All I see's a X," I says.

"That's because we don't know the exact amount," he says.

I want to ask him how come he just don't write question mark instead of X but I can tell the way he's holding the paper that he learned to write that X in college. Uncle Teddy, when he writes his name, makes a X too.

"Here's everyone's name and here are the percentages that they're due," Homer says. "Your name is at the top. You get the lion's share. That means more than half. Let's say fifty-five percent. The remainder will be divided up between the rest of us."

"How much you getting?"

"Fifteen percent," he says. "That's pretty fair."

"We can't afford to give you but five percent," I says. He smiles and cocks his head, looking at my belly then looking back at his paper, but not saying nothing.

Mother said she was gonna get rid of the baby she was carrying. It was big in her belly already. She had bought some herbs from somebody. She didn't say who. We left Dill's in the middle of the day. We took all our stuff so I knew we were going for good. She ate the herbs while we was driving and she would pull the car over every once and a while and get sick. I was ten years old and thinking every time she bent in two and spat up that the baby in her she didn't want would come out of her mouth with her puke, like it was in her stomach and all she had to do was spit it up. But the baby didn't come out. So she got a better idea. She said when we got to Miz Candy's she was gonna fix herself. It weren't hard, she said. She told me to say "good riddance" to the baby while we drove along. She said we'd be free of our troubles and looking at palm trees by the end of the week.

Homer wedges his hand gently between my legs.

"I can't give you more than five percent," I says.

"I could live with that if you gave me something to go with it," he says.

"I don't wanna get with you, Homer," I says.

"Don't play holy, honey, I know you got a wild nature," he says.

We pass a sign.

**You Are Now Entering
The Town of Deming, New Mexico**

I twist my hips and make a face at him. He takes his hand away. We get through the town then I pull off the road. I put my head down on the wheel but I don't cry.

ROOSEVELT BEEDE

Up ahead Billy pulls the truck over and we pull over behind her. She's got her head on the wheel and Homer's saying he's sorry.

"Lemme drive," I says and Homer gets out the truck and goes back to his car. I open the door and Billy scoots over and I get behind the wheel and we head on out that way. After a minute, Homer, with his foot heavy on the gas pedal, cuts around us to lead the way even though he don't know where the hell he's going.

"What'd Homer do?" I ask, but Billy ain't listening. She's got that picture of Willa Mae out of her purse, studying it, looking from the young woman in the picture to the young woman in the truck's side mirror.

My father died in World War I. I was four years old. Willa Mae was two. I got a picture of him wearing his uniform. His hat looks like a tin plate.

"I bet there ain't no treasure," Billy says.

"Sure there is," I says.

"You mind digging her up to get it?"

"I done resolved myself to it," I says. "Maybe we'll take her back home with us. The truck's got room."

"Maybe," Billy says. She puts the picture away and reaches underneath the seat, taking out a loaf of bread wrapped in wax paper.

"You want me to stop and get you something to go with it?"

"I got a taste for it plain," she says.

She's already opened it up and she's eating a slice with nothing on it. When Willa was pregnant with Billy, Willa had a taste for dirt.

We pass a sign. "Read that for your Uncle," I says.

"'Red Mountain, elevation five thousand feet.' There was a Black Mountain a few miles back," Billy says.

She's still working on that loaf, eating it slice by slice. There's bread crumbs on her belly.

"You think we was wrong doing that ring trick?" she asks.

"We needed the money," I says.

"But it's stealing and you ain't no thief."

"I guess I am now," I says. I'm driving a truck pretending it belongs to me and I pretended to be a Driver who pretended to lose a ring with fake rubies so we could get some money that didn't belong to us so we could get a treasure that does. I don't know. I look up into the sky where I was taught God stays at. I ask God to forgive me. Several miles back, June said the desert looks like what the ocean would look like if the ocean didn't have any water in it.

"It musta hurt losing yr church," Billy says. She's looking down into her loaf, not at me.

I don't got nothing to say at first. Her and me don't got much practice talking. "It weren't too bad," I says finally.

She turns towards me. I lift my chin up. A gal starts as a virgin and then one day she loses her virginity. Maybe it's the same with a man losing his church.

"What happened with you and Homer?" I ask.

"He's toying with me, is all."

"I'm sorry," I says.

"It weren't too bad," she says. "Homer can go to hell."

When Willa Mae came back to Lincoln, jilted, but with that new car and sporting her diamonds and pearls, she had a photograph too, of her rich Carmichael the third fella. She'd ripped the photo into three almost-equal pieces and then Scotch-taped them back together so his face looked wrong but you could still see enough of him to see he was handsome, well-dressed, and white-looking.

"He looks white cause he *is* white," Willa Mae said.

Once I was over visiting her and Dill and Willa Mae got drunk and fed that ripped and taped-back-together photograph to one of Dill's hogs.

"That rich bastard can go to hell," Willa Mae said, watching the hog eat the fella's picture. She'd been jilted but she was tough about it, like Billy, jilted by Snipes and toyed with by Homer, is tough about it now.

"Homer can go to hell and Snipes can go right to hell with him," Billy says.

I want to tell Billy how she's just like her mother, but that would be like picking at a scab.

We pass another sign.

"Read it to me," I ask her.

" 'Continental Divide,' " she says.

WILLA MAE BEEDE

The first few months I was with Dill I thought she was a man in the most regular sense of the word which is to say I thought she had a man's privates. We wasn't never nekked together in the daylight and some people might think that's strange, but I been with enough different men to know that just cause you don't get nekked in the daylight with him it don't mean nothing. Most men like the lights out. Most men like to keep part of they clothing on. Some gotta do it with their shoes and socks on. Some keep they pants on. Many keep they shirts on and buttoned up. Son Walker liked to wear his hat. There ain't nothing normal when it comes to Men and Relations. Dill liked the lights off and the clothes on. I had a roof over my head and our Relations were good. One night we was going at it and I got bold. I felt around down there and then I knew and Dill knew that I knew but we didn't mention it.

I found what kind of a man Huston Carmichael the III was when he jilted me. I found out what kind of man Dill was by feeling around in the dark. I found out but I didn't tell nobody for a long time and when I did, I felt bad but once words leave your mouth you can't get them back in. I know cause I tried. I went around trying to take back what I'd said about Dill Smiles but the words had already run down the road. It weren't no use.

DILL SMILES

Ma's out in the field working with Even on her bareback. Even don't got a knack for it, though. My half-sister's heavyset and can't stand on the horse even though he's got a swayback and ain't moving. After working on it for a while, they quit for the day. Ma looks tired, Even looks let down. The horse, though, looks happy, standing tied to the clothesline, eating his dinner.

"Come on over here," I tell them, "I'll teach you how to shoot."

"We already know how to shoot," Ma says.

Even wants to practice, though. Maybe she'll be better at shooting than she is at riding.

Laz lines up the cans and they shoot. Ma's good. Even's aim ain't shit but she can twirl the gun around and when she do hit a can she blows the smoke away from the gun barrel like a Saturday-morning cowboy. Laz gives it a try, squirming up his face and standing to one side with his arm straight and steady as a board. He's the best of the three.

I hear the sound of a car stopping followed by a sound that could be my truck, but we're too far away from the parking lot to hear good and the row of pink rooms blocks our view. Candy and Even figure they got customers and walk toward the house to greet them. If it's Billy and them I got my gun.

"Billy comes near this grave thinking she's gonna dig and I'ma shoot her dead," I say to Laz but he ain't listening. He's watching Even walk back toward the house.

"How was she?" I ask him.

"How was who?"

"Even."

"She's yr own sister. Show respect," Laz says.

"I asked you an honest question," I says.

"I got my mind set on Billy," Laz says. He punches his chin out when he says it.

"Billy don't got no love for you," I says.

"She will," he says.

My .44 revolver is loaded and in my pocket. I remember I got Willa's ring in that pocket too so I move my gun to my pocket on the other side. The wood handle curves out. My pockets are as good as any holster.

Willa Mae was in Room 33. There was blood in the bed. She was under the covers, so just glancing at her from the door, you couldn't tell she was bleeding. That's how come she bled for so long. From the door of the room it looked like she was just laying in the bed with the spread up to her chin. The blood had soaked down—spreading out and going down through the mattress. When she told Ma to call me they didn't think she was dying. Her voice just sounded tired, they said. By the time I got there they were worried. They couldn't get ahold of the Negro doctor though and Willa had the door locked anyway saying she was fine, just tired. Billy had been standing in the corner for two whole days.

"I got my mind set on Billy," Laz says, "there ain't nothing can change my mindset." He pulls his cap down over his glasses then pushes it up again. Once upon a time I had me a romantic mindset like Laz's got now. I ain't telling him that, though.

"You ain't told me how Even was," I says.

"She was nice," Laz says.

"How nice?"

"She was a lot better than my hand," he says.

Around the corner of Room 33 someone comes walking. A fella I don't know, followed by Teddy. Behind Teddy is what looks like Billy Beede.

HOMER BEEDE ROCHFOUCAULT

I'm coming around the corner with my spade on my shoulder, ready to dig. Uncle Teddy and Billy are right behind me. Miz Candy said there'd be trouble but I'm not scared. The way I see it, I gotta make a good impression, else Billy will get more mad at me and take back my five percent we agreed on. Making a good impression means doing most, if not all, of the digging.

There's a long fella sitting at what must be the grave. A second fella, about my height, is standing beside him. I add things up pretty quick. "I ain't afraid of no Dill Smiles," I yell. I've got to give it to her, though. From here, at first, I took her for a man. Laz, seeing us, comes running over.

"Dill's a good shot," Laz says. His face is sweating.

We all stop walking. I stand as tall as I can and point my chest out. I stick the tip of my spade in the red dirt, telling Billy and Uncle Teddy and Laz, with the way I'm standing, that I've got things under control. But I'm not just going to run over there. The bulldagger's a good shot.

"Hey, Dill," Uncle Teddy says waving. Dill doesn't say or do anything.

"How was yr ride?" Laz asks Billy.

"It was long," Billy says.

Laz looks me over. "You Billy's new man?" he asks.

"Hells no," Billy says before I can get my answer together.

Laz pats the sides of his pants and stands a little taller. That's probably his baby she's got. He looks at Billy but Billy's looking at Dill.

Miz Candy and Even and Aunt June come around the corner to stand with us in the fat triangle of shade thrown by Room 33. Aunt June has her little shovel. They're all waiting for somebody to start.

"We've come to dig," I say, yelling at Dill.

"You ain't come to dig nothing," Dill yells back.

Just the sound of that lezzy's voice makes me take a step back and all of them behind me follow suit.

"Dill ever killed anyone before?" I ask.

"Not yet," Billy says, and we all laugh nervously.

"Go head and laugh," Dill says. "Laugh all the hell you want."

I can feel fear coming up. I need to make a move before fear grabs me and someone else takes the lead and I lose my five percent. I walk forward a few steps. Dill raises her pistol in the air.

"Willa Mae wanted to provide for Billy," Uncle Teddy says, but the pistol doesn't come down.

"We came all this way," a woman says. I turn to see who spoke. It was Aunt June.

I take another step forward, Billy steps forward right behind me as does Laz. Billy's got her spade on her shoulder, holding it steady with one hand while her other hand is pressed into the small of her back, balancing the weight of her belly. Teddy is just behind Laz. June's behind him with Miz Candy and Even at the rear.

When we were pulled over by that Deputy I was scared. I could see that white man taking my car and lynching me and Uncle Teddy just for sport. When he didn't do any of that, I saw the fingerprints and that picture he took of me as things that would be a bad mark on my career. The white man was doing what he could to keep me down. But Dill tops that white man. He did what he could to thwart me on my road to the Senate but that Senate seat isn't mine, it's just something I want. The bulldagger wants to thwart me from getting a five percent that's right-fully mine.

I reach into my hip pocket, slow, like I was reaching underwater. I take out my piece of paper, where I got everything figured out, opening the paper up slow and holding it in front of my chest like the sense it makes can stop bullets.

"We can all profit from this," I say, taking another step forward.

Dill shoots her gun into the air. The horse they have gets up on its rear legs, pulling at the chain but not breaking it.

"Keep going just like yr going," Billy says. Her voice has a nasty edge to it. I'm still in the lead but she's right behind me. The others have moved back into the shade. Billy smiles at me and gives me a thumbs-up sign. It isn't a real smile, though.

"I don't know you, but that don't mean I can't shoot you," Dill yells in my direction.

My five percent will pay off my father's debts. Then I'll be the true man of the house and mother will have to let me go to any college I want.

I take another step. Then another. Dill points the pistol right at us and we all hit the dirt. A shot rings out, popping the side of the house.

"Deliah, what the hell you doing?" Miz Candy yells.

"Don't you Deliah me," Dill yells back.

"You don't got to shoot," Miz Candy says.

"They stole my truck," Dill says.

The record that Deputy's got on me will be a bad mark somewhere in the future but Dill Smiles wants to kill me right now. I stand up, walking backwards with my hands up in the air.

"I'm going to sit in my car," I tell Dill and everyone.

My paper and my spade are just laying on the ground. The wind comes and floats my paper across the field. I back up, passing Billy still laying in the dirt, past all of them huddled in the shade, before I can take a breath again. I take a few good breaths, getting my voice back.

"You Beedes figure out what you want to do. I'm happy to help dig, but I don't need to get killed," I say walking away.

This must be what my mother meant by Beedeism. Jewelry buried in the ground. Gals needing husbands. Bulldaggers with pistols. I would head home right now and wash my hands of the whole thing if it weren't for my five percent.

JUNE FLOWERS BEEDE

If that Dill Smiles thinks we gonna stand out here in the heat with her playing shoot-out at the O.K. Corral, she got another thing coming.

Homer went to sit in his car. We all stand around until Candy says she's got food for us and eating will help us think of what to do.

We sit at her picnic table and she takes a brand-new pink tablecloth out the package, spreading it down.

"All them times you wrote, we woulda sent you something if we could," Teddy says.

"June wrote me pretty letters," Candy says smiling, "at last I get to meet you."

"Wish we were as fancy as my handwriting," I says.

"Hush," Candy says.

I'm a pretty good cook but Candy's got a four-burner gas stove with a oven and a big ice box. We sit at the picnic table with her and Even playing waitress. They bring out smothered pork chops in brown onion gravy, steamed cabbage, a fresh loaf of Wonder Bread, and macaroni and cheese. They got lemonade to drink and for dessert there's chocolate layer cake. Teddy gets two jars of Cousin Blood's liquor from the truck. Homer's working on jar number three.

"We made it this far," Teddy says serving the food onto our plates.

Candy reaches out her hands, taking ahold of my hand on her one side and Billy's hand on her other. She dips her head and we do too. Nobody speaks. After a minute I look up. Candy's looking at Teddy.

"You gonna say grace?" she asks him.

"Thank you for this food," Teddy says.

I squeeze his hand and smile at him. He ain't gived much of a blessing since he lost his church. He lets my hand go and picks up his fork.

"Willa Mae said her brother was a preacher. Guess she was talking about some other brother," Candy says.

Teddy's got a forkful of pork chop on the way to his mouth. He holds it there, then sets it back on his plate. The fork touching down makes a little clattering sound. He's got a look on his face I been looking at for many years. Not when I met him. It came on his face when he reminded me he was the husband and we turned back from California. It became the face he had when we was in Tryler. I thought the face was just a look and I figured he'd shake it, but in the thirty-odd years we been married that face has become his face and it's the face I married that's lost.

"Stand up, Teddy," I says and he stands up.

"I'm at a loss for words," he says. He goes to sit down but I give him a look that won't let him sit. He clears his throat.

"Thank God we made it this far," he says. I think that's all he'll say but he keeps talking. "I guess we could ask for your help as we hoping on getting Dill to lay down her sword and shield but we ain't asking you for that. We just saying thanks and Amen."

"Amen," we all say. Teddy sits down. We eat quiet, complimenting Candy and Even on they cooking, but not saying much else.

Laz finishes first. "Me and Dill rode out here together," he says. "I can talk sense to her cause we's friends." He gets up and walks around the house.

When he's out of our view there's several shots. Billy stands up but the rest of us can't move. Laz comes back around the house. He's OK.

"There's plenty of food," Even says and we settle back down and heap up our plates again. I don't know what anybody else's thinking, but every time I cut me a piece of pork chop I pretend like I'm slitting Dill Smiles' throat. Homer's in his car drinking Blood's moonshine and singing along to the radio. Before long we're through. Billy has a third plate full. We sit there watching her eat. Laz got his elbows on the table and his head propped up in his hands like it was his child Billy's got.

"Anybody got any ideas?" Billy asks.

"I'll think of something," Even says.

"We got time," Laz says. He don't want to rush Billy's eating.

"Me and June gotta be back by Wednesday," Teddy says. He's thinking of Sanderson coming. Here it is Monday evening. When we get back I'll have a new garden. Teddy helped me pull up flowers by they roots and I wrapped them in wet rags.

"If we dig or not, they're plowing on Thursday regardless," Candy says. She gets up and opens the first jar of the liquor and passes it around the table. We each take a sip. It occurs to me at that moment how lucky Willa Mae is. She may be dead but at least she is dead all in one place. When I go they'll bury me someplace, and my leg, long gone, will be in the ground someplace else. One time Willa Mae called me "one-legged" so I called her "fast." But maybe it was me who did the name-calling first.

Teddy's got something to say. He stands up. Maybe he'll give another blessing. When Billy's through wiping her gravy up with her bread he speaks.

"I'ma talk to Dill. I think she'll hear me out," he says.

I lift my hand up, taking hold of the hem of his coat. Before I lost my leg I felt something bad was gonna happen, something bad that I couldn't stop from happening. The yard is studded with weed grass. The breeze going through makes the grass look silvery. Dill Smiles is around the corner with a loaded gun. I should feel something bad coming but I don't. Teddy pets my hand and I let him go. We all watch him walk around the house.

ROOSEVELT BEEDE

Me and Dill talk a long time.

She sees me walking up to her and lets me keep coming. She tells me the headstone's at the wrong end but she didn't lay it. I say her truck rode good and that I'm sorry for using it without permission. She folds her arms acrosst her chest. I ask who she's got watching them thirteen piglets. Joe North, she says.

She sits in her chair. I sit on the ground. Not at her feet but close by. "I'ma have to go head back to Lincoln tonight," I says. "I gotta get back in time to clean up the place and whatnot."

"Laz'll be happy to drive you," Dill says.

"We'll have to drive straight through to make it in time, cause you know if I ain't there for Sanderson's inspection, that bastard'll fire me for sure," I says.

Dill looks over at the tractor. "A man needs employment," she says.

Me and Dill have, over the years, had long conversations about Sanderson. The actual amount of money in Sanderson's bank accounts, the "fairness" of Sanderson's forefathers who treated their share croppers, once a month, to hotdogs and picture shows instead of just giving them good wages. Me and Dill together have calculated the smallness of Sanderson's dick. But not today. Not as long as we're in LaJunta and disagreeing at this grave.

"I said grace over dinner. It felt good."

"You told me you'd never preach again," Dill says.

"It was just the blessing," I says.

"Maybe you'll build yrself another church," she says. There's a snarl in her voice.

"We all got dreams," I says.

Her and me sit there quiet. The horse, at the far end of his clothes-line, evacuates.

Dill shifts her gun in her lap. "I don't got no dreams of nothing," she says.

We sit there for a minute more. Even comes around and feeds the horse then brushes him down. Then the rest of them trickle out through the office and onto the back porch, watching us. Laz and Billy sit close together, talking.

The day has gone. From morning to afternoon. From afternoon to evening. The sun slips behind the western hills.

June stands up. She taps her crutch on the cement steps. She taps just once. I know what she wants to know. *If we's going home we better get going, right?* I shrug my shoulders at her without moving. My wife heads inside. A minute later Billy, Laz, and Even head in too. Candy's still out there watching us.

"It's late," Dill says. "You'll have to drive hard."

"I know that," I says.

The lights go on in the office. Billy and them, clustered together, watch us from there. In Room 22, the light is pink from the lampshade. June stands in that window watching alone.

"I'ma turn the Bird on," Candy says, and goes inside. A minute later the pink flamingo, all rimmed in matching neon, lights up, making the ground look pink and silver-blue.

Someone comes stumbling around the corner drunk and talking trash. He opens his pants and urinates. It's Homer.

"I'ma kick your bulldagger ass," he shouts.

Dill goes over to where he's zipping up his pants and hits him square in the face. She stands there, waiting for him to get up. He don't. She walks back to her chair and sits down.

"There ain't gonna be no digging," she says.

"I guess that's it then," I says. I get up, brushing the dirt from my pants, and head back inside. I thought if Dill turned me away that I would feel lost, but I don't.

From the window June watches me cross the field, but when I come in the door of number 22, she's got the lights off and's in the bed.

"Dill didn't budge," June says knowing.

"Nope, but we had a good talk," I says. "Maybe she'll change her mind in the morning."

"We got to head back tonight," June says.

"Why you in the bed, then?" I ask.

"It's a nice bed."

I don't take my clothes off but I get in the bed too. It's soft but not too soft. And it's king-size and new-smelling.

"Whatchu think?" June asks.

"It is a nice bed," I says. I get up, undress to my undershirt and shorts, and lay back down again.

"Candy's got all them letters I wrote her saved," June says.

"Howabout that."

We lay there quiet.

"Whatchu thinking now?" June asks.

"I'm thinking maybe we should chance it," I says. Maybe Dill will change her mind and we'll use our share of the treasure to start over. June knows what I'm thinking of, but she don't say nothing and I don't neither. We lay there, looking at the ceiling. The next words are on me and we both know that.

When I do speak, I apologize to June for turning around. I apologize for losing my calling. I apologize to her for making her old, and for never coming through with her leg. I don't talk for long and I end things on a question.

"How about we go to California?" I ask her.

"I got a husband who's a preacher," she says. "You sound like him."

"I am him."

"You could be anyone, laying up here next to me in the dark," she says.

"Whatchu think of California?" I ask again.

For a minute she don't answer. I imagine living out in Oakland under her father's thumb. Maybe it won't be so bad. I'd miss Texas, though.

"Tell me what my daddy tolt you, that time you two was in the river," June says. She turns to look at me but I keep looking at the ceiling.

"It was complicated."

"I ain't stupid."

I breathe in deep. What her daddy said was simple. "He made me swear I'd love you," I says.

We both lay there just breathing.

"California's California, but Lincoln's where yr from," June says.

"You think I could try preaching again, in Lincoln?" I ask.

She takes my hand in the dark. "Let's chance it," she says.

CANDY NAPOLEON

Only me and Billy are still awake. We're sitting at the kitchen table. Dill's out there in the dark lit pinky-blue by the flamingo. Laz is sleep in the corner on the floor. Even's gone to bed. We got the lights off in the office so we can see Dill but Dill can't see us.

"We oughta get Dill drunk," I says. I tap my nails against a mason jar full of liquor. It's quiet cept for my tapping on the glass.

"Good idea only Dill don't drink much," Billy says.

Outside Dill stands up, stretches, and sits back down. She raises her hand in our direction. Maybe waving at us to come dig, maybe giving us the finger.

"If she don't drink much, getting her drunk'll be easy," I says.

"You go out there with that mason jar, she'll be suspicious," Billy says.

"I got some special whiskey glasses," I says. "They're collectibles. Dill thinks they're real interesting."

"I dunno," Billy says. But I'm already up, going over to the cupboard by the sink. There's plenty of spill-light from the sign for me to see what I'm doing. Billy pulls up a chair for me and I stand on it, towering over the room, my head almost at the ceiling. I hand her down the glasses one by one.

"They're of every state in the union," Billy says, looking at each glass.

"I don't got all the states but I got quite a few. I got them when I was touring with the rodeo," I says.

I put the glasses all on a big round tray. I got about thirty. Billy pours each one full. "I'll take the tray out to her," I says. "I'll make like it's a party in celebration of her triumph and you all's defeat."

"Dill might be meaner drunk," Billy says. But Billy don't know Dill like I know Dill.

I head on outside.

"It's just me," I says, crossing the back porch and walking towards the grave. Dill can see I got something on the tray.

"I ain't hongry," she says.

"They gave up," I says. "You and me are gonna celebrate."

I put the tray on the ground and take up the Minnesota glass, sipping from it.

"I ain't drinking," Dill says.

"You gonna let yr mamma drink alone?"

"You got yr special glasses out," she says.

"Cause we're celebrating," I says. I take another sip.

"Willa liked to travel just like you," Dill says. Her voice sounds like my little Deliah but I don't tell her that.

"Here I am drinking alone," I says.

"I'll have one with you," she says. I raise Minnesota a little higher. She picks up what looks like Oregon.

"Here's to Mr. Dill Smiles," I says.

DILL SMILES

She called me Mr. Smiles. I'll drink to that. Just one or two. I deserve that much. I been out here all day doing what's right. I kicked that fool's ass. Not Laz. The cousin that come out here with them, he come around here whipping his dick out and pissing in the yard, thinking he could beat me and he got beat instead.

"My glass is from Minnesota," Ma says.

I've picked a glass that's nubbly blue with one of them tall wide pine trees on it. It says Oregon.

"There ain't gonna be no digging here," Ma says. We drink to that.

I ain't never been to Oregon. I left Dade County for Texas and I ain't never left there except to come out here. I moved away from home. That was enough moving for me. Not like Willa Mae or Ma. They was both always moving.

"How you been keeping yrself?" Ma asks.

"I been all right."

Maryland next. Marry-land. Maryland with a crab and a black bird wearing an orange sash. The glass is full. Nothing spilling.

"Shit," I says. It burns going down my throat.

To keep her I let Willa Mae do whatever she wanted but what kind of life is that? It weren't so bad. She respected me. Respected me enough to say that the first baby she was carrying might be mines. She sat in our front room telling me that. Shaping her hands around her belly that after seven months of growing she couldn't hide no more.

"This baby might be yours," she said and I nodded appreciating the respect she was giving me even though it was just a shambles of a real respect, not no way completely genuine. We both knew the baby was Son's but still I nodded to what she said. I nodded in thanks. Ten years later, when the second baby came along, Willa tried saying the same thing and I beat her for it.

Ma's lips are wet. I can out-drink my ma. She picks up the empty Maryland glass, running her tongue around the inside.

"You and Willa ever get married?" she asks.

"Oh sure, quite a few times," I says.

Ma turns the tray around, putting each new full liquor glass in front of me so I won't have to reach.

She's got two from Florida. One with its green alligator. One with its pink flamingo.

"Dade County," I says. We both drink to that. She asks how my pigs are and I tell her I can't complain but I don't tell her about my thirteen piglets and no runts. I tell her instead about this pig I read about in the newspaper. A pig who was trained to count, but one day turned on his master and ate him up. They had a picture of the pig in the paper next to a picture of the man that was ate.

"Shit," Ma says.

"Shit is right," I says.

I get up. "You take the chair, Ma," I says.

"I'll drink to that," she says. She raises Florida again but don't throw it back. She takes the chair and I sit on the ground.

Georgia is busting with peaches. Idaho's got its potato. There's no glass saying Texas. Not yet at least. Willa Mae said she loved me. She said the first time she looked at me she loved me. What was she looking at.

I've heard of Idaho but I ain't heard of it in a real way, the way you can hear of something and match it with something inside of you that you already know, something inside of you that makes sense. But the potato helps. I seen plenty of potatoes.

"Did you love my daddy?"

"No."

"Did you love Even's daddy?"

"John Henry Napoleon, King of the Cowboys," Ma says.

"What kind of answer is that?"

"All the answer yr getting," she says. Her voice is thicker and her nose is large with a pointed tip. She is pretty far gone. I ain't never been much of nowheres but Dade County and Texas and here. I go all the way through Idaho. Ma turns the tray. Now I'm in Utah. The orange shapes Ma says are mountains. The painted square of blue that stands for the sky, the skull of a cow. Drink Utah. Drink Colorado with its snow-white mountains. Drink Missouri, the show-me state.

"There's folks that shoot theirselves for love," Ma says. "I hope you don't end up like that."

"I'll end up like I want."

"You was always so hardheaded."

"That's cause you thought you could train yr daughter like you trained yr damn horse."

There is a squat glass with a chip on the rim. I have got as far as Ohio. Ma has on a wig. When she takes off her cowgirl's hat, her wig comes off too. Underneath the wig she's got little gray plaits. They got something painted on Ohio that looks like a bean.

"That's a buckeye," Ma says.

Texas has a picture of itself and a boot. Tennessee has a guitar. I drink.

I spent the pearls but I still got the diamond ring in my pocket. I could give it to Ma to give to Billy and them right now and they all would leave me be. I put my hand in my pocket but don't take the ring out. I just feel the ring sitting there inside the dark pocket cotton that's softer and more private than the outside of my pants. I fiddle the ring around.

Maine has a red cockroach with whiskers.

"I ain't drinking from no red cockroach cup," I says.

"That's a lobster," Ma says.

I lay stomach-down in the dirt, my feet resting on the white-chalk grave-marking stones. I know what Ma is thinking. She's thinking there's my daughter topping her woman one last time.

"There's worse things," I says. But I don't know what is worse than whatever I was thinking before I went to Maine or Tennessee.

Ma's teeth have disappeared and her skin has grown smooth. She looks young, like a child. I am a man, but an old old man, and Willa Mae, six feet underneath the top of the ground, unfolds her hands from where I laid them crosst her chest and, with a smile, takes me in her arms.

WILLA MAE BEEDE

This song's about someone who didn't have much but gived me all they did have. I call it "Promise Land" and it goes like this.

> My man, he don't got nothing
> So you must understand
> He never takes me nowhere
> Cept to the Promise Land.
>
> When he takes me there,
> We may be walking
> But love ain't secondhand
> When me and mines is heading
> To that sweet Promise Land.
>
> You keep your riches
> You keep your castles
> They'll turn to dust and sand
> Me, I don't want for nothing
> Cept my old Promise Land man.

I went down to Blackwell County once. I met Old Daddy Beede. He had married Willameena Drummer around 1875. They was married fifteen years before they had they first child, then they got going and had sixteen altogether. Twelve boys, four girls. They named them after presidents and philanthropists, you know, rich folks that like to give money away, and they named them after words they liked saying. Old Daddy had the name of every one of his children wrote out on the side of his house.

Beede and Willameena
Washington
Jefferson
Adams
Pierce
Quincy-Adams
Buchanna
Liberty
Freedom
Prosperity
Lincoln
Johnson
Grant
Rockefeller
Carnegie
Justice
Fortune

Don't do whatcha see me do
Don't walk nowhere I lead
My middle name is Trouble
First is Sin and last is Greed
Wise up, child, turn yrself around.

Can't tell you right from wrong
Cause wrong looks right to me.

The game yr Mamma's playing
Keeps her full of misery.
Wise up, child, turn yrself around.

Once, when me and Billy went to Galveston, we had our shoes off and
was walking in the wet sand. Billy walked behind me putting her feet
prints where my feets had already made a mark. Good Lord, I thought,
my child's following in my footsteps. But I tried not to worry. The way
I see it, you can only dig a hole so deep.

BILLY BEEDE

It's early. Not light yet. Dill's laying facedown on the grave. I was gonna run out here when Miz Candy got Dill drunk but I fell asleep and Miz Candy didn't wake me.

I stand over Dill looking her up and down. I kick her gun away. To dig I got to move her so I pull at her feet. She wakes up, wiping her face and steeling it, making her features bullet-hard, like she wants to shoot herself at me, but she don't move or reach for her gun.

Dill's got a Hole in her heart.

"When them tractors start working they're gonna dig Willa up and scatter her all which away," I says.

"Serves her right," Dill says.

"Her legs'll be over there, her head over there, her body someplace else."

"She won't feel it."

"She might."

"So what if she do?"

"My mother don't deserve to be scattered to the winds like that," I says.

Dill rolls over to lay on her back. She looks at the sky. In an hour or so it'll be daybreak. She gets up slow. Her body's stiff from sleeping on the ground. Her whole front's covered in dirt but she don't make no move to brush it off. She's got her hand in a fist. I close my eyes cause I know what's coming next. She will hit me.

"God damn her," Dill says. She kicks the gravestone rocks. I hear em scrambling and scattering. I open my eyes to look. Dill's already picked up my spade and started digging.

LAZ JACKSON

I hear the sound of digging. A sound I know pretty well cause I done heard it so many times. You hear a lot of digging sounds in my line of work. I hear Dill Smiles cursing but I don't expect to see her digging, but there she is, digging, and Billy is digging too. There's barely enough light to see. I come out to help. I make sure my shirt is tucked and my pants are buttoned right and my coat's not too wrinkly. They've dug a good bit already. Long way to go still, though.

"Y'all digging?" I says. I'm just making conversation.

Neither of them look at me. Neither of them speak. Like if they broke the stride of what they was doing they might quit. It took so long to get started, if it's quit now it'll never get started again. I go to the truck and get two spades. One I stab in the dirt and hang my coat on, then I roll up my sleeves and loosen my collar and get to work.

There's a certain method to digging a grave. You don't just pop the spade to the dirt willy-nilly, there's a certain method to it. You mark your four corners, the boundary of the thing. You line out your plot. Then you dig down in layers. Keeping it smooth and even all the while, not doing like they doing, scrabbling into the dirt like a dog would. Digging's hard work. Especially out here where the dirt is hot and baked. I dig slow and steady and neat. I toss the dirt over my left shoulder. They see how I'm doing it and follow suit and soon we got a good rhythm.

I don't get much call to dig peoples up, but when you gotta do it, you dig them up the same way you would dig them down. Walter Little buried his father and his mother within the same week. The next week he come running to us in the middle of the night with a shotgun talking bout how they weren't really dead and we had buried them alive and me and my daddy was gonna have to get up out the bed and unbury them right now or he was gonna be a orphan and a murderer too. So we dug them up for him. By the time we hit the two boxes he had told us to forget it. We went and opened the boxes anyhow. And the smell was something else. We made him look. Then he went home. But that don't happen too often.

Billy rests. Dill and me dig without resting, without speaking. We get it almost all dug up by the time the others wake. Each of them, Roosevelt and Homer and Even, help a little. Candy helps too and June moves the dirt with her trowel while Roosevelt helps her stand without her crutch. When we hit the coffin they all get real quiet. They're hoping for a chest of diamonds from the looks on they faces. I'm just hoping she don't stink. It's been six years. She won't stink.

I start to pry off the coffin lid. Everybody moves back. The lid's still in good shape. It weren't expensive, but the dry heat's helped it hold up. Dill stands frozen and not looking down, but watching me. They all know I know what to do.

The lid comes off in two pieces. Willa Mae Beede's remains is laying quietly in the box, wound up in a quilt. Everybody is watching me, letting me touch the ragged quilt and move it aside, letting me get the first look at the bones, then they look too, once they see, through me, that Willa Mae's dead corpse can be looked at and stomached.

There ain't no treasure. Far as I can tell.

"Motherfucking undertaker stole the jewels," Dill says. She kicks at the pile of dirt we dug out, speckling Willa's remains with it.

They all watch me move aside the tattered quilt, showing the bones at their full length. The skull's got some hair around it, all the flesh is rotted away, but there is a nice pillow of brown hair, good brown hair. Around the neck bones, where Dill said the pearl necklace would be, there ain't nothing. And on the fingerbones of the hands laid cross the chest, there ain't no ring of no kind. Suddenly everybody that was crowded around to see the treasure sees what's really there: just a bunch of brownish-colored bones dressed in rotten scraps of a red dress, wrapped in quilt tatters and laying in a cheap pine box.

"I buried her with her jewels. The motherfucking undertaker stole em somehow," Dill says again. She curses and kicks more dirt. The others, except Billy, are looking at Willa Mae. Billy is looking at the tractor in the near distance.

"Motherfucking goddamn thieving undertaker," Dill says.

"All undertakers ain't honest, I guess," Teddy says.

"I'd appreciate getting my goddamn keys back," Dill says and walks away towards her truck.

"Guess someone stole it all," Teddy says. There's a strangle sound in his voice, like he will cry but not now. He will cry good and hard, but not now in front of other men and in front of his wife. He will cry later and maybe do something more than cry.

"We did our best," June says.

"Cover it back up," Homer says, sounding disgusted.

"We'll decide where to rebury her a lot better with some breakfast in our stomachs," Candy says and the promise of food gets them to move inside, all at once, like a herd. They don't like looking at dead folks but dead folks don't bother me none.

Billy ain't said nothing yet and she ain't moved. She's sitting at the top of the grave, like a headstone, looking like I think an angel would look, watching the rest of them go inside then, when they've gone, looking at where they went, but not down at her mother's bones.

Even comes back outside. She's got a newish quilt which she spreads alongside the grave.

"Miz Willa Mae oughta have a new shroud," Even says.

She helps me lift the bones up out of the coffin. The old quilt underneath Willa Mae holds together just long enough to get her up. When we clear the grave it makes a ripping sound. She makes it out in one piece though. The coffin is wedged too tight in the ground so we just leave it where it's at. The bones and their old shroud lay on the new quilt in the sun.

"I heard plenty of times when an undertaker would steal a wristwatch or a brooch," I explain to Even and Billy, but only Even's listening. "Dill coulda been digging the grave and the undertaker coulda been stealing the jewels while Dill was digging," I says.

Now Billy's looking at her mother's bones. Her eyes flick over them quick. Then she looks at the grave.

I wrap the remains gently up in the quilt, folding the edges carefully in, like I'm tucking in a baby.

"We got a nice cemetery down the road. Miz Willa Mae might like it," Even says.

"I'd like to take her back to Lincoln and bury her there," I says. "If it's all right with Billy."

Billy don't speak.

Me and Even look at the bones wrapped in the new quilt. The quilt pattern is called wedding ring. "My mother and dad got one on they bed that looks just like it." I'm looking at the quilt so Even notices before I do: Billy is crying. Even goes inside and leaves us alone.

I ain't never seen Billy Beede cry. And I ain't never seen no one cry like she's crying now. She may as well be fighting someone, the way her arms move around in the air and the tear-water washing her face like sweat and the stuff coming out her nose. She's saying things I don't understand. Words threaded through with a long private string of goddamn yous, the kind of curses that's said between mother and daughter, I guess. She goes on like that till she can't breathe. Then she stops and sits there, licking her lips with her tongue and running her arms across her face to dry it.

"I'm gonna take your mother back to Lincoln," I says. "I'm gonna get her a new coffin, a nice one, and a nice angel headstone. I'll put her in the ground real good and all at my expense."

I expect Billy to smile or say thank you or something but she is looking hard at the wrapped quilt, thinking. There's a part of the dress, just a little bit of the hem down at the bottom edge, that didn't get tucked in.

"Look where the hem of the dress is at. Sometimes she kept stuff in the hem," Billy says.

I unpart the quilt down near the bottom. I don't want to expose the skull again. The shoes still hold the feet. The hem of the dress is a line of fabric folded over twice and still neatly stitched. I don't know what I'm looking for exactly. I am looking for a wife, I am looking for Billy Beede's hand in marriage. And there it is. In what's left of the hem of the dress I find the diamond ring.

WILLA MAE BEEDE

Don't the Great Wheel keep rolling along
Don't the Great Wheel keep rolling along
I stopped in yr town this morning,
But tonight, this gal, she's gotta be gone.
Don't the Great Wheel keep rolling right along.

BILLY BEEDE

It didn't turn out like we planned.

We got back to Lincoln all right. Uncle Teddy drove Dill's truck the whole way with Aunt June sitting beside him. I sat by the window, watching the land go by but looking at Mother's ring mostly. It was big for my finger which surprised me, but it twinkled good in the light and Laz ran it across a piece of glass showing us all how diamonds could cut.

Laz knew a man in Dallas, a jeweler friend of his daddy's. When we got back to Lincoln, Laz and his daddy took the ring and came back with sixteen hundred and twenty three dollars and fifty-nine cents. It was enough to give everybody something and Laz had a new ring for me. Not a diamond, just a plain wedding band, but it was nicer than diamonds, I thought.

When we rode back from LaJunta, Dill rode in the truck bed. She didn't want to drive and she didn't want to talk. Every once and a while she would take something out of her pocket. She reached up and ran the thing across the back of the truck cab window. It didn't cut the glass. Teddy and June didn't see but I seen. It was a diamond-looking ring Dill had. Then I knew Dill had tooked it from Mother and if Dill had tooked that ring then she had tooked the pearls too. Maybe real pearls maybe not real pearls, we never did find no kind of pearls at all, but I wasn't gonna ask Dill about them while we was riding back home. I wasn't never gonna ask her. Dill and Mother had something between them and now Dill and me got something between us. If Dill stole

things I don't got a need to talk about it. The truth, whatever it is, is
gonna stay secret.

Homer drove his own car back. He had a busted lip from where Dill
hit him, but no broken teeth. Next time, he said, when he challenged
Dill, he'd be sober and she'd better watch out. When we passed Pecos his
car peeled off the road and he shouted goodbye and tooted his horn. I
didn't want to send him nothing but when Laz and Mr. Jackson came
back with all that money, Uncle Teddy sent him ten dollars and Aunt
June wrote a thank-you note.

We didn't get all what we thought we'd get. Aunt June got her leg,
though. She walked her first steps the same day as her first grandbaby did.

Folks take after they folks. That's the law of nature. The thing about
not watching my mother get old is that I wasn't never sure what I was
gonna get, cause if you don't got yr folks to look at, if all you got is a little picture of a woman standing beside a cactus, a picture took by a man
who weren't even your daddy, then you don't got a good idea really of
where yr headed. When I seen her bones I knew what we all knew, that
we's all gonna end up in a grave someday, but there's stops in between
there and now. Right now I got my first child running around in the
yard and another one on the way. Five years from now Laz gives me
Mother's diamond ring back. He'd never sold it in Dallas. The money
he brought back was from his savings. Dill's hog farm is going pretty
good. Uncle Teddy's got another church. There's lots of things between
now and them bones.

Riding back to Lincoln, looking at my ring, I could feel the baby inside me. I hadn't never really thought of a name for it, but riding home I
felt like I could. Not pick out a name though, just let one come to me
without thinking. Like it had a name already, and if it had a name already
then it already was. And if it already was then it was always gonna be.

My belly sat in front of me. In front of my belly, beyond the hood of
the truck, was the back of Laz's hearse with Mother's body riding inside
and the road unrolling out ahead.

Going back home we made good time. I think we did all right.

ABOUT THE AUTHOR

SUZAN-LORI PARKS is a novelist, playwright, songwriter, and screenwriter. She was the recipient of the 2002 Pulitzer Prize for Drama for her play *Topdog/Underdog,* as well as a 2001 MacArthur "genius grant." Her other plays include *Fucking A, In the Blood, The America Play, Venus,* and *The Death of the Last Black Man in the Whole Entire World.* Her first feature film, *Girl 6,* was directed by Spike Lee. A graduate of Mount Holyoke College, where she studied with James Baldwin, she has taught creative writing in universities across the country, including at the Yale School of Drama, and she heads the Dramatic Writing Program at CalArts. She is currently writing an adaptation of Toni Morrison's novel *Paradise* for Oprah Winfrey, and the musical *Hoopz* for Disney. She lives in Venice Beach, California, with her husband, blues musician Paul Oscher, and their pit bull, Lambchop.

ABOUT THE TYPE

This book was set in Granjon, a modern recutting of a typeface produced under the direction of George W. Jones, who based Granjon's design upon the letter forms of Claude Garamond (1480–1561). The name was given to the typeface as a tribute to the typographic designer Robert Granjon.